THE ENERGETICS, BOOK 3

NIXIE
AND THE
HEALER

ELLEN BARD

NIXIE AND THE HEALER
The Energetics Series: Book 3
Ellen Bard

Copyright © 2019 Ellen Bard
All rights reserved.
EllenBardAuthor.com

Please consider leaving a review wherever you bought the book, or telling your friends about it, to help me introduce it to new readers; it makes a huge difference to me.

Many thanks for reading!

ISBN-13: 978-0-9934394-4-5
Published by Parchment Publishing.
ParchmentPublishing.com

Dedication

For my Fox,
for all your support.

The Chakras and their Energies

Muladhara: The Root Chakra – Earth Element
The energy of nourishment and home, family and safety.

Svadisthana: The Sacral Chakra – Water Element
Fluid and adaptable, the energy of movement and connection, of practical and physical creativity. The energy of pleasure, sexuality and sensation, and emotions.

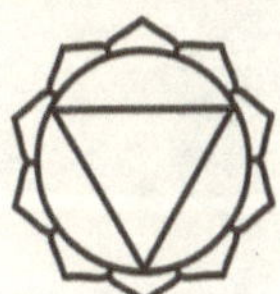

Manipura: The Navel Chakra – Fire Element
The energy of the individual; of confidence, of proactivity and of drive and passion. Playful and proud.

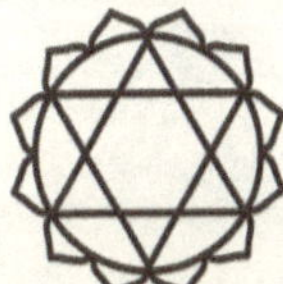

Anahata: The Heart Chakra – Air Element
The energy of healing, and of balance, located in the middle of the body and the seven Chakras. The energy of love, of relationships, of devotion. Of compassion and empathy.

Vishudha: The Throat Chakra – Ether (Space) Element
The energy of communication, of conceptual creativity, and of truth. Of expression, and of listening.

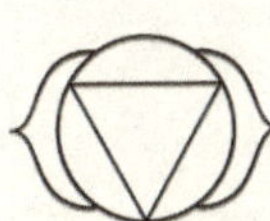

Ajna: The Third Eye – The Mind
The energy of imagination, of visualizations, and insight. Of clarity and wisdom. Of dreams and intuition.

Sahasara: The Crown Chakra – None*
The purest of all the energies. Only experienced through the Grace of the Source (the energetics' name for the creator, the divine).

*Neither a dominant nor auxiliary Chakra for energetics

1

Jeb came to on the wooden floor of his office. His muscles cramped and his body burned with pain. He retched. The energy rose again and he fought to suppress it, but it was strong. He'd had a hold on it for decades, but recently it was harder and harder to keep it bound.

His body spasmed as he fought the internal battle to keep his auxiliary energy, Svadisthana, locked down. It was too dangerous for him to use. He'd learned that the hard way.

He tried to pull on Anahata, his dominant energy, to bind it. The energy wouldn't stay contained. His pulse raced as some energy escaped and found a nearby source of liquid, the water glass on his desk – which exploded. Shards of glass shot across the room and a few embedded themselves in the arm he'd thrown up to protect his face.

As Jeb was senior Maven for the Cairo-based Anahata Major Guild, the study was warded against all energies getting in, and his students' Anahata energies getting out. But the wards were less effective against other energies. His mistake.

Another pulse of energy wracked his body, and he had to grit his teeth against a shout of pain. What was going on? Why was it so much harder for him to keep his Svadisthana energies bound? He lost the thought as more energy leaked. As fast as he drew on his dominant energy from the ether, the auxiliary burned it away, a war between two opposing sides within his flesh. Anahata, the healing energy of air and of love. An energy Jeb was at peace with – unlike his Svadisthana energy.

Which disgusted him.

The energy of water, of practical creativity – and of sex. Once, he'd used all aspects of that energy assuredly. And then, he'd used it to murder innocents.

He'd vowed never again.

Had bound the energy, with help.

And had considered that part of him, that despised energy, gone.

It had taken a will of iron, a will that he drew upon now. He used his Anahata to create a glowing shield around his body to contain any further energy leaks. Then he went inside himself. He spun Anahata energy into a second shield tight to his skin. When it covered him, and he had the two shields in place in addition to his regular shields, he relaxed a fraction.

All hell broke loose.

Svadisthana exploded from inside him, and raced around the room. He felt as though he'd been punched in the abdomen, the area where Svadisthana Chakra was located, and he curled up in a ball to lessen the pain.

The energy sought to ground itself. With no other humans in the room, it couldn't find a sexual outlet, so it found the drops of water from the glass, as well as the beads of blood that had been created by the glass breaking Jeb's skin, and it worked with those.

A fine mist of blood and water began to form around Jeb, while the energy continued to shoot around the room. The walls and floor had a spray of blood misted over them. But worse, the energy was calling to the weather outside. Egypt was a dry land – one reason why Jeb was happy to stay in the Guild's headquarters here – but there was water, with the Nile so close. When Jeb raised his head, groaning, to look out the window, he could see a cloud forming outside, tiny drops running down the glass.

Jeb lay on the floor, his body convulsing as energies that had been kept inside him for decades escaped. He managed – just – to keep some shields up, but he wasn't sure how long he could maintain it. If he stopped balancing the destructive Svadisthana with Anahata, the scales could tip, and the energy he'd tried so hard to keep hidden would be loosed. Done in an uncontrolled manner, it could pose a danger to all the Guild buildings – and everyone inside them.

There was a knock at the door. A soft voice came through the wood. "Jebediah-san? May I enter?"

Source. It was Aiko, the Head of the Guild. This was a blessing and a curse. On the one hand, Aiko was exactly the person to help him. On the other hand, if she came through that door without knowing what she was walking into, his escaping energy could slam right into her, which could have some nasty consequences. He could enthral her sexually, or hurt her physically with his energy wild and uncontrolled in the room.

Another knock.

The moisture at the window ran down in rivulets, blurring the view of the sky. A couple of books were dislodged from the shelf, and thudded onto the floor.

The door opened cautiously, and Jeb made a heroic effort to draw on Anahata in order to strengthen his Svadisthana shields. Cold sweat bled through his shirt onto the wooden floor, only to be immediately swept up in the mist around him.

He opened his mouth to warn her, but only a croak came out, his throat parched.

"Jeb?" Aiko peeked around the door, caught sight of the room, and stepped inside smartly. She shut the door behind her, and studied Jeb.

Closing the door on the rest of the Guild was a wise move, though from Jeb's perspective she was now on the wrong side of it.

He felt her draw on Anahata to protect herself from the sexual energy he was exuding, and he rasped a sigh of relief.

He curled into himself, trying to focus, trying to find his voice to ask for her aid, but more energy escaped, and called to the water outside. The window shattered, and glass flew. A piece sliced across Aiko's arm and she cried out, her hand flying to the wound, blood sliding down the arm to stain the white top she wore. Her shields wavered and Jeb's stomach tensed.

He needed her help, and he needed it urgently. But what if she became lost to his water energies, and two of the most powerful members of the Guild lost control?

There was going to be a hell of a lot more damage than a broken window.

Nixie stretched, cat-like, and purred in satisfaction. Life on her Thai island was good. She rolled onto her back. "Mmmm. Thank you."

The tousled-haired youth beside her was still breathing hard, and nodded weakly, his body sprawled inelegantly beside hers.

They'd been seeing each other for a week or so, and Nixie was thrilled that they'd finally slept together. She tried to keep a little discipline, and rarely had sex with anyone on a first date. She loved the buildup, the intensity, the butterflies in her stomach as she anticipated what their physical connection would be like. To make it last she had a personal target of waiting at least a week.

Okay, sometimes six days.

She shrugged internally. It wasn't her fault that she liked sex. A lot. She glanced back at the lean, long-limbed twenty-something she'd just very much enjoyed a couple of hours with. He stared up at the ceiling, eyes wide. She'd made sure he'd had a good time too. Sex was something she was passionate about in all the ways, and she was skilled in bringing pleasure to her partners. White, with dark hair curling around his ears, he wasn't that much younger than her — she was in her early thirties in human years – but in life experience, given she was a part magical being who was likely to live for hundreds of years, they were worlds apart.

Nixie's energies were Svadisthana and Vishudha. The first was where her love of sex stemmed from, in addition to a love of swimming and her creative talents. But Nixie was a romantic at heart, despite the fact that she had no Anahata in her energies. She blamed her parents. Marius and Fai had been together centuries – true soulmates.

Nixie wanted that. She wanted someone as strong and as fearless as her father, a bear-like man, who made his tiny but fierce wife Fai look delicate by standing near her. They were strong individually, but even stronger as a couple.

Nixie had bathed in their love all her life, sharing that love with her cousin Blaize who had moved to Thailand and joined their family as a child when her parents died. Blaize was a best friend and sister in one.

Nixie propped herself up on an elbow, and ran a finger down the man's flank. She liked the play of his muscles. They would look good sculpted in a pale stone, perhaps. She tipped her head, idly considering his body.

Nixie had never thought that Blaize would find her perfect partner before she did. Blaize had reluctantly gone to be trained in her auxiliary energy by a Maven called Cuinn, and then fallen in love with him. Nixie scowled briefly, then shook it off. She was pleased for Blaize, she was. She just…wanted to find her own soulmate sooner rather than later.

In the meantime, she told herself, she was auditioning men for the part. After all, you needed to spend time with someone to really decide whether they were right for you.

The guy lying next to her was human. It was possible for energetics to fall in love and marry humans, but it was rare as the human had to pass your Guild's approval to share their world's secrets.

She looked at Ben, the man in bed beside her, and sighed to herself. He probably wouldn't pass muster. And Nixie didn't think she could live her life with a secret that huge from her partner. She wasn't big on secrets. They were too much like hard work. Much like sculpture. She saved those for only the most interesting models.

Ben would make a fine subject for a life drawing, however.

"What's up?" he asked.

She smiled.

"Nothing. Unless…?" She looked suggestively down at their tangle of naked bodies.

He grinned back. "Sure. Give me a minute or two. And in the meantime, why don't we talk?"

Nixie's forehead creased. "Talk?"

That's not what they were here for. She ran a hand down his back, kneading the muscles there, reminding them both of their physical connection.

He lifted a shoulder. "You know, talk. I don't feel like I know that much about you. What's going on with you?"

Nixie recoiled a fraction. She couldn't help herself. She wasn't a fan of sharing. She was a realist, and knew men were usually attracted to her for her looks. She was fine with that. Her deep relationships were with her friends and family, not her various lovers. They came to her for fun, and sex, and she made sure all parties had both. He caught her expression, and hurt flashed across his face. He spoke quickly. "Or not. It's fine."

"It's not that, I just…I don't know what to say." She couldn't exactly tell him that her plans for the future were currently suspended, as she'd been included in a prophecy which potentially foretold the end of her race's world.

That was the problem with humans. Things got complicated quickly.

"What do you do for a living?" he said.

"Business graphics," she said. She had set responses for questions like this, designed to be as boring as possible, to stop this type of conversation developing into something too personal. Not that many pursued conversations with her. They were usually too swept up in the physical pleasure she could provide, a mutual connection that was more than enough.

"Okay. What do you like to do when you're not working?" he said.

She was impressed – and surprised – at his tenacity. But what could she say? That she practiced what he would see as magic in her spare time, using the energy from water. Huh, water. That would do it. "I like swimming."

"I guess you do live on an island. Makes sense." He was a traveler to Koh Somdun, the island where she lived off the west coast of Thailand, there for a few months to enjoy life in paradise on his way round the world. Another reason it wouldn't last.

He was looking at her expectantly. Apparently he needed more.

"I sometimes do archery. And I like art. Drawing, painting, that kind of thing." She had a sudden feeling of panic. Talking of which – she was supposed to be driving her parents' car down to the dock to collect Blaize and Tierra. Her parents were away travelling and calling on friends in Europe, and Nixie was looking after their house.

Blaize was here so Nixie could use her artistic skills to help with some of the details of the prophecy, and Blaize could have a break. Plus it was well past time for Nixie to catch up on Blaize's love life.

She felt a brief flicker of unease about the prophecy and she quickly stuffed the feeling down inside herself. She was involved, but not really *involved*, in the same way the others were. She knew Blaize wanted to discuss that with her too, but Nixie saw herself as support, a friend, for those who were the main actors.

Talking of which, she rolled over to the bedside table where her phone was lying and picked it up. *Shit.* She was cutting it pretty fine. Nixie tended to operate on 'Thai time' – after all, she was half Thai – but Blaize most certainly did not. Blaize would not be happy if Nixie left her standing on the dock in the sun for half an hour.

"Now what?" There was a touch of irritation in Ben's voice.

"I forgot I have to pick up my friend from the dockside, and I need to go home and get the car." She'd ridden her scooter to Ben's house. She should have brought the car, but she hadn't thought of it. Nixie was more of a big picture girl than someone focused on the details.

"Right," he said. She couldn't figure out what his tone meant, but she didn't have time to explore it. She bounced out of the bed and scrambled into her clothes. She should probably shower, but there wasn't time.

Ben lay on the bed watching her. She couldn't interpret the expression on his face either. Never mind. She tended to keep things flexible. Casual. He was fun in bed, and she'd like to see him again, she was sure of that. Ben had had a great time, she'd seen to it. He didn't need to know her deepest self to enjoy sex with her again. And who knows, maybe things would develop.

After all, she knew her soulmate was out there somewhere, and she was willing to do a lot of experimentation to find him.

C H A P T E R

2

Nixie sped home on her bike, grabbed the keys to the car and drove as fast as she dared to the dock. As she'd thought, Blaize was already there, frowning, green eyes stern. Her red hair gleamed in the sun, porcelain skin indicating she'd been away from Thailand a while in the cold Canadian spring.

Both Blaize and Nixie were in their thirties, but neither had chosen to fix their age yet, something all energetics were able to do through a ritual. It could be changed again with effort, but most of them opted for more sleight of hand tricks like type of clothing, hairstyles and make up to change their age for the humans around them. Or moved location and started again.

Blaize, Tierra, and a surly girl Nixie didn't recognize, who must be Ai, stood under the only bit of shade on the dockside, and as there were no other people waiting with them, Nixie had to assume the boat that they'd come in on had docked a while ago. Nixie squirmed as she drew the car up next to them. She hadn't meant to be late. She knew it frustrated Blaize. Luckily Blaize could never stay annoyed at her for long, and especially not when they hadn't seen each other in an age.

She bounced out of the car, and threw her arms around Blaize, who stiffened before she sighed and put her arms round Nixie in return. "Hey, Nix."

Nixie exhaled in relief and dropped her arms. "Sorry, B! I got caught up."

Blaize put out a hand and tugged on Nixie's jade-colored top. "Oh yes?"

Nixie looked down and flushed.

"Oh." She'd put her top on inside out and back to front. Blaize had the label between her fingers, underneath Nixie's chin.

"In a rush to get dressed, were you?" Blaize's tone was dry.

Nixie grimaced. "Sorry, really. I lost track of time."

"Mm hmm." Blaize rolled her eyes. She likely had a good idea of what Nixie had been up to. "Anyway. Let me introduce Tierra, Cuinn's cousin."

A woman as short as Nixie, but a great deal curvier, stepped forward. She had dark hair and brown skin, and with her near-black eyes sparkling she gave Nixie a sunny smile.

Nixie made a noise of delight. "Tierra! So wonderful to see you."

"Oh, I forgot you knew each other," Blaize said. "Great."

Blaize gestured to the girl on her other side. "This is Ai. She's hanging out with us for a while, and she's never been out of Canada before, so we thought she'd enjoy the trip."

Ai was an Asian teenage girl already taller than Nixie. Tierra and her Manipura Warrior partner, Fintan, had met her when they were tracking a Rogue in Vancouver as part of the prophecy. The girl was an energetic – but had had no idea of her heritage, as she'd been orphaned young, and ended up in the foster system and then homeless for most of her teens. She was streetwise, but wary. Right now she looked somewhat sweaty in skintight black jeans and a black T-shirt with a skull on it, a cell phone welded to her hand.

Nixie smiled at her. "Hey, Ai. Welcome to Thailand."

Ai looked up briefly, and nodded stiffly. "Yeah. We've been here a while already."

Nixie's shoulders tightened. She usually got on well with everyone, but perhaps she hadn't made the best first impression. She glanced at Ai's cellphone screen. "Crystal Bust, I play that sometimes. Nice."

"Crystal Bust is so three years ago," Ai said, scorn lacing her voice. "This is Sonic Caverns. It came out last week."

Nixie's cheeks heated. She suddenly felt old, which was not a feeling she was used to, as she spent time with younger men all the time. And it wasn't like she was old herself. Okay. She'd try again later. She could build rapport with a teenager, it was no problem. One of Nixie's gifts was supposed to be charm after all. She was just tired.

"Now we're all caught up, can we go home?" Blaize said.

"Of course," Nixie said, and opened the trunk of the car for their luggage. They packed the cases and themselves into the sporty little Mazda, and Nixie drove them home.

Set back in the forest on the island, the three traditional Thai-style wooden houses were clustered in a clearing – close enough to walk between them, but far enough for a little privacy, important given the fact that the heat was such that windows and doors were rarely closed.

Nixie loved living here, with nature and the sea so close by, and her parents within walking distance. Nixie was excited to have Blaize back. She wanted to tell her all about the art pieces she had on the go.

She hadn't had anyone to share her art with for a while now, and Blaize, while not appreciating art in quite the same way Nixie did, always listened. In turn, Nixie had always listened to Blaize's goals and whatever she was focused on achieving next, and been her cheerleader.

This trip, Blaize had given up her two bedroom home, closed up for the months she'd been away, for Tierra and Ai. These latter pair had formed a close bond, and Ai was still fragile, though she would never admit it. Blaize would sleep in Nixie's spare room.

Which Nixie was thrilled about. Blaize wasn't only her cousin, but her best friend, and she had sorely missed her in recent weeks.

Plus, Nixie really really wanted to hear about the sex Blaize was having with Cuinn. He sounded hot.

Jeb uncurled his body and began to drag himself over to Aiko, worried about her slashed arm, wanting to heal her, but she threw up a hand to stop him.

"A minute," she said, tightly. Blood trailed down her arm, but she ignored it.

Ah. Yes. If he came closer his escaping energy could affect her more. He shook his head to clear it. She closed her eyes and the room shivered with energy as she rebuilt her shields. Thank Source she was so powerful.

A box fell from a shelf with a bang. Papers fell and scattered across the floor. He jolted in reaction. What could he do? How could he help Aiko?

Distance. Right. Distance, so she could focus and regain control. She wouldn't leave him while he was like this. She knew what was happening with him. He managed to get up onto his hands and knees, but he wasn't strong enough to fight the energy and to stand at the same time. He slumped against his antique desk, holding the energy, no longer trying to stop it.

The energy that had already escaped still bounced around the room. The cloud of blood and mist followed him, and soaked the side of the desk he leaned on. He simultaneously drew the moisture from the desk – and heard the wood creak and crack.

"I need you to – to hurry," he managed to grind out, his jaw aching with the effort of keeping the energy under some semblance of control.

Moments later there was a snap, and the desk split across the middle, the wood as dry as bone. His possessions – pens, notepad, laptop – fell to the floor in a crash. He grimaced. He'd been fond of that desk.

Dark clouds gathered at the window. He heard a soft patter and rain hit the glass, falling into the room where the pane was broken. Jeb's stomach tightened. If he didn't get a handle on this, it wouldn't take long for the rain to get torrential. His power was thirsty.

Aiko's delicate figure stood above him. He heaved a sigh of relief. He was lucky he could count on her. "Aiko. Please. Help me lock it down."

She nodded sharply and dropped down next to him. Ignoring the rain of blood that soaked her tan skin and her pin-straight dark hair, and the not insignificant slice on her arm, she put a hand either side of Jeb's head, and cradled his chin and cheeks in her small hands.

Aiko's power ripped into him, and he welcomed the pain with relief. Her Anahata healed his shields even as it drew the errant Svadisthana back into Jeb. It wasn't an easy process for either of them, and sweat beaded on Aiko's skin while Jeb's jaw clenched and unclenched as Aiko's energy tore through him. The cramps were back, and his body felt as if it was being turned inside out. He squeezed his eyes shut and stars burst inside his head. It probably took only minutes, but Jeb felt as if he were back in a war zone, bombs exploding around him, as his head filled with noise and light.

And then there was blessed silence as Aiko drew her hands carefully back.

He threw up.

Aiko didn't flinch. She moved her body out of the line of fire, and pulled some tissues from a pocket. After Jeb had heaved everything out of his stomach onto the floor he leaned back, blank, onto the side of the desk. Which was no longer there, as the wood had fallen in on itself when the desk split. He toppled over.

Aiko grimaced as she stood up and dragged him to prop him against the wall.

"You're okay." She knelt next to him. "May I check you over?"

He nodded, too miserable to speak. Aiko touched his arm and he felt a tendril of her Anahata energy, a healing balm this time, thread its way around his system. She was checking to see there was nothing else wrong with him. Wasn't what she'd seen enough? *What could be worse than the psychic wound he'd been bearing for so many decades?*

After a minute or so Aiko opened her eyes and settled back on her heels, at ease. For an energetic with so much air, she was surprisingly grounded. "There's nothing wrong with you that some healthy sex wouldn't fix."

Jeb spluttered.

Aiko waved a hand. "Or another appropriate use of your Svadisthana. It's gone far enough. Something's shifted in you. The energy was harder to bind this time. It doesn't want to stay locked down, and it's fighting you and the bindings to be free. It's not natural. My advice both as a Healer and your friend is for you to re-integrate the energy as soon as possible in a controlled way."

It had seemed worse than previous leakages. And he had no idea why.

She rested her hands in her lap, her shoulders back. "It doesn't set a good example. Energetics are about balance. If a student doesn't suspect that you're holding your Svadisthana in check, rather than that you are weak in that energy, as you claim, another member of the Guild will. In fact, anyone who knew you before the war must surely wonder."

They'd had this discussion before.

"No one but you sees this," he rasped out. "It has to be this way."

She shook her head, the straight drop of hair that framed her face rippling. "It really doesn't. This is something we do to punish people, or to restrain Rogues. Not to normal, healthy energetics who could be using their energy for the good of the race."

He didn't answer. What was there to say?

She helped him wash up in the bathroom, then physically locked and energetically warded the door behind them while she escorted him to his quarters. They didn't want anyone else seeing his room after what had happened. He was going to have a lot of cleaning up to do tomorrow.

She briskly helped him into bed. His body sagged against the pillows, and guilt permeated his being.

She paused at the door on her way out. "This isn't a sustainable solution, Jeb. One day, you're going to want to leave the Guild. Or to have a relationship again. If it's the former, then I might not be around to help you. If it's the latter, unless you're careful, you're going to release decades of pent up Svadisthana energy onto one woman all at once. And that could easily overwhelm her system. If she's not someone you have a connection with or a strong energetic, at best you could end up influencing her to do something she doesn't want to do. At worst, you could kill the both of you."

3

Long after Nixie had grilled Blaize about Cuinn – until Blaize had finally thrown a pillow at her and ordered her out of her room so she could nap – Tierra, Nixie and Blaize gathered on Nixie's balcony. Ai was sleeping.

"We don't have to do this now," said Nixie. "If you guys need to rest, it's fine. Jet lag can be a bitch."

"The sooner the better," said Blaize. "We need to work out who the twelve people are in Cuinn's vision. If we can identify them, we can talk to them. We can find out if anything weird's been going on with them, and warn them."

Cuinn had started everything when he'd received some disturbing prophecies. As part of Blaize's Ajna training, he'd shared the images with her through their minds, and then taught her to be able to project them into the mind of someone else, as to this point only the two of them had seen the faces in the prophecy shards.

Nixie would start with faces. It wasn't a beginner level task for Blaize, but luckily she was powerful, if new to training in her Ajna energy, the energy of the mind.

Blaize lay in Nixie's hammock, which was strung across a corner of the broad balcony surrounded by wooden balustrades. Tierra chilled comfortably on a pink beanbag, watching, and Nixie sat on a cushion on the floor.

Nixie nodded. "Okay. How's it going to work?"

"I don't think it should be too hard. For you, anyway. We'll need to touch," said Blaize. "I'll use Ajna to project a figure into your mind, and then we need you to draw it."

Nixie patted the sketch book and pencils next to her. "No problem."

"Sometimes it can be a bit blurry. I'm still learning how to do this, but it's a priority."

"I could've come to you in Canada, you know," Nixie said.

"I know. But Ai needed a break," Blaize replied.

Blaize and Tierra exchanged glances and Tierra continued. "She's never really spent much time in the countryside, and she was getting spooked really easily at Cathair Cuinn. She might have grown up on the streets, but it was an urban landscape, and even the tough lifestyle she's had to deal with hadn't involved people trying to kill her with magic till now. She's been in some shock. We thought a change of scene, and getting her out of Canada, might help her settle into our world. Plus Cara's helping Cuinn, and Adam's in the area if he needs him."

Adam was Tierra's brother, and a Protector with Muladhara Guild, and Cara, one of Tierra's closest friends, ran a Rehab Centre off the west Canadian coast. Both were included in the prophecy along with the others.

"Alright," said Nixie. "How'd you want to start?"

Blaize swung her legs over the hammock to sit up, and planted her feet on the floor, about half a yard between her feet. "Bring your cushion here. How long do you need me to hold the image for?"

"I'm not sure. Depends on the quality. It's not like drawing from a still life, I can't quite tell how I'm going to switch between the image and the paper." Nixie shrugged. "Let's try it and we'll see."

She went and sat between Blaize's knees, facing away, her sketch pad in her lap. Blaize put her hands on Nixie's shoulders.

"Relax," Blaize ordered.

Nixie laughed. "I'm not sure the best way to help me relax is to boss me about."

Blaize gently bopped her on the head. "Whatever, nong sao."

It was the Thai for little sister, and was a term of affection she had used for many years.

They both closed their eyes. Nothing happened for a few minutes. Nixie began to feel sleepy. She'd had a busy day.

Nixie didn't have either of her energies in common with Blaize, so couldn't tell if Blaize was doing anything or not, until suddenly an image appeared in Nixie's mind.

Nixie jumped and opened her eyes, jerking forward and breaking the connection between them. "Oh! Sorry."

Blaize looked at her flatly. "Nix! Concentrate. I'm not as good with Ajna as Manipura."

Nixie bit her lip. "Sorry. Really, I am. It was just a surprise."

"I didn't think I'd ever say this for real," Blaize said, "but if we don't work out what is happening, and why, and stop it, then it could truly be the end of the line for the energetics. I need you to concentrate."

Nixie's eyes widened. *Shit.* That kind of pressure was definitely not going to help her relax, which was when her best drawings came. Though Blaize had never had a tendency to exaggerate. Nixie flexed her drawing hand. This wasn't quite as fun. On the other hand, the sleepy feeling had been entirely chased away.

They settled back into position, and Nixie tried to focus. She did tend towards the distractible, it was true. But drawing was something she loved, and she wanted to help.

It took another minute or so, but the image appeared again, small at first, as if it was at the end of an out-of-focus telescope. Nixie concentrated. She could tell it was a male figure, but that was all so far.

The figure flickered, and slipped away again. Nixie took a breath to speak but Blaize said, in a tight voice, "Stay still."

Okay. Patience. Nixie did as she was told, and within a few more moments, the image was back. Blaize's fingers were digging into Nixie's shoulders, and it was clearly taking a great deal of effort on her part.

Nixie focused on the man as the image stabilized. *Hmmm.* Nice enough looking, she supposed, though nothing special. He was slender, but his shoulders were filled out, and his body was toned.

His chin was covered in stubble, but not the well manicured beard that her lover of this morning, Ben, had had, but more the sort of beard that suggested that the figure had a tendency to forget to shave. In fact, the man generally was sort of scruffy.

Under the stubble though, the guy had some killer cheekbones. Nixie studied the picture. Whoever he was, he was not making the best of himself. She looked at the image again, past the scruff and the bland clothes.

And then she raised her eyebrows, as the image wavered and shifted, and when it came back into focus, the pure, unadulterated carnality in the man's eyes had her gasping for breath. Suddenly his scruffy look had her panting.

"Woah," she muttered.

Blaize's hands squeezed down hard.

"I know, I know," responded Nixie. She hadn't moved, had she? She hadn't even opened her eyes.

The image shifted again, and his eyes changed. The sex had gone, and now his dark blue eyes held a deep sorrow, and the almost-hobo look was back.

She was confused. It was the same man in both images, and yet he was so different. It was as if there were two versions of him. In one, you'd pass him in the street without noticing him. He blended in, unless you caught his eyes and saw how sad he was. Something terrible had happened to this man, she was sure of it.

And then there was the other version. The version that smoldered and could stop traffic if he chose. But which was the real him? She knew which she preferred.

For now, she was ready to start drawing. She opened her eyes slowly, wondering if she'd still be able to see the image at the same time, but it disappeared. *Oh well. That would have been too easy.*

Blaize kept her hands in position on Nixie's shoulders, and all Nixie needed to do was close her eyes to remind herself of the face as she drew. She picked up the pencil and sketch pad and began.

She first sketched out the man's proportions with faint pencil marks. She blocked out the head, his torso and the top of his legs, and then his upper arms. No detail yet, just the outline of his shape, and then the lower legs and lower arms. She would close her eyes every ten to twenty seconds to catch another glance.

She nibbled on the end of her pencil, considering. She'd leave the clothes for later. The face was the important thing as they were trying to identify the figures first off, but they'd discussed it being worth doing the whole scene in case there might be other clues the wider group could piece together. Which version would she draw? She closed her eyes for a longer look.

Nixie was all business now. She concentrated, seeing the detail, the lines on his face, the mixed colors in his hair, the angles and planes of his face.

But the image was like a flipping coin, changing every handful of seconds. Sexy. Sad. Sexy. Sad.

Which version?

She went for sexy.

Well, duh.

She sketched for thirty minutes, Blaize's hands on her shoulders the entire time, the image ready and accessible for Nixie whenever she shut her eyes. After that time, Tierra, who had moved to the table to work on her laptop, intervened. "I think you should take a break."

A faint crease appeared between Blaize's eyes. "Why?"

Tierra smothered a smile. "Because you have smudges under your eyes that weren't there an hour ago, and because I think Nixie has something for us."

Nixie nodded absently, gazing down at the paper in front of her. She had scratched away with the pencil until she was satisfied that the sketch pad held a reasonable representation of the man from the image.

She wasn't sure going for the sexy version of the man had been the right decision. Because she couldn't stop staring at him. He wasn't at all her normal type – even the sexy version seemed much more serious than she was usually drawn to – but there was something magnetic about him. He had depth, she decided. As if she could spend time with him, and never be bored. And Nixie was quite often bored. She had a need for variety and for new experiences, and that went double for relationships. This man seemed like someone who might be both interesting, and also interested in sticking around for something in addition to the incredible sex she could provide.

"So?" said Blaize.

"Hmm?" said Nixie, her eyes not moving.

Blaize put out a foot and gave Nixie's leg a shove. Nixie looked up to see Tierra and Blaize both looking at her.

"Oh. Sorry." Nixie handed the pad to Blaize, a little reluctantly.

Blaize took it. Her hair was sweaty, and her breath came a little quicker than normal, as if she'd run a hard race. "That looks pretty good. Well done, Nix. Now we need to distribute it to our friends and see if anyone knows who it is."

Tierra got up and stood behind Blaize, and she gasped. "We don't need to. I know him. It's Jeb. Jebediah Gale. He was my Maven for Anahata, a century or two ago."

Tierra craned her neck over Blaize's shoulder to get a closer look. "I saw him a couple of weeks ago – he helped us with finding Ai's parents. But there's something odd about the drawing. Can I see?"

Blaize handed the pad up to her, and Tierra took it out of the shade of the balcony into the sun. "Huh. That's odd."

"What?" said Nixie. There was nothing wrong with her sketch, she was confident. It looked like the guy in the image. The not-miserable version, anyway.

"Well…" Tierra hesitated. "It looks like Jeb used to look, when he was my Maven, and before World War II."

"World War II?" said Blaize. "Why? What happened to him?"

"The details don't matter. But what does matter is that after the war, he sequestered himself in Anahata Guild, and he hasn't been out of there since."

Nixie drew in a breath, shocked. "Never? How can he live like that?"

"There's more. Jeb's auxiliary energy is Svadisthana."

"Well that makes sense," said Nixie. "I mean, look at him. He's not that attractive, but he's very, very sexy."

Blaize tipped her head to the side. "I guess."

Nixie poked her in the leg. "You're distracted. Cuinn's all you can think about. You don't count."

"Anyway," said Tierra. "After the War, for various reasons, he decided that he would ignore his auxiliary energy. Bind it."

Blaize and Nixie's heads snapped round at that.

"What?" said Nixie. "What does that mean?"

"He swore off relationships, and all that comes with them," said Tierra.

Nixie's mouth fell open. *Wait, what?!* Surely Tierra didn't mean what Nixie thought she meant. "Everything?"

"Uh huh," Tierra said. "Everything."

Nixie goggled. Enforced celibacy was hard for anyone. Harder still on an energetic, and harder again on a man, surely. In fact, if she'd had to say, she'd have considered it physically impossible for Svadisthana energetics. Especially male ones.

So, wow. She had to ask. "What kind of guy doesn't have sex?"

After a restless night Jeb was up early. He needed to clean his workspace as quickly as possible so rumors didn't spread. In a Guild, especially within the teaching areas, strange things often happened, but blood-spattered walls weren't typical of the Anahata Guild. He'd cancelled his first few lessons, but it was still possible for people to drop by unannounced.

His body felt weak, but under his control again. Whatever Aiko had done had bound the Svadisthana energy again, thank Source. *But would it last?*

He had already borrowed a new, simpler table from the Guild's stores before he opened the door to his study. He'd get a replacement desk later. He shuffled the table inside the room, then rubbed a hand over the back of his neck as he looked around. It was worse than he'd remembered. The floor was covered in a fine mist of blood, and the wild energy that had escaped before he had controlled it had knocked things off the wall.

While he lectured in the larger halls, he spent much of his time in these rooms, and seeing his personal space like this was almost physically painful. His gaze caught on the broken wooden box that had fallen from the shelf, and the breath went out of him in a whoosh, his stomach clenching. He stepped over the debris and squatted next to it. Cards and photos had fallen out in a heap. This cedar wood container was one of the most precious things in the office to him, filled with the photos and notes from people he had helped since his actions in World War II had caused so much devastation. The contents didn't balance out his actions, but it soothed him a little. He gently scooped up the papers and laid them back inside the box, putting the box back where it belonged. He rested a hand on it for a moment, his head bowed, then swallowed and went into his attached bathroom to fill the bucket he'd swiped – along with a mop and cloths - from a cleaning supplies cupboard on the way to his study. He began to clean.

He'd tried so hard to make the right choices. To not make any further mistakes, or bad decisions. It seemed, however, from the havoc he'd caused in his study, he was no longer able to do even that right. He felt powerless.

By mid-morning, he felt that the room was decent enough. He cleaned the older, broken desk, and got help from a passing student to take it to the garbage room. A couple of hours later, showered and in fresh clothes, he decided to go into the grounds of the Guild for some air.

Jeb was used to the pollution and the intense heat, over 100°F at this time of year. He hadn't left the grounds since he'd come here after the war to recover from his energetic and physical wounds.

He walked to one of his favorite places in the grounds, a shady garden with wrought-iron benches, surrounded by palm trees.

He sat on one of the benches, rested his elbows on his knees, and propped his face in his hands, deep in thought. *How can I prevent last night from happening again?*

There was a buzz from his pocket, and his phone rang. He straightened, and took the phone out. Seeing it was Tierra, he answered it. After exchanging greetings, Jeb frowned. Something was off. "What's up?"

There was a beat or two of silence before Tierra spoke. "I'm so sorry to share this with you Jeb, but Cuinn's seen you in the prophecy. You're one of the twelve energetics involved."

Jeb stood up in one swift movement, the phone clutched to his ear. *That's ridiculous.* "He's wrong. He's never met me, how would he know?"

"He and Blaize have shared the images, and Blaize was able to project it into her cousin Nixie's mind. Nixie's an artist, and she drew you."

He was shaking his head over and over, despite the fact she couldn't see him. The implications of what she was saying, if it was true, were not something he was prepared for. "Tell me exactly what she drew."

"Your figure, with detail on the face. You're one of the twelve. There's no doubt. You're standing along with the rest of us."

He didn't want to ask the next question, but he had to. "Am I on my own?"

If he was in a romantic relationship – a full, true relationship, with love, sex and all the things those entailed – then there would be no way for him to keep his Svadisthana bound any more.

"It's hard to tell. Obviously Blaize and Cuinn have come together as a couple, as have Fintan and I. But we don't know that all twelve of those we can see are romantically linked. We still have several blurred figures, though we do know that there are six men and six women."

Something tight loosened around Jeb's chest. "There's been no clear indicator that the prophecy needs six couples?"

"No. It's a possibility, but there's nothing to say it has to be like that."

Well, that's something. Although being involved was bad enough. Jeb was happy to support Tierra and her friends, but he wouldn't – couldn't – leave the Guild. This was the safest place for him to be. He probed further. "Are there any clues about the physical location?"

"Not that we can work out so far," Tierra answered. She understood what he was asking. "And it might not even be that we need to be in the same place as a group. The image might be a metaphor for us working together."

The band around his chest loosened further and he took a deep breath. "Okay. I'll have to see what I can contribute from here. Which I would do anyway, you know that."

"I know," Tierra said, her voice soft. "Though when you feel ready, we'll help you acclimatize back into the world. If you need it."

"I'm not –" he stopped, realizing how sharp his voice sounded. He tried again, matching her tone. "I'm not leaving the Guild. I need to be here, where Anahata is strongest, and I can keep my other energy under control."

Although it wasn't, was it? He shook that thought off, and began walking back to his room. He had a meeting with a student scheduled, and he should prepare. "Is there anything else I should know? Or anything I can do to help?"

"No," said Tierra. "We'll let you know if you can. Thank you."

They ended the call.

What did it all mean?

He'd aided Tierra and Fintan when they had come to the Guild for information on a teenage orphan they'd come across as part of the search for answers around the prophecy, and they had also asked him to identify the murder victim. The latter, especially, had taken it out of him, as he'd had to use his telemetry on a photo of a dead girl, and from that photo he'd re-lived her death, a traumatic and draining event. But it had been something he could do. And he'd continue to do whatever he could to help, of course.

But there were two things that the prophecy could ask of him that he could never do.

Form a romantic and sexual relationship, and leave the Guild's grounds.

And if they needed him to do that?

They'd already failed.

Elrian gripped the shoulders of the thin young man at his feet, and dug his fingers into the scarce flesh there.

The bland surroundings of the guest bedroom they were in were an odd contrast to what he was about to do. It had the benefit of isolation, however. The Seattle safe house was out in the lush, cool forest that surrounded the city. Orderly and clean, this house wasn't as nice a place as he had had in Vancouver, the place he had had to abandon when his son's friends found it. Elrian preferred more luxurious quarters. But it would do. After Tierra's mysterious escape from his main home, and the work he'd had to do to remove the incident from Cassidy's memory, he'd decided not to bring subjects there any more. He was reluctant to spend too much time in Vancouver.

Not that it was easy to find leeching candidates. There were never that many energetics in an area, and the American Pacific Northwest was no different. He tried to take runaways, or other energetics who wouldn't be missed, and the information he'd been getting from his lover had helped with that. Energetics were such a clannish race that they tended to have strong family ties and cluster together.

He had had to send Dagon, one of his enforcers, all the way to Portland to capture the youth. Aeros, he was called. White, with untidy, shoulder-length hair and nondescript blue eyes, he wasn't especially remarkable in any way as far as Elrian knew. A loner by nature, the young man's energetic family was in New York, and he hadn't been in Portland long enough to establish a routine and friends who might miss him.

He was perfect.

Dagon stood to the side, patient and motionless. Elrian let Dagon take energy sometimes, but his enforcer was more interested in the captives for other reasons. Elrian didn't ask – as long as Dagon didn't damage their energy too much, Elrian didn't care what he did with their physical bodies. It tarnished their energy a fraction if Dagon played with them too close to Elrian's ritual, but it was worth it as payment for loyalty.

Sitting on the edge of the bed, Elrian centered himself and closed his eyes, preparing himself to siphon the other man's energy. Weak and already drained, Aeros struggled momentarily in place on the floor, fear widening his eyes. He was bound and gagged, and there was nothing he could do about what was going to happen. By now Elrian had come to enjoy the fear a little. What had started as a practical exercise had become delicious in more than one way.

The energy of another energetic helped Elrian overcome some health issues he'd been experiencing. Yes, it was a forbidden use of energy, but only fools obeyed the rules when there was power and bounty there for the taking.

Leeching wasn't all he wanted from his victims. He needed them so that he could create remnant stones. Without these, he wasn't going to be able to ensure that the prophecy went his way.

He gritted his teeth as he remembered how he'd had both Ai and Tierra in his hands, and both had slipped through his fingers. He could have leeched from one or even both of them, and their deaths could have provided the basis of a remnant stone each, if he'd had sufficient strength and control. Now, this youth was the only victim they currently held.

However, his latest prophecy dream had indicated that one of the energetics on the opposing side was sick, and there was a strong possibility that they would die. He bared his teeth. That might be enough, but now there were two established couples, Elrian was concerned the death of only one of them might not be enough.

At some point soon he was going to need to invest some serious time and effort into seeking prophecy in the dreamscape. There were so many gaps in what he could see ahead. A new energetic couple would be likely to meet soon. He still had four chances left to ensure things came true in the way he wished, but he was not happy that he'd already missed two opportunities.

In the meantime, he had dropped his focus on the twelve and was concentrating on himself. He'd finally admitted to himself that he needed the energy that leeching provided. Not as badly, perhaps, as his former Adherent, Indigo, had needed the energy. He hadn't sunk that low. He shuddered. She'd practically been a junkie.

He reached inside Aeros's body, delicately. Today he wanted to draw from the boy's Ajna, to replenish Elrian's own store, but eventually he might use up Aeros's auxiliary energy, his Vishudha, to create a remnant stone. Elrian also needed to replenish the remnant stone ring he wore, that had been a gift, and worked as an emergency back up external store for energy.

He had to be careful, and take things more slowly. Siphon the boy's energy, and keep him alive as long as possible, unlike the last victim whom Elrian had killed accidentally by taking too much, too fast. That had drawn attention he hadn't wanted, the Guilds' top people hearing about it, not only those ranged against him in the prophecy. It couldn't happen again.

He tried to keep his own consumption limited, sipping at the energy of those he captured like fine wine, until he was ready to use their death for remnant stones. He also gifted his people, like Indigo and his bodyguards, with energy in this way, but that meant more energy was needed.

Perhaps it had been best that Indigo had been killed by Blaize. Indigo had became a little peculiar at the end, and he had needed to feed her a great deal of energy. He may have pushed her too far. He was glad he was stronger and wouldn't have that issue. Her own weaknesses led to her demise.

He took in a breath and tugged on the incandescent streams of energy that he could see in his mind's eye. The boy's struggles were irrelevant now.

Elrian clamped down and tore the energy out of him.

Aeros' eyes bulged as he tried to cry out, but the cotton scarf stuffed in his mouth prevented him from making too much noise. Not that there was anyone to hear.

Elrian barely registered the youth's muffled screams.

CHAPTER

4

Nixie had been glad to help Blaize, but it had soon been time for the new arrivals to crash. The next day, Tierra had declared they should start the day with some relaxation, so they'd all gone down to the beach. Tierra was so friendly everyone wanted to please her.

Nixie's friends had opted to lie on the sand, though they approached it in different ways. Blaize, unselfconscious about her body, stripped off to a skimpy bikini, and basked in what was left of the day's sun. Tierra had said she was tired, and had decided that lying on a towel was preferable to any kind of exercise in the sea, and Ai had joined Tierra on the beach, unwilling, it seemed, to be separated from her for the moment.

"It's a lot hotter than the last beach I lay on," Tierra said. "That was on Vancouver Island, Canada, with my friend Cara, and the best you could say for the weather that day was…almost warm. We definitely didn't go in the water."

She smiled, though she seemed subdued.

Nixie loved water. Her energy of Svadisthana was linked with that element, in the same way as Blaize's Manipura was linked with fire, and Nixie adored the peace of being underwater. She was a PADI certified Divemaster – easy enough to achieve on the islands – and had also done a lot of free-diving.

She floated on the surface of the sea, and bobbed up and down with each wave, trying to quell the disquiet that she felt. While Tierra had called this Jebediah guy, Blaize had filled Nixie in on all that had happened since she'd gone to start her training in Vancouver in the last few months. Not the details about Cuinn – well, okay, some of those – but details about how much danger Blaize and her new friends had been in. Danger which apparently was now coming for Nixie.

Nixie didn't take life too seriously. She was likely to live for a long time, and didn't have Blaize's ingrained sense of duty and responsibility, which probably came from the tragic start Blaize had in life when her father, Aden, killed her mother, Aria.

Nixie wanted to enjoy life. What was the point of it otherwise? And while she searched for her perfect mate, she wanted to have fun.

This situation did not seem like fun.

A hand pressed on her shoulder, and Nixie slipped under the water and came up spluttering. Blaize floated in front of her, smirking. They had a definite tendency to regress to a younger age when there was any chance of playing a joke on the other. Nixie was usually more of a brat though, naturally taking the younger sister role in their relationship over the years.

Nixie swiped her hands over her hair to stop the water flooding her eyes.

They chatted for a while, treading water and luxuriating in the sun. Blaize was happy to tell Nixie all about Cuinn and their relationship, which sounded sexy and intense. Nixie loved it.

"How's Cuinn doing given Tierra's discovery that it was his father behind the attack on you, and Tierra's kidnapping?" Nixie asked. She couldn't imagine. She knew she was lucky to be so close to her parents.

Blaize's mouth twisted. "Not great. He doesn't like to talk about it. They were estranged a long time ago, but I can see it still hurts him."

That seemed eminently reasonable to Nixie. She couldn't imagine what pain would drive someone to go to the lengths Elrian, Cuinn's father, was going to. She nodded, then tilted her head. "Why is he doing this? Elrian?"

"We don't know," Blaize said. "Power, we think. But we don't know how, exactly."

"Tierra seems quiet. Is she always like this? Or is it part of what she went through?" Nixie asked. Tierra had been taken by Elrian, held captive, then released by a mysterious woman called Cassidy in Elrian's household, who had wiped Tierra's memory of where the location was.

Blaize fingered her bracelet. "She's not great. She puts on a brave face, but she's been having headaches, and I've caught her staring into space several times. She's usually more grounded. Fintan and Ai have helped. Fintan keeps an eye on her, and given his role as a Warrior, he knows a lot about dealing with the aftermath of trauma. Ai gives her someone to look after."

Fintan's dominant energy was Manipura, and he'd been a Warrior for a hundred years, perhaps more. His current role was as a troubleshooter, someone sent in to solve problems that might also need some muscle, or to capture more unusual or difficult Rogues when he might also take a team with him. Nixie liked him. He rarely took life took seriously, and enjoyed jokes and pranks.

She and Blaize swam in silence for a while. It felt like a lot. So much had happened in a short time. But what could Nixie contribute?

"What's up?" Blaize said. She was well attuned to Nixie's thoughts. This was awkward, though. How did you gracefully back out of a potentially world-changing prophecy?

"I'm not a Warrior," Nixie blurted. Alright. Less on the graceful side, so far. She kicked her legs in agitation, and circled Blaize, who followed her with her gaze.

"Okay? I mean, I'm aware," Blaize said. "Why are you telling me this now?"

"This prophecy. Are you sure you saw me?"

Blaize frowned. "Of course I'm sure. You're my best friend, and hardly someone I'm going to mistake for someone else. I'll show you, if you want. Once we've identified a few more of the unknown figures, we can do you. We should get everyone on paper in case there are clues in the visions that Cuinn or I have missed."

"I'm not sure why I would be involved. I don't have special skills, like you or the others." Nixie ducked her head under the water to cool down, then broke the surface.

"You can fight well enough when you can be bothered," Blaize pointed out. She lay back in the water, floating gently. "Or when you're not distracted by the beauty of an ant on a dead leaf or something."

"If Mum and you weren't Warriors and hadn't made me practice with you, I wouldn't have gone anywhere near it." Nixie was too agitated to relax and float. She wasn't an intellectual, a fighter, or even a healer. She was an artist. And how could that help?

"The prophecy seems to want all kinds of skills and energies, not simply fighting," Blaize shrugged, water cascading over her pale shoulders as she moved them in and out of the water.

"It's hard to see how being an artist is going to prevent the end of the world," Nixie said.

Nixie had studied art rather than academic subjects, and her only ambition was to be happy, and to find love. Her motto in life was 'go with the flow,' and she liked it when she was able to do that. Rules, structure, boundaries – none of these excited her.

She frowned, and brought her legs into her chest in the water so she could execute a gentle forward roll, turning in the water. She popped up for a breath, and then dived back down into the underwater silence.

When she came up again for air, Blaize was still floating in the same place. She cocked her head and looked at Nixie.

"What?"

"You're part of this," Blaize said. "It's not something you can pretend isn't happening. It's too dangerous to ignore."

Nixie pressed her lips together, and tried not to sound as surly as she felt. "Sure. Maybe I'm the light relief."

Nixie was better at cheering people up than serious stuff.

"I love you, Nix, you know that, but maybe, just maybe, it's time to grow up a little." Blaize's tone was gentle, but she had fixed Nixie with a look that said arguing was pointless. This certainty was typical of Blaize. It had got Nixie – a follower more than a leader at the best of times – into trouble on numerous occasions when they were younger.

Nixie was cut by Blaize's words. Nixie was an adult. She made an income through her graphic art, and she was helping with the prophecy.

"I don't think there's anything wrong with living lightly. With not getting too attached to things. With fun." Nixie thought about the image on the sketch pad, which wouldn't leave her alone.

"That guy I drew today, seemed like he could do with cheering up." Nixie wrinkled her nose. "Imagine deciding not to have sex. Or relationships."

"Yeah, okay. I mean, it's not a path I'd take, and you wouldn't last more than ten minutes. He must have good reasons, though. Maybe his Svadisthana wasn't that strong to begin with?" Blaize didn't sound convinced.

Nixie shuddered. It was almost unthinkable for any energetic, a race much more relaxed about sex than your average human. But for someone with Svadisthana energy to decide that was unheard of. What did he do with it all?

Maybe she could help him with that too. She grinned. She wasn't sure about the serious version of this Jebediah, but if he was the sexy version, she could definitely help him with his sexual energy.

"Nixie! I know what you're thinking," Blaize said, laughing. "He's a real person, who obviously has issues. Sex isn't the answer to everything, you know."

Nixie blew out a breath and mock-pouted. "I don't know what you mean."

To be fair, for most Svadisthana energetics sex *was* the answer to many things. She scrunched her nose up. It was one of the key ways they contributed to the balance. When energetics used their magic, they brought energy into the world from the ether, energy that helped the world function and was part of their race's duty for Source.

"Race you back!" Nixie kicked her legs, and tore off through the water, strong strokes of her arms bringing her back inland. Blaize groaned but launched into the waves behind her.

Nixie was ready to start drawing again. But in the meantime, she'd enjoy being, um, creative with her mental vision of Jebediah, daydreaming about how she might persuade him to own his sexual energy once again.

Now that might be an adventure she could get on board with.

Nixie hit the beach a few seconds ahead of Blaize, and they staggered over to their towels, laughing and dancing over the hot sand so their feet didn't burn. Nixie was ahead, but stopped short at the sight of Tierra, head in her hands, eyes closed. She'd moved to the shade of a tree.

Ai hovered protectively, and glared at Blaize and Nixie. "Tierra's not well. She needs help."

"What's up?" Blaize asked.

Tierra shook her head vigorously, then grimaced. "It's fine. I need more sleep, that's all. I'll skip lunch and head back to the house for a rest."

"What's wrong?" Nixie said.

"I'm not sure. I feel exhausted, and achy." Tierra shrugged. "It's probably jet lag. I haven't done much travel outside Canada in the last few decades. My body's adjusting to being away so much recently."

Blaize looked unconvinced. "You never complain about your health. And you're really pale."

36

"It's time for us to go in, anyway," Nixie said. "We can eat, then Blaize, you and I can have another session and Ai can tell us if Tierra needs us."

Ai nodded. "Alright."

"Let's see how you feel after some rest. It's unusual enough that you might need to see a healer if it continues," Blaize said.

Tierra looked rebellious, but given the slow way that she got to her feet as they packed up, Nixie thought she probably didn't mind that much. Nixie didn't know Tierra that well, but she liked her. Tierra was a kind person, with a tendency to put others first.

Nixie felt a stab of guilt. She didn't always remember to put others first. She meant to, she really did, but sometimes she got distracted. She'd make plans with friends or family, then go off for the day and paint, and lose track of the time. Her auxiliary energy, Vishudha was partly the cause. It was the energy that linked to the element of space, and its energetics tended to be abstract and not great with time – time was a relative construct after all. Nixie's Vishudha wasn't strong, and she hadn't started her training in it yet, but it was definitely there. She tried, she really did, she was just so distractible. A couple of weeks ago she'd gone to pick her mother herbs, telling her parents she was popping out for ten minutes, and hadn't returned for five hours, having gotten caught up in the charm of a flower she'd seen and wanted to capture in her sketch pad. There were so many objects of beauty in the world. She wanted to encapsulate them all in her art.

Nixie trailed after the others up the beach. She'd admit, she was worried about the danger they all seemed to be in. Physical danger was fairly alien to her. She'd have to refresh herself on updating her bungalow wards. Nixie hadn't done that for a while. She grimaced. She'd rather be drawing.

Tierra headed back while the others stopped for a quick late lunch. Blaize led the conversation over their food, grilling Ai about what she had read so far in the energetic texts Tierra had set her. The girl had a quick mind, Nixie would admit. And despite the fact she seemed to be playing games on her device the whole time, somehow she was also learning about her new world.

Sated, they walked the rest of the way home. When they reached the cluster of houses, Ai went in one direction to sit with Tierra, while Blaize and Nixie headed back to Nixie's place. Nixie slipped her arm through Blaize's.

"I missed this," she said. And she had. Blaize had been a constant presence in Nixie's life, and even when they'd been far away from each other, at university, or when Blaize was working in a different country, they'd emailed or texted pretty much every day.

But since Blaize had left for Canada and met Cuinn, things had changed. Blaize hadn't been in touch as much, and Nixie had missed hearing about the small things in her day. Nixie was glad Blaize had met Cuinn, but she wished it hadn't impacted her relationship with Blaize. Nixie's relationships had never come between her and her friends and family.

Blaize squeezed her arm back. "It's good to be home, Nix."

Nixie felt lighter as they got to her balcony. Blaize's words earlier had been hard to hear – Nixie was used to being the little sister bossed around by Blaize, but her criticism had gone further than that. Nixie knew it was because she cared, though, and usually Blaize's words didn't cut quite as deeply. But Blaize had had a lot on, after all. Not just the romance, but the prophecy, and Blaize's own part in it. It was understandable.

They got into position on the balcony, both sitting on the floor cross-legged this time. Nixie picked up her sketch pad and pencil again, ready. Instead of turning to a fresh page, she turned back to the picture of Jebediah. "Would it be possible to see the image of Jebediah again? I want to fill in more detail."

Blaize put a hand on one hip. "Why? We know who he is. We can move onto the next person."

"I think there's more in there. Don't be so task-focused." Nixie poked Blaize in the stomach. "It's good practice for both of us. We can start on a new figure tomorrow when you've had some sleep."

It was good practice. But she also wanted to make sure she'd got all the details of Jebediah down first. There was something about him, something that she was missing.

And she wanted to try drawing the sad side of him. Just his face. She'd start with the eyes. Those sorrowful, spellbinding, midnight blue eyes.

"We have another eleven to do," Blaize said.

"Please? In case there's a detail I've missed." Nixie flicked to a new page, ready to capture the darker side of the man.

Blaize shook her head and then, at Nixie's pleading look, reluctantly relented. "Fine."

They began the process, and after a minute or so, Blaize was able to project the image of the man back into Nixie's mind.

Nixie shivered as she took in the sad version of Jebediah. She opened her eyes, and her pencil flew across the pad. Time rushed past as she and Blaize worked together, until eventually Nixie came out of her creative trance enough to notice that Blaize was shaking.

"Oh!" Nixie's hand shot to her mouth and she dropped the pad on the floor. "I'm so sorry."

Blaize shook her head, though the fine trembles continued. "I'm fine. Are you done?"

Blaize wasn't fine. She was exhausted. Nixie had a hollow feeling in the pit of her stomach as she realized that without Tierra to keep a check on things, Nixie had pushed Blaize too far.

"Yes, I'm done. Go inside and wash up. Do you want food before you sleep?

Blaize shook her head.

"Okay. Then get ready for bed. Let me clear up here. I'll be right behind you," Nixie said.

Blaize staggered to her feet and went inside.

Nixie bit her lip and stared after her. *Shit.* That's why she needed someone like Tierra as a spotter. Nixie adored Blaize, but Nixie got lost in the flow sometimes. And she was doing this for Blaize. Being focused was her way of doing a good job for her cousin.

She sighed, and looked back down at the pad in front of her. Jebediah was complex, that's for sure. On the one hand, the only thing that was different about this version of him was the eyes. But he seemed like another man. Abject. Despairing almost. *What's his story?* She'd like to ask him.

She flicked back to the first page, and traced a finger over the picture with the tip of her forefinger, then stopped abruptly. It wasn't only the eyes that were different.

Huh. I don't remember drawing those.

The first version of the man had two details that didn't appear in the version she'd drawn most recently. In the first – the sexy – version, Jebediah had a plaited bracelet on his right wrist, and in the far distance of the picture, there was a bird of some sort freewheeling across the sky.

She jumped up and ran into the house. "Blaize!"

Blaize came out of the bathroom in a hurry, her toothbrush still in her mouth. "What? What's happened?"

Nixie showed her the two pictures, excited. "Look!"

Blaize looked at them, one at a time, blankly.

"See?" Nixie said. "I saw two versions of him, like the two sides of a coin. Did you see him like that too?"

Blaize frowned. "No. What do you mean?"

"I saw a very, very sexy version of him, with the bracelet, and then the sadder version of him without."

"That's strange," Blaize said. "If I'm the one transmitting the image, how can you see something different?"

Nixie considered. "Artists often see things others don't. Just because you didn't see it doesn't mean it wasn't there all along."

Blaize's forehead creased even more. "That doesn't sound very logical."

"Does it have to be?" Nixie said. She paused for a moment. "The bracelet. The bird. What do they mean?"

"Huh. Well, it means that Jeb was probably wrong about him never having another relationship," Blaize said around the toothbrush, then held out her left hand to show Nixie a very similar plaited bracelet.

"What do you mean?" Nixie went to look.

"Hold on," Blaize mumbled round the toothbrush, and disappeared back into the bathroom. Nixie flopped onto the bed in Blaize's room, holding the pad above her head and looking up at it. She'd felt a twinge of – what? Something, anyway – at Blaize's words.

Was Blaize saying the man in the picture would look like this again? Sexy and sensual? Which of these pictures was the future, and which was the past? Or were they both possible futures?

Blaize came back into the room without the toothbrush. "Cuinn and I have paired bracelets, that are the colors of both our Chakras plus white for Source. So do Tierra and Fintan. We don't know why they appear, or what they do, but they are gifts from Source. Cuinn thinks there are powers in them we need to unlock somehow. Either way, they have indicated a romantic relationship so far. Everyone in the vision is wearing them, though they're blurry enough we can't tell whose matches whose."

Nixie rubbed at her left wrist. So she had a bracelet in the vision too? Did that mean that her soulmate was one of the men in the vision? Her chest felt tight at the idea. She suddenly had a lot of questions. She needed to see the vision of herself, and soon.

Before she could ask more, the thud of someone running up the wooden outside stairs startled them both.

"Blaize!" It was Ai, and she sounded terrified. Blaize ran outside to meet her, Nixie hot on her heels, her stomach churning.

"What's the matter?" Blaize spoke quickly, but she was in control. She was good in a crisis. Much better than Nixie, who wanted to go and hide under a blanket.

"There's something the matter with Tierra. She's having some kind of fit." Ai ran back down the stairs, beckoning them, and they all flew across the scrub between the bungalows.

"What were her other symptoms?" Blaize demanded. Then she tossed over her shoulder "Nixie, are there any healers on the island?"

"I don't think so," Nixie stuttered. "I can call people and check."

"Do it."

Nixie pulled out her cell and rang round the two or three other energetics on the island. There was no healer visiting any of them, and a human doctor would bring the risk of exposure, and would be very unlikely to be able to help if it was an energetic illness, which it almost certainly was. Energetics rarely got human illnesses — from colds to STIs, they were resilient to most diseases and infections.

Blaize had disappeared into Tierra's bungalow, and as Nixie followed her, she gasped at how ill Tierra appeared. She was unconscious, her breath coming in heaves. Sweat dripped off her. Blaize sat on the bed next to her, holding her hand and talking to her, but Tierra wasn't stirring.

Blaize looked up, swiping her free hand across her forehead. "She's stopped fitting, but there's something seriously wrong."

Nixie felt helpless. What could she add in this situation? Poor Tierra. She looked awful, her usually brown skin pale and clammy-looking. She'd like nothing better than to flee, but she could never leave Blaize alone to deal with this. Tierra, too. Nixie would do what she could.

Blaize's hand clenched into a fist, and Nixie realized Blaize felt as impotent as Nixie. Blaize was trained to fight her enemies, but this wasn't something she could fight with fists or feet.

Nixie stepped across to Blaize and put an arm round her waist.

"She's going downhill far too fast, and her vitals are thready. We need to call Fintan, and we need to get a healer. We don't have the abilities between us to diagnose her, let alone cure her." Blaize swallowed. "The only one of us that could have helped her? Is her."

5

"It worries me," the Guild's elderly Records Keeper, Feng, said. He'd been in the position since Jebediah had first visited the Guild hundreds of years before. Of Chinese ethnicity and slender, he was vague in everything apart from his work in the archives, where he was laser-focused. As he spent more time with records and books than people, it worked okay. "As a race, we're already stretched thin. A number of the Rehabilitation Centers have asked for more staff."

Jeb nodded grimly. The birth rate of the energetics was down, and the number of Rogues was increasing, putting strain on Rehabilitation Centres that looked after Rogue energetics and restored them to health. It was also a problem because too much dark energy upset the world's balance, the maintenance of which was part of the energetics' purpose from the Source.

Jeb had ample experience in the field dealing with Rogues, imbalanced energetics whose energy had twisted, and who had been taken over by the dark side of their emotions and Chakras. One such case had been where Jeb's journey into espionage had begun. An

Anahata's love energy had twisted to hate, and he had become so destructive that he had become involved in human affairs, finding ways to express his energy in horrific ways. Living in Constantinople during World War I, the energetic had denounced some Armenians who had been in hiding, leading to their deaths as part of the Armenian genocide. He'd been caught by Protectors in the Muladhara Guild, who had handed him to the Rehabilitation Center Jeb had been working in.

Jeb had been horrified at what the man had done, while it had also brought the frightful acts that were being committed by the humans to his attention. He'd asked if he could do more to help the efforts of the Guilds to end the War, and that had led to him becoming a spy.

Had he done any good in that role? He'd thought so, at the time. But the final consequences of his acts hadn't been worth the rest.

These days, Jeb advised Rehabilitation Centres on their Rogues remotely, as one of his many roles in the Guild. He was also in charge of the Maven-Adherent pairings, and of the education of Anahata energetics, lecturing and teaching in the classroom and one-to-one. As one of the senior members of the Guild, he supported Aiko on special projects. Today he was working on one such activity. Aiko, who oversaw all the Rehabilitation Centres, had noticed trends in the data from recent decades and asked Jeb to look into the issue. For all the energetics' sophistication and knowledge, there were some big gaps in what they knew. Like how Rogues came about in the first place. They knew what happened, but not why.

Jeb pulled the first of the pile of texts Feng had found for him towards himself. Moments later, Jebediah realized that Feng had continued to hover. "There is another option, if our research doesn't help."

Jeb cocked his head. "Yes?"

"You could go and see Damir." Feng flinched as he said it, as if expecting a negative reaction.

Jeb caught it, but while he was able to stop himself hitting the table with his forehead, he wasn't quite able to suppress a groan. "I'd really prefer not to do that if at all feasible. The man is impossible."

They called Damir 'the Hermit', as he'd chosen for the past several centuries to live in the Cairo Necropolis, the Egyptian city of the dead, away from other energetics.

The man was clear-sighted and knowledgeable, but was rarely prepared to share his wisdom and insights with those from the Guild. He preferred to live humbly in the slums with some of the poorest humans in the country, which would be admirable if the man wasn't such a huge pain in the ass.

"But he knows such a lot!" Feng exclaimed. The man really did love knowledge in all its forms. Despite living alone, he remained well-connected with other energetics, exchanging frequent letters with those he thought were worthy, and had a constant stream of rare texts delivered for scholarship purposes.

Jeb hadn't been out to deal with Damir since World War I, but the memory of the last time was seared into his mind. In exchange for the knowledge that Jeb had wanted, something about a specific way of purifying water to prevent the dysentery that plagued the armies of the allies, Damir had lectured him for an hour on why the Guild system was doomed, how energies were being used wrongly in the modern age. Damir had derided Jeb for his work helping the allies, suggesting that his efforts would be better placed helping the non-military personnel affected by the war, rather than their armies. At the time, Jeb had thought his own efforts critical, and considered himself, if not a hero, then something close.

That hubris had brought a tragic end to innocent lives.

Facing Damir now, nearly a hundred years later, would bring that up, and if the man knew anything about what Jeb had done – and damn the man, he always seemed to know everything – then it would reopen all Jeb's emotional wounds. Jeb didn't feel that would be good for anyone. The Hermit was better left alone.

"The man is graceless and purposely offensive, and is as likely to hold back the information out of spite," Jeb said. "We have plenty to read through. This library is second only to Ajna's in terms of the texts we have. There's bound to be information that can help us here."

Jeb's phone buzzed, and he wandered outside to take the call. It was Fintan. Jeb had liked him when Tierra had brought him to the Guild. He'd had a playful air despite the difficult topics they had consulted him on.

He wasn't playful now.

"Tierra's sick. She had a fit for no reason, and lost consciousness," said Fintan, at the end of the phone. "We need your help urgently. There's no healer on the island, and something's very wrong. You need to get on a plane, now."

Jeb felt cold. Tierra, sick. His mouth was dry as he forced out the next words, knowing Fintan would react badly. "I can't come. You know that. I don't leave the Guild. But I'll find someone experienced to come and examine her."

It wasn't even a question. After his recent loss of control, the Guild was the only safe place for him, and for anyone near him. But he would do whatever he could to help Tierra. She was as dear to him as a sister.

"How many Anahata energetics are as powerful as you?" retorted Fintan. "I don't want to waste time with someone else. We need you. You're one of the best. And we need you now."

Fintan's breath came quickly on the other end of the line. Jebediah rubbed a hand over his chin and closed his eyes.

"I can't leave the Guild. But I'll find you someone, I promise. I'm sorry."

"What would it take?" Fintan asked. "Name it."

"It wouldn't help. You don't understand what the consequences could be."

"You're right. I don't understand," said Fintan, flatly, the sound of an airport public address system in the background giving out the last call for a flight. "You know where we'll be if you change your mind."

Elrian shuddered. Energy came from the captive in a rush, and Elrian drank it in greedily, feeling his own stores replenish. The energy circled through his body, and with some effort of will, he released the boy's head. He mustn't take too much. He needed to save the kill for when they were making a new remnant stone, a process which took great effort and preparation. The youth slumped to the floor, tears leaking from his eyes.

Pathetic.

Elrian wiped his hands on a pristine handkerchief from his pocket, and pointed at the boy. He addressed Dagon. "Clean him up and put him back."

A hint of a smile appeared on Dagon's face. "Sir."

"Don't damage him."

"Of course." Dagon made a little bow. Elrian turned away, absentmindedly smoothing a crease from his pressed white shirt sleeve. He went into the room he used as a study here in Seattle. He settled into an armchair, and decided to use the energy he'd gained to dreamwalk.

Like his do-gooder estranged son Cuinn, Elrian was Ajna-Muladhara, and was able to dreamwalk in the ether to gather and interpret prophecy.

Elrian himself had been senior in the Guild for much of his long life, until he'd gone off the radar after his wife, Cuinn's mother, had been killed in World War II.

That death had confirmed in him a hatred of humans, and also been the last nail in the coffin in his relationship with his son. The son that had encouraged his mother to help the weak humans, using her gifts in a hospital – a hospital that was bombed, so his beloved wife died along with the useless humans she was trying to heal.

His lips tightened as he remembered. But now was not the time for that. He lay back in the chair and put his feet up on a stool. He took several breaths and closed his eyes.

He went through the usual relaxation process fast, and in a short while he was in his Haven, his personal safe place in the ether, or the dreamscape.

Elrian had updated his Haven several times over the years. These days it was a slick and modern monolith of concrete, glass and steel. He didn't need all twenty floors; only the top two were built out, the rest empty space.

His work space was on the nineteenth floor, and his living space was on the twentieth, where he also had an outdoor area with gardens. The Haven, with its manmade-looking exterior, was in part a show of power – not many Muladhara energetics would enjoy being so high up, without access to earth, even in the dreamscape. But Elrian wasn't a coward. The dreamscape was a place he could make and remake around him. He influenced it, not the other way round.

He took the lift down to the ground floor and walked out of the glass doors. His Haven extended far into the distance. But now he needed to hunt.

He drew on the energy of the dreamscape, created a bow and arrow, and jogged into the forest. When he was surrounded by trees, he paused. He walked forward a few paces, then stopped.

He wanted the rabbits he was hunting to hear him, and be startled from the ground and bolt. They weren't real, exactly. They were parts of the wild ether, drawn into his dreamscape by his desire and shaped by his requirements. A way of seeking prophecy.

He walked a few more paces, paused. He looked closely at the ground for signs of movement, or the telltale glisten of eyes.

He stalked through the forest, pacing, pausing, pacing, pausing. Watching.

He enjoyed the hunt. The knowledge that there was a creature out there who would soon meet their end through his actions. But not through the ease of a gun. No.

There was a rustle off to his right, and he turned his head silently. There.

He raised his bow and arrow, and drew his arm back slowly. If the rabbit bolted, he'd probably miss it. They were fast.

He could see the dark glint as he loosed the arrow, and the rabbit, catching the sound, streaked away. But not fast enough. The arrow caught it in the hindquarters, and the rabbit faltered and dropped to the ground, screaming in pain.

When Elrian got to it, he picked it up by the ears, its pulse fluttering. It dangled in front of him, its belly heaving with panic and pain.

He wrung its neck.

It took him a few minutes to jog back to his building, rabbit in hand, and take the lift up to his workspace.

He was skilled in haruspicy, or the reading of animal entrails. There were other ways to discover prophecy in the dreamscape, but this was his current preferred method. Understanding the future demanded a sacrifice. He knew Cuinn, his ignorant son, preferred to go outside the safety of his Haven – building and lands – into the wild energy and gather prophecy shards himself. But why risk it?

There had been a time when this was Elrian's approach too, but no longer. Now he let prophecy come to him.

He put the rabbit on the clean, wide steel table he used for this kind of activity, and filled his lungs. He drew on the dreamscape, activating his Ajna energy. He relaxed his shoulders.

He took a sharp silver knife from a leather sheath, and raised it, pausing for a moment with the tool in his hand. Then in a smooth movement, he brought the knife down and slit the rabbit's belly, letting the entrails fall out onto the metal table.

He put his hands into the entrails, careful not to disturb the arrangement, closed his eyes, and opened himself to their message.

He saw images flicker across the inside of his head. Jebediah and the girl Nixie dancing around each other, with a strong sexual chemistry, but their personalities so different they had no way to connect. His lips flattened as he saw them with matching bracelets as part of the twelve who ranged against him.

He asked the entrails what he could do to change this image of the future. He saw the man and the woman naked, wrapped around each other. He was puzzled. Surely this was what he was trying to avoid?

But the image developed, and the orange of Svadisthana surrounded the couple, who writhed and moaned, their bodies pressed tightly together. But the energy grew and grew, feeding on the sexual activity of the couple, and feeding it in turn.

The moans changed in tone from sexual to anguished, and a huge burst of sexual energy was unleashed. The female slumped in the male's arms, her heart stopped.

And Elrian understood what he needed to do. Instead of splitting this couple up, as he had tried with the others, he needed to encourage them to be together. He needed the death of two energetics, the entrails told him, but it was achievable. Jeb's attempts to dam his auxiliary energy – a stupid thing to do – would create a pressure that his growing attraction to the girl would shatter when he finally gave in to the attraction, destroying her in the process.

Elrian smirked, well pleased.

Because the death of another innocent would finally devastate Jebediah's spirit, and ultimately, Jebediah would destroy himself.

6

Nixie sat on the floor, head in her hands, next to Tierra's unresponsive body. It had been a long twenty four hours for them all. She'd tried to help where she could, but she couldn't offer much. They hadn't had time to invest in sketching more of the twelve figures when Tierra was in crisis.

Blaize had spent a lot of time on the phone to Cara, also involved in the prophecy and Tierra's friend. Given her role managing a Rehabilitation Centre, Cara was a good choice to consult about medical matters, but she hadn't been able to give them much more help than in dealing with some of the symptoms.

Fintan, Tierra's partner and a scruffy surfer-type, had arrived in the morning, and told them someone was coming to help. He'd tried to get the man that Nixie had drawn to come, but despite the fact he had been Tierra's Maven, and Nixie's picture had shown he was part of this, he'd refused to join them. Perhaps she'd been wrong about his kind eyes.

Nixie heard a car draw up, its headlights cutting through the night outside. With everyone else occupied, she headed out to meet the visiting healer. Sounds from one of the regular jungle parties drifted through the night, and Nixie peered through the trees to see if she could catch a glimpse. At around nine p.m. it was early for a party, and if it was anything like usual, it would only get louder from this point on. She bit her lip. For a moment, she longed to be there, to shed the responsibilities of the prophecy and Tierra's illness, and lose herself in the music. *No.* She brought herself back to reality and turned back to the man who had disembarked from the taxi.

The healer Jeb had sent was a delicate man, with the olive skin and dark eyes of Egyptian heritage, and he smiled warmly at Nixie, greeting her with an embrace despite the fact they'd never met.

"I'm Heka."

She greeted him with her name. "Do you want to wash up? Or have something to eat?"

"I'm fine. I'd like to see the patient," he said.

Nixie nodded and led him to Tierra's room, where Fintan sat vigil, and Ai was slumped against the wall in a corner, almost blending into the shadows due to the black clothes she always wore.

The healer came over to the bed and politely asked Fintan to step back. "I need a little space for diagnostic work."

Fintan scowled, but stepped back into the corner of the room with Nixie, who stayed to see what he would do.

There was a screech and the music outside was cranked up. It was as loud as if it was coming from a speaker inside the room.

Heka pressed his lips together but gently folded the sheet back from Tierra, who was wearing her panties and a T-shirt, and ran his hands slowly from her feet to her head.

Nixie didn't know that much about Anahata, but it was Fintan's auxiliary, though he didn't have enough skill with it to heal Tierra from such a serious illness himself.

"What's he doing?" she whispered to him.

"He's scanning her. Using his Anahata to probe inside her physical and her energetic bodies to see if he can find out what's wrong. An infection, a break or tear, her immune system, anything."

Nixie nodded and squinted, trying to see if she could spot any of the Anahata energy. She saw nothing. Heka was no inexperienced teenager, energy leaking everywhere.

The music swelled, techno beats drumming through the room. This must be a spontaneous gathering, because Nixie didn't know of any parties that were regularly held this close to her home.

"It could be a while," Fintan said quietly. "Jebediah told me this guy's very skilled, but he's going to need to do a thorough exam."

But moments later Heka stopped and said to them, "The noise is distracting. Could one of you see what's happening? If there's anything you can do? I'm going to need you to step outside anyway and give me some space as I'm getting traces of other energies as well as Tierra's own Muladhara and Anahata, and I think your energy might be mixing in with hers. I don't want the diagnosis confused."

"I'll go," Nixie tried to subdue her eagerness. She wanted to help, and she was a lot more suited to going and checking out a party than she was sitting in this room.

Nixie hated waiting. She wasn't a patient person. She tended to gratify her desires immediately. After all, why wait? You could be dead tomorrow.

Fintan looked mutinous, but nodded. "Alright. Nixie can go check the party. Ai and I will be with Blaize next door. Let us know when you're ready, Heka, or if you need anything."

Nixie slipped on her sandals at the bottom of the raised bungalow's wooden stairs, and headed towards the music. She had only gone a few hundred meters through the humid forest before she started to see blurred shapes writhing and twisting around each other. She got closer and could see they were dancers. A cornucopia of noise, sound and light assaulted her senses.

The revelers had set up a portable sound system and she could see fire dancing, hula hooping, and participants with fluorescent paint on their bodies and faces, a popular trend at the island parties. It gave the gathering a tribal, earthy feel, but the dancing was rhythmic and sexy, and her Svadisthana thrummed at the sight of so many bodies enjoying their sensuality.

The scene was the polar opposite of the serious, tense sickbed she'd left behind moments before. People twirled and spun in front of her, whooping and chanting along to the music and beat. Bodies rubbed against one another and it was hard to tell where one person ended and another began.

She'd use an abstract style to represent it, oil paints, wild curved brush strokes of bright colors curling around each other and swirling around solid trees, depicted more naturalistically. The strokes would represent the people, but also the music, and the primality of the scene.

Oh, she wanted to join them so much. The natural energy of the humans captivated her, made her want to lose herself in the gathering as she had so many times before. It was easy for an energetic like her to become a center of gravity in such a group, and she had never, ever failed to take a man home when she'd decided to. The pounding primal music called to her, the jungle by the sea, the wild celebration of life her natural habitat, the temptation of escaping for the rest of the night hard to resist.

She wrapped her arms around herself and stood watching. She could talk to them, to ask them to turn it down, but she couldn't get distracted. Couldn't give in to her desire to lose herself in the music, even for a moment.

Another handful of people spilled out of the other side of the forest and joined the group, which was up to about thirty. She spied drink, and given the joy and abandon on faces, it was likely some other less-than-legal substances were involved. It was pretty unlikely even her powers of persuasion were going to get them to turn the noise down.

What else could she do? What did the healer actually need? Did he need the party to stop? No. He just needed quiet. And though she wasn't highly experienced in her auxiliary energy, Vishudha, with some effort she could create a small silent zone for him to work.

With a long exhale, she turned her gaze from the party, and jogged back to the house, where she updated Fintan and Blaize. When she suggested she would work with her Vishudha to mute the sound for the healer, Blaize looked doubtful.

"Are you sure you can?" she asked.

Nixie winced internally. "Mai benn rai." *No problem.*

She went inside the house, and told Heka what she was going to do.

"Alright," he said. "I can account for more of your energy when I diagnose. I'll pause while you get it set up."

She nodded. She folded herself into a cross-legged position on the floor, her back to the bed. She didn't train with her energies much. She had a tendency to be a little leisurely in her practice. She had completed her training to be a Practitioner in Svadisthana, but she hadn't had Blaize's drive to start training for her auxiliary energy yet. There would be plenty of time for that.

She closed her eyes and felt for her connection to the ether, the place where Source provided infinite energy, energy that was bounded only by the amount the energetic in the physical world could contain.

As an artist she loved color, and the strong orange of Svadisthana was her favorite, with the bright blue of Vishudha close behind. It was easy for her to draw the latter from the ether, sculpting it with her mind into a smooth ball inside her.

She made the sphere dense with energy, the sides smooth, until it was almost heavy inside her throat, the seat of the Chakra. Once she was satisfied with it, she took a handful of deep, deep breaths. Now was the delicate bit. She put her hands on her throat, and she sang out a long, clear note.

As she did, she increased the size of the energy sphere, which expanded around her. It took some effort. She really should practice more with her energies. When the sphere covered her body entirely, silence fell, as if she was in a padded tomb. She sucked in another breath, a bead of sweat at her temple, taking a moment before she was ready to expand it further. Another breath, and she gritted her teeth. She wasn't going to let Blaize and the others down. She saw blue flickers in her vision, and she shook her head to clear it. She pushed again, to encompass the bed, Tierra, and the healer. She opened her eyes to peek and check that it was working.

Heka's eyebrows twitched, and he gave Nixie a nod. Okay. Good. It was working. She considered the size of it. She should make it a little bigger, so Heka had room to work. Another deep breath, and she expanded her chest and diaphragm. She used the large exhale to inflate the sphere to cover most of the room.

There was nothing but hush.

It wasn't a state that Nixie was especially familiar with, and after only a few minutes she became uncomfortable, left alone with her own thoughts. She preferred to live in the now. When she reflected on the hundreds of years she might live, and the expectations she, as part of her race, should live up to, she became overwhelmed. Better to live in the present, and experience life through the senses, not the intellect. Though her 'now' was equally full of responsibility, it seemed, with the prophecy looming over her and her friends.

Heka continued to examine Tierra, but there was no one else in the room to distract Nixie. She held the bubble of silence for another forty-five minutes, an age, until Heka finally gestured. It was a test of emotional as well as mental and energetic prowess, and she'd heard that holding silence like that for several days was part of the Practitioner test for Vishudha. She could see why. Left alone with nothing but your own thoughts, no other sound or input to distract you, was disorientating. She'd heard that when their eyes were also covered, some energetics almost tipped into madness from the solitude. More practiced energetics had more control, and were able to shut out external noise without dampening the sound inside the orb, but she didn't have the training for that.

She dropped the bubble gratefully, and the sounds of the jungle rushed back. Animals, night birds, the party, music, Heka's footsteps, Tierra's breathing, Nixie connected to them all and bathed in them.

Heka had called the others, who filed in around Tierra. Heka cleared his throat and cracked his knuckles. "There's something very strange going on here."

He addressed Fintan. "Tierra's energy is Muladhara and Anahata, correct?"

"Yes," said Fintan, tightly.

Heka rubbed the back of his neck. "I found traces of all six energies in her."

They all stared at him.

"You mean…like everyone else?" Nixie asked. The Chakras were present in every living thing, including humans and animals. But usually they were only activated in energetics, and only ever two, a dominant and an auxiliary.

"No. All six are active," said Heka. He gazed down at Tierra, and tapped a finger against his lower lip.

"What are you talking about? That's not possible." Fintan's arms were crossed, his jaw clenched.

"Her dominant and auxiliary as you describe them are there, very strong, but the other four are also there. Active. Very weak, but there. It's…peculiar."

It was more than peculiar. Nixie had never heard of such a thing. It wasn't supposed to be possible.

"Is this causing her illness? How can we stop it?" Fintan asked.

"I don't know why this is happening," Heka admitted. "I can stabilize her, give her a healer's shield, and I think I can bring her out of unconsciousness, but I don't know if this energetic anomaly is what's causing the issue or whether it's something else. So I still need to talk to colleagues at the Guild once that's done and see if anyone has come across this before."

"Do it," Fintan ordered.

Blaize laid a hand on Fintan's arm.

"Please," she added.

The healer nodded. "Can you lift her up? I need to sit with her head in my lap so I can concentrate."

Blaize put an arm underneath Tierra's back and lifted the other woman's limp torso, steadying her head while the healer got on the bed and crossed his legs. He gestured and Blaize rested Tierra's head in his cupped hands.

"Do you need us to go?" Blaize asked.

Heka shook his head. "As you like. But I will need quiet so I can concentrate."

He raised an inquiring eyebrow at Nixie.

She breathed deeply. It wasn't an easy magic. But she nodded, and raised the sphere of silence again.

The healer's eyes closed and his face went blank. Nixie couldn't see what he did for the next thirty minutes or so, but she figured Fintan, who had Anahata as his auxiliary, could from his eyes, which moved up and down Tierra's body as if following something.

But when Heka created the shield, they could all see it. A glowing green light surrounded Tierra, at first in a bumpy ovoid, then moving to cling tightly to her skin. It shone brightly for a few minutes and then disappeared into Tierra's body, leaving a dark afterimage.

The healer slumped a little, then opened his eyes, which were blurry with fatigue. "It's done. The shield I have created is a general one, to protect against illness and the symptoms of what she has. She should wake up naturally in a few hours. I brought the materials for a glucose drip, and I'll put one of those in too to prevent dehydration in this heat. But it's not over. Whatever this odd infection of energies is, her body can't defend against it. It's simply not used to all six energies being activated, and it's going haywire trying to deal with what it considers an attack. And because I don't know the cause, I can't create a shield that defends against that."

"So what do we do?" demanded Fintan.

"We get more help. Or it's going to happen again."

"I have information," Imogen said. The attractive blonde wore a pencil skirt, heels and a white blouse, her heavy blue-green pendant hanging between her small, high breasts and contrasting with skin the color of milk. She'd chosen to look in her early thirties, but she was centuries old, a Master in one energy and a Maven in the other.

She'd entered the room at the safe house without Elrian noticing, and he raised his head wearily. He'd drained a little too much of the energetic that Dagon had brought him, and his system had felt the overload. After his trip into the ether, he was letting it settle within him before he did anything else. He'd have to take less next time. The energetic had survived, perhaps more through luck than by judgement. And that was very unlike Elrian, whose judgement was always level.

"What is it?" he asked. He didn't rise to his feet. He was too tired. He was devoted to her, but she was unpredictable, while it was his nature to be careful. She shouldn't be here. She should be at the Guild given everything that was happening.

They didn't know her as Imogen there. She'd long since taken another identity while she re-climbed the Anahata power structure after her first fall from grace, and subsequent retreat. As far as he was aware, he was the only person who knew her true name and her dark past. A hidden Rogue in the heart of Anahata. What sweet irony. More so when you considered the double meaning of the name she'd taken.

She had said she'd come to check on him, and take care of him, but there were times when she added to his work rather than helped. She had access to great power, and while it took a lot out of her she was somehow able to use it to transport herself instantly between locations, though she hadn't revealed the mystery of how to him yet. She was full of secrets, and she was hard to predict, both in action and mood. He sighed. Having said that, he wouldn't be on this path without her.

"It's about Jebediah," she said. "The Anahata-Svadisthana energetic who's the next in the prophecy to couple."

"Yes?" The back of Elrian's skull rested on the armchair he sat in. Study was too grand a name for this room, but it had a desk, a chair, a lamp and the armchair. There was little decoration apart from a five foot dragon tree in a terracotta pot that stood in the corner of the room opposite the armchair. Elrian's Muladhara energy needed something growing around him.

Imogen stalked to the chair at the desk and swung it round so the seat faced Elrian. She sat gracefully in the chair, her ankles neatly crossed, her hands loosely clasped.

"Do you know Jebediah's story? Why he's stuck in the Guild?" she asked Elrian.

He shrugged. "Something about a woman and his Svadisthana? An inappropriate use of his energy? He contravened their rules about the use of influence."

She nodded. "Correct. But I have new information."

He waved a hand for her to go on.

"The woman Jebediah influenced was the person who then gave the Germans the location of the hospital where your wife was working. The information that led to its bombing."

Elrian stiffened. "What?"

She smoothed a hand over her already perfect hair and settled back with an exaggerated casualness. "Jebediah is the person who got your wife killed."

All tiredness left Elrian, his system electrified. Rage sang through him and he jerked upright. He was dedicated to Imogen, and she was his lover now, but his wife was the reason he had started on this path in the first place. The reason he craved revenge on the humans. The reason he wanted power, to cleanse the world.

"You need to do better this time," Imogen said. "The prophecy needs to turn our way. So I will help you. Together we will ensure the deaths needed."

Elrian swallowed. That was … a mixed blessing.

"What is your plan?" she asked.

He mentally shook himself. He needed to put fatigue and fury aside and focus.

"My dreamwalk tells me the male is unsteady, easily shaken, and has a great deal of pent-up sexual energy waiting to explode. I need to get the couple together. The female is wild, out-of-control, and has no boundaries around sex. Once they're in the same place, they will only need a small push to get them together, and then –" He waved a hand. "Boom."

"Good." She recrossed her ankles carefully. "I have hired a mercenary to help us. I want you to talk to him about what he can do on the island. I've also been jabbing holes in Jebediah's Svadisthana wardings for weeks. It's causing his control to slip, and he has no idea why. It's getting worse, and he thinks he's losing his mind. A couple of days ago I was able to push him to a point where he nearly razed his study to the ground."

Elrian's pulse quickened. She was taking action without him. That wasn't part of their plan. They were supposed to work together, to be a co-ordinated team. "Alright."

"And it's time to get Cassidy involved. I talked to her on the phone yesterday, and she still seems to be resisting your influence on her. Would you like my help?"

"No," he said, quickly. He had been so careful to keep the two women apart. After Imogen, Cassidy was the most important person in the world to him. She wasn't resisting the influence because he wasn't really using much influence on her. She was a powerful Ajna influencer herself, and he told himself it was because she was a difficult target, but really it was a line he hadn't wanted to cross with her. She still had most of her free will, and he'd worked around her, nudging her only when he really needed to, or when the time came to hide things from her. "I'll manage her."

"She's an asset, my love," Imogen reached out and stroked his cheek. "We can't be sentimental when we have so much to do before our power base is settled."

Hellfire and negativity, no. "I'll keep her in line. It's not a problem."

He loved the beautiful, hard-edged woman in front of him, it was true. And he was confident that by the conclusion of this prophecy they'd rule the Guilds together.

But if he used too much influence on Cassidy she might end up losing her sense of self, her personhood. And he wasn't ready to let go of Cassidy quite yet.

Jeb was concerned that Heka, an experienced healer, hadn't been able to restore Tierra to health. He went down to the archives to research the issue to see if other Anahata healers had encountered anything similar in the past. He walked to Feng's desk. The slight Asian man smiled at his approach. "I don't have anything new for you on the Rogue issue yet."

"I'm not here for that," said Jeb. He explained the situation to Feng, whose long face fell as Jeb told the story.

"Poor Tierra. She's such a wonderful woman," Feng muttered. "That's very unusual. Very unusual indeed. If it's in the archives, we will find it."

Jeb nodded. Tierra made a positive impression on most people she met. "She's important to me too."

Feng was already walking into the stacks. "Do you want me to ask anyone else for help?"

Jeb hesitated. Given all that was going on, he thought not. Though he would tell Aiko when he got the chance. He'd already asked Heka to stay quiet about it for the moment. If it was connected to her breaking the energy sharing taboo with Cuinn, they needed to keep it quiet as long as possible. Cuinn and Tierra could face consequences if others knew.

"No. Unless there's something specific we find, or you think someone has information that would be helpful, let's keep it between us."

The next day, Fintan stayed with Tierra. Nixie and Blaize had made him and Heka up a bed in Marius and Fai's house, as Nixie's parents were away visiting their in-common Guild, Svadisthana, but Fintan wouldn't leave Tierra's side, preferring to sleep on a mat on the floor next to her. Heka was grateful for the bed, and took rest after his work.

Tierra thus safe under watch, Blaize asked Nixie if she would spar with her. Nixie made a moue of distaste, but agreed despite her usual reluctance. Blaize was taller, more muscular and better trained than Nixie, and these bouts never went well for her. But even Nixie could see that Blaize was worried about her sick friend, and Nixie wanted to cheer her up. And not much cheered Blaize up more than kicking someone's ass.

Blaize was also more comfortable with the odd bruise than Nixie, who tried to avoid pain wherever possible. This time Nixie lasted all of fifteen minutes before she pulled on her Svadisthana energy and drenched Blaize in the equivalent of a bucket of water.

Blaize stood in front of her, her auburn hair dripping down her neck, and actually growled. Nixie burst out laughing.

Blaize bared her teeth, which made Nixie giggle harder. Blaize swiped out an arm, which Nixie "eeep"ed at, and jumped backwards. Then she slipped on the water, and ended up flat on her back on the training mat, still laughing.

A slow smile spread across Blaize's face even as she shook her head. "Nong sao, you can be a pain in the ass."

"It's why you love me, right, pee sao?" Nixie gasped for breath even as her body continued to be wracked by giggles. The laughter had released tension she hadn't even known was there.

Blaize shook herself off, and used a flare of Manipura heat up and down her body, which evaporated the water in a puff of steam. Then she stepped carefully around the puddle, and threw herself down next to Nixie. They were in a shared outside gym area between the three houses.

Nixie lay on the floor and looked up at the blue of the sky. *Like an upside down ocean.* Perhaps she would go for a swim later to clear her head. The two of them lay in a companionable silence, both looking up at the sky, their heads close together, bodies pointing away from each other.

"How's Cuinn?" Nixie said.

Blaize's lips twisted. "I spoke to him yesterday. I miss him. He's been having nightmares recently, and we don't know why."

"Something to do with the prophecy?"

"We don't know. They actually seem like more ordinary nightmares."

"From what you've said, there's a lot of stress. Could it be that?"

Blaize shrugged. "There's a lot we don't know in this situation, and not much we do."

Nixie wriggled on the floor, and let the blue above her fill her up. She tried to think of nothing, but her mind kept turning over everything Blaize had told her, as well as the situation with Tierra.

"Blaize?" Nixie asked.

"Hmm?"

"I'm frightened. I don't think I'm cut out for this kind of adventure."

"It's not an adventure, Nix. We're fighting for our lives here. And perhaps more."

Nixie felt cold. "That's what I mean. I'm not a fighter. I'm an artist. I don't see what my role is."

"You're already helping with the identification. We'll work on that some more until we have pictures of everyone who Cuinn has seen clearly so far, and also any important images he's seen. It's a good use of time, as I can't dreamwalk for prophecy like Cuinn, so he's trying to find more pieces while we do this."

"And then what?" Nixie said.

"How'd you mean?"

"How else can I help?" Nixie persisted. "You're used to danger from your Warrior training, but I'm not. I'd freeze if someone attacked me."

Nixie felt a thickness in her throat, and moisture prick the back of her eyes. She didn't like admitting to this, but she didn't want Blaize to rely on her when Nixie knew she couldn't deliver. "I'll help where I can, like with the images, but I can't fight. I'd panic."

Blaize pushed herself up to lean on one arm, and stroked Nixie's hair. "It's okay. I know you. The real you, not the side you show to most people. You've always been there for me when I needed you. This won't be any different."

A tear leaked out of Nixie's eye. She'd do what she could. But Blaize was wrong.

"What're you going to do next with your life, Nix?"

Nixie blinked at the change of topic. "What?"

"You did your initial training in Svadisthana, but what about Vishudha? Are you going to stay on the island, living next to your parents? What's next for you?"

"Why does there need to be a next? I like my job, I like my house, I like my life. There's plenty of time for more training later. People are always looking at what the next thing is, they never enjoy what they have now. Then when they reach the next thing, they move the bar again. I want to enjoy the beauty of the moment. To be present right now, here." The heat of the day suddenly felt stifling, rather than comforting, and the ground underneath her was hard and unforgiving, no longer cradling.

"I love the island, you know I do, but right now we have a problem a lot bigger than this moment." Blaize half sat up and rested on one arm, contemplating Nixie's prone form. "I can see you're frightened. Me too. But we – I – your friends need your help. You can't just coast past this one and expect it all to work out."

Ouch. What was this, lay into Nixie day? She wished Blaize would stop. Nixie had forgotten this side of Blaize, the persistent, moral, driven person whose total faith in Nixie was a double-edged sword.

"I guess I got used to living down to people's expectations." Nixie sat up and wrapped her arms around her knees. "Tired of people judging me on my appearance."

Nixie was attractive, she knew, by the current standards of society, but she had no control over that. She was so much more than her body and face. Getting others to see past them had been exhausting, and eventually, she'd given up. She dressed to please herself. She'd pursued graphic art, a human career that didn't involve people seeing – or judging her on – what she looked like. She worked from home, kept her gender hidden from readers, and kept her work boxed off from the rest of her life. She'd been so discouraged by jealous hints that she wasn't serious enough for study at her auxiliary Chakra Guild, Vishudha, she'd put her energetic studies on hold indefinitely.

"Let's try more sketches while Fintan looks after Tierra," Nixie said. "We can do whichever you find easiest so it doesn't drain you too much."

Nixie would offer what she could to help her friends. Blaize knew about her past, but also knew Nixie had no interest in talking about it these days. She was happy as she was. Nixie accepted herself, and had no need to chase anyone else's acceptance.

But dammit.

Blaize's words had opened up an unpleasant possibility. If Nixie hadn't been skating along on the surface of life for the last few years, if she'd bothered to bite the bullet, weather the storms, and start her Practitioner training in Vishudha?

Maybe she'd have some help to contribute right now, more than the odd drawing. Be a useful chess piece, rather than a pawn who had no skills or abilities better than a hundred others.

But she hadn't. And now it might cost her friends their lives.

8

"I need you to tell me what is happening to Tierra." Fintan's voice was gruff with emotion. "Please, Jeb."

Jeb and Feng had spent the day searching deep in the stacks of the archives, following references like breadcrumbs from one to another. Now Fintan wanted an update.

"We haven't found much" Jeb said. "A reference in the diary of an energetic from the fourteenth century, the leader of a small energetics community in southern France during the plague they called the Black Death. She was able to protect herself from the sickness, but didn't have enough power to save the humans around her."

"Alright. And?"

Jeb continued. "She was an Anahata energetic living together with a small community of other energetics and running a human orphanage. She was married to a human, and their own children died in infancy."

"She'd watched the spread of the plague and realized how bad it was – in some places in Europe, sixty to seventy percent of the people died from the disease. She wanted to protect the orphans but she wasn't strong enough on her own."

"So what happened?" Fintan was becoming more and more frustrated.

"When she saw the plague nearing her community in 1349, she asked her brother, also an Anahata dominant but without the same healing powers she had, to break the taboo and share some of his energy with her."

Could Fintan see what was coming? When Feng had told him earlier, this had been the *oh shit* moment for Jeb.

"Tierra told me about breaking the sharing energy taboo with Cuinn, to save Blaize." Jeb had been uncomfortable, shocked even, but he'd understood her motives. For Tierra, rules were important, but people came first.

"Yeah," Fintan said, winter bleak. "I tried to stop her. But you know what she's like."

"They shared energy, and at first, everything was fine. Ninety percent of the children survived the plague. However, she became very sick after a few weeks."

"Why did it happen? What caused it? And more importantly, how did they cure it?" Fintan asked.

Jeb ran a hand through his hair and stared at the wall of books. "They didn't. And they didn't know why."

There was a silence. "Fix this. Please, Jeb. She looks so small in that bed."

Fear for Tierra had crept into Jeb's heart. If he couldn't find the answers they needed, what would happen to Tierra?

Feng hastened in.

"I'm on the phone to Fintan," Jeb said, his brow wrinkling in puzzlement. The refined Feng rarely rushed anywhere.

"I have something to share with you both," Feng said.

Jeb put the handset down, put the call on speaker and gestured to Feng, who introduced himself.

"It's a case study written up by an Anahata Rehabilitation Centre in 1902. A Muladhara-Anahata energetic was captured by two Manipura Warriors because of serial leeching. He was caught because the last of his victims had been his lover – who had been willing when they were together, but when she'd found him cheating on her, she'd reported him to the Guild," Feng said.

Leeches were a type of Rogue. Feng went on to describe the rest of the story. The Leech had been taken to a Rehabilitation Centre. These weren't like human prisons. In them, Healers worked to untwist the energy of Rogues that had become tangled and used in a dark way. They also gave Rogue energetics the opportunity to repent, but this Rogue had shown no remorse for his actions.

Jeb pinched the brow of his nose, thinking. How did all this connect?

"He was powerful, and appeared to have access to other energies," Feng said. "He told the Healer that he'd taken energy from six people. The first time had been an accident, when he took energy from a lover during sex. It felt good and he chased the feeling again, but the next woman sickened and died. He'd travelled to areas where no one knew him, and experimented on other women, siphoning off different amounts of energy and noting the results."

Feng's tone was hushed, and horrified. "The Leech worked out how much he could take on a regular basis without killing his lovers, and then met the woman who had eventually turned him in. He told her what he was doing, and together they'd turned outside their relationship to other energetics, leeching from victims and having sex with each other while their victims looked on."

Jeb's stomach turned.

Feng continued. "It was only when the Leech slept with someone outside the relationship that the lover had turned him in, perhaps hoping to be seen as another victim."

"But what happened to him? Did he live?" Fintan said.

Feng hesitated before speaking. "He got sick. And his symptoms seem to echo Tierra's. He fitted and lapsed into unconsciousness. They didn't know how to help him, and he died six weeks later."

"I found the case study in the sealed, classified papers of the Guild," said Feng.

There was a long silence.

Jeb's stomach churned, and he rubbed his upper arms. He felt a chill that was from more than just the air conditioning of the temperature and humidity controlled archives.

"Tierra has the same mix of energies as the killer," stated Fintan.

"Yes."

"But she wasn't the recipient of the energy when she shared it with Cuinn, she was giving," Fintan said. "So how can it be the same?"

His tone was desperate, pleading. Jeb didn't have the answers he wanted.

"Somehow, in opening herself up, she seems to have triggered something. She's activated her other Chakras," Jebediah said slowly. He was working it through as he talked.

"How can this be possible?" Feng asked.

Jeb was too busy reeling from the information to answer. If it was possible for energetics to have more than one Chakra activated, then it put into question everything they knew. The fact that energetics had one dominant and one auxiliary Chakra wasn't only a core part of what energetics were, it was a fundamental truth.

"I don't know," Jeb said. His mind raced. He needed to take this to Aiko. This fundamentally shook his understanding of the Chakras and how they worked in energetics. It was overwhelming, and he needed her counsel.

"You need to get here," Fintan said, his voice cracking. "Do not let Tierra down."

He hung up. Jebediah rubbed his forehead, talking to Feng. "Put this somewhere safe, away from others' eyes. I'm going to talk to Aiko."

When he arrived at her office, he knocked and walked in. She sat on one of the armchairs in the corner of the room, a headset on. When she saw Jeb she pulled it off, looked him up and down, and cocked her head.

"What's the matter? More trouble with your Svadisthana? Or is it Tierra?" She gestured to him to sit in the other armchair.

He sat and leaned forward. "My energy's fine, and Tierra is stable, though I am worried. Even more so now."

He filled her in on what Feng had found in the text. Her eyes widened as he talked her through it, the only sign of her shock.

"Never have I come across this," she said, when he finished. "This could change everything we know about our energy and our power. It brings up so many questions. Is it possible for everyone to access all six Chakras? Or only some people? And if it's possible, why don't we see more energetics who have access to all six? I will admit, Jeb, I'm worried about Tierra."

"And can it be done without negative side effects?" Jeb asked grimly. "So far, people have either died, or the energy has been too much for them and it has twisted."

Aiko leaned forward and put a hand on Jeb's knee. "I'm sorry to ask this of you Jeb-san, but you need to go to Tierra. She's not the only factor involved here now. We need to know more about the situation. How was it triggered? And how can we keep her alive and untwisted?"

Jeb reared back. "Don't ask this. It's too dangerous for those around me. What if I make things worse simply by being there? There must be someone else."

Aiko's face softened.

"I'm sorry. We cannot let others know about this yet. The Guild seems unsettled at the moment – Maya came in only last week with a complaint about a decision I had made, and seems to be stirring things up. She's already Guild leader for her Minor Guild Anahata-Ajna, but it's not enough for her. I think she wants my job." Aiko sighed.

Jeb's eyebrows drew together. He hadn't heard that. Maya could be a challenge, true, despite the Anahata being the Guild associated with love. There were as many politics here as in any other Guild. "You should have said. I might be able to help smooth things over. Maya and I get on fine."

"It's just one of the challenges of running the Guild. I wouldn't even mention it but it means I don't think it's a good idea to share the information you've discovered until we know more. Maya and others like her may use it to stir people up because I don't know the answers," Aiko said.

Jeb tried once more.

"Is there no one else?" The stress of leaving the Guild made his entire being tighten, and he could feel a dull ache between his shoulders. How would be protect others from his energy if he left the Guild?

Aiko shook her head.

"What about my Svadisthana energy? What if it..." he trailed off. They both knew the risks.

"We'll work together now to bind it again. You're very disciplined, and you have iron self-control. You come into contact with new people all the time here, and you've kept it locked down for decades. You've proved you can do this. Why would going outside the Guild be different?" she asked.

Jeb pursed his lips. He looked out of the window and thought, breathing deeply, trying to center himself. Why was it different?

When he'd first arrived at the Guild, he'd been angry and guilty, and devastated at the loss of innocent life his actions – his use of energy – had caused. He no longer felt quite so angry, but he would never get over the guilt at what he had done during the war. His Svadisthana wasn't safe, and he would not use it again.

But perhaps Aiko was right. Perhaps there was no difference between being here and being outside. Now his energy was bound, and he'd controlled it for so long, he no longer needed the safety of the Guild. If he and Aiko could be confident that his energy was locked up tightly, then being outside might be no different from being here.

Plus, he'd be among friends. It was a good place to be, Koh Somdun. He'd never been before, but he knew it was small, with a tiny population, and he'd have plenty of space. He tried to visualize it in his mind, to see himself safe, his energy locked down, and on the island.

He knew if Tierra didn't survive and he hadn't tried to help her, and he truly was the only one for the job, he would never forgive himself. Perhaps it was the right thing to do, despite the risks.

Source, am I actually considering this?

"I need more time to think," he said.

"We don't have that time. It's a flight or two away, and we don't know how long Tierra will stay stable. You need to talk to her to make sure you have all the information you can extract in case anything happens. If we don't take care of her, she may become a Rogue."

Jeb's heart jolted.

"I'm sorry, Jeb. I hope very much that you will be able to help Tierra, and Feng will continue the research here in the meantime – I will give him support for his other duties. But if she dies, we need to ensure we know everything that has happened, down to the last detail," Aiko said.

Jeb shook his head. "I won't let her die."

"If you are with her, that is more likely to be true," she said. "It's time to leave the Guild."

Cold eyes met Elrian's. There was plenty of confidence in them. Elrian tried not to sneer at the Rogue mercenary-for-hire his lover had sent him. Called Trent, a Svadhistana-Ajna energetic, he had an angular face and strong jaw. Muscular and rugged, he was the epitome of tall, dark and handsome.

He was also chewing on a toothpick, which to Elrian's mind was disgusting. It wasn't even disposable, but made from eighteenth century carved bone. Trent had told Elrian matter-of-factly it had once belonged to a pirate king. Trent had murdered the most recent owner for it. Elrian thought it likely the only time the toothpick was out of the man's mouth was when he was actually consuming food. The idea made Elrian shudder in distaste. Why was good hygiene such a difficult concept for people?

"How do you want me to proceed?" Trent asked. They sat across a table from each other in the bar in Seattle. It was raining outside, and Elrian felt the cold in his bones. He tried to smooth down his white shirt, which, usually immaculate, had become creased on the trip into town.

He ached with exhaustion. This journey he and Imogen were on was supposed to be more energizing than this. When only one or two couples had formed, he'd only needed to destroy one person from among them. Now he had three couples bonded, he would need to kill two of the energetics from their ranks to thwart them enough for his version of the prophecy to win through. If, Source forbid, there became five or six couples, he would need to kill three individuals.

That would not happen.

He was focused on killing both members of this couple to be sure, and perhaps killing Tierra, his niece, who'd just been the bait at first, might also be worthwhile. There was safety in contingency planning. So much power was within reach.

"Follow them, and look for an opportunity when they are alone together," Elrian instructed. "If you see a chance, weaken his shields. He thinks he's protected, that his sexual energy is locked down, but the vision I saw indicated that she can break through them. Help it happen."

"Understood," said Trent. He had shown no emotion. No pleasure, displeasure, enthusiasm, nothing. Simply stared at him with those coal black eyes.

"I will also give you a carved jade charm to place near Tierra," Elrian continued. "It doesn't need to be in the room with her. Within about ten meters should do it. This will speed the draining of her energy. It's tied to her, so it won't affect anyone else."

Trent nodded.

"The money is in your account." The man was paid well for his services, paid for his loyalty.

What was Trent's relationship to Imogen anyway? How did they know each other? If it came to it – and Elrian was sure it never would, but, still, he couldn't stop the thought from worming into his mind – whose orders would Trent follow? Elrian's? Or hers?

He shook it off. Trent was a tool to be utilized, nothing more. The tool that Elrian needed to tip the already vulnerable Jebediah over the edge.

Whilst Jebediah thought it was Tierra who was the sick one, it was actually Jebediah who was most at risk.

Because with the right trigger, Jebediah would destroy both himself and Nixie.

CHAPTER

9

Jeb stepped off the boat and into the clinging wet heat of Thailand. He was used to hot weather as he'd lived in Egypt for seven decades. But Thailand was humid, and within moments of leaving the air conditioned boat his shirt was sticking to his chest and a rivulet of sweat ran down his back.

The journey had been tiring, exposing Jeb to new technologies that he'd only seen on television. Usually, energetics were used to the world changing around them, and learned to adapt quickly to social and technological changes, taking the progressions – and regressions – of the human world in their stride, just as the elements ebbed and flowed around them. This much change at once, however, was draining. He was grateful for the island's gentler pace.

The dock was pretty basic, and brightly colored traditional fishing boats were moored opposite where the commercial passenger boats drew up. Beyond them lay the clean white sands of the beach, and then the changeable blue of the sea.

Jeb had missed the sea. He might have locked down his Svadisthana, his water energy, but it was still part of him.

A motorbike pulled up. Not the usual low cc scooters you saw on this sort of island, but a proper sports bike. Jeb had never learned to drive a car, sequestering himself as he had before cars were common, but he had learned to drive a motorcycle around the time of World War I. He'd always enjoyed the speed and the feel of the road underneath him.

The male rider got off the bike and without saying anything handed Jeb a helmet he produced from underneath the seat. He lifted his own plastic visor and turned cool blue eyes on Jeb.

"Fintan," said Jeb. Right. It would be him who came to pick him up.

"Thanks for coming. Get on." Fintan steadied the bike, closed his visor, and waited for Jeb to do up his helmet. There was no sign of the lightness that Jeb had seen in Fintan when he'd visited the Guild. The man was closed up tight.

They weren't going to catch up first then. *Lucky I only have a rucksack.* Jeb pulled the straps over his shoulders and hopped onto the bike.

Fintan gunned the engine and drove the length of the dock, past stray dogs, children fishing and street food carts selling everything from corn on the cob to unidentifiable meat on a stick. They drove through the small town that was bunched around the dock: cafés, hotels, travel agents, and the ubiquitous 7-11. A few miles and they were onto a sandy road edged with coconut palms, where few scooters and fewer cars passed them.

After about twenty minutes they turned down a track that Jeb would have missed if he'd been looking for it alone. The lane was not much more than a couple of ruts in the sandy earth, and Fintan had to slow the bike as it bumped along. A clearing came into view with a cluster of traditional Thai bungalows spaced for privacy. Each was raised on thick wooden posts.

Fintan parked his bike underneath one of them, and Jeb got off.

"Thanks for the lift," Jeb said. He and Fintan had got on well when he had come to the Guild with Tierra. And Jeb was here now, wasn't he? Not that he was sure he could help. He pushed that thought away.

Fintan looked at him, his fists clenched by his sides. He was angry, that was obvious. But he wasn't only angry at Jeb.

"I'll do everything I can to help. I know you're worried," Jeb said, his voice soft.

"Don't read me!" Fintan was a tinder box looking for a spark.

"I'm not. I'm worried too. Tierra is important to me." Jeb felt as if he was talking to an injured wild animal.

"Not so important you came sooner. What if that was the difference between her being well and –" Fintan broke off and looked away.

"I wouldn't have known any more than Heka did. If Feng hadn't found the information on past cases, I wouldn't have known what this was either. We haven't come across it in the modern age."

Heka had left for another emergency elsewhere once Jeb had made it known he was on his way. They'd spoken on the phone so Jeb could understand what had happened so far.

He stepped forward. "Take me to her, and let's see what we can do."

Jeb followed Fintan up the stairs, stepped onto the large wooden balcony, and stumbled when he saw what at first his addled brain took for a fairy sitting on the floor.

A very sexy petite fairy in a white summer dress that set off liquid brown eyes and black hair.

Jeb's Svadisthana energy roared into life, and smashed against the bars of the cage of shields and wardings that he had created with Aiko. There was an orange flash as a little energy escaped before he could clamp down on it, and Jeb staggered and fell to his hands and knees, the wood grazing his skin where he hit it.

He clenched the energy inside him like a tight fist, and swallowed. It took a few moments, but he got it under control, patching the gaps in his shields. *It must have been spending that time on the boat. Too much exposure to wild waters.*

He got up slowly, carefully. The journey had tired his physical body, but also his energy, as he'd been hyper-vigilant the whole way. This was exactly what he had been worried about.

"Are you okay?" Fintan asked. There was a crease between his eyebrows. He stuck out a hand to help Jeb up.

"Fine," said Jeb, taking the hand and pulling himself up. "I tripped on the step."

That excuse would hold unless they had seen the orange flash. He wasn't going to think about it now. Tierra was his priority.

The black-haired woman rose to her feet, and bit her lip. "Can I help?"

He shook his head. "I need to see Tierra."

"Come in," she said. Her voice was musical, seductive. This was a lot to deal with on top of Tierra. He needed some rest, and to work through what to do about this, and who to tell, if anyone. He rolled his shoulders to soothe the ache there. He missed the peace of his study.

All three of them went inside the house, where Tierra was propped up in bed on several cushions, conscious but wan-looking. A fan stirred the heat of the day into a cool breeze onto her face, which disturbed her dark hair so it moved gently. She talked in a low voice to Blaize, who sat next to her, their heads close together. At the sound of the door, they both looked up.

"Jeb!" said Tierra, obvious delight in her voice.

There was a twist in Jeb's belly. He had already let her down – and she didn't hold it against him. He came over to the bed and dropped a gentle kiss on her cheek. She held her arms out for a hug.

"I don't want to hurt you," he said.

"Don't be silly! I'm fine. Well, I'm not squashable, at least. Give me a hug, then tell me what you've discovered so far."

He sat next to her on the bed and wrapped his arms carefully around her small curvy body. He would fix this.

Fintan and the dark-haired woman stood behind him, and Blaize sat in a chair the other side of the bed. There were a lot of people in the room. "Am I telling everyone here?"

Tierra nodded. "All of us here have been featured in Cuinn's prophecy. It's hard to believe this illness isn't connected in some way. But we really don't have any idea of how at the moment. Tell us what you know."

He gestured them all in, and the fairy dropped to the floor and sat with her legs crossed, while Fintan went over to stand next to Blaize, his arms folded across an intimidating chest.

"I don't know —" Jeb gestured politely to the woman he didn't know.

"Oh!" said Tierra. "This is Nixie. She's Blaize's cousin. They grew up together."

He put out his hand to shake Nixie's, but she'd already given him a Thai-style wai, the palms-together bow that Thais used to greet each other. His hand stayed awkwardly in front of him until she realized and grabbed for it. But by that time, he'd already begun to pull away.

He colored under his stubble, heat washing over his face. "Sorry. Hello."

He was usually better than this. Empathy was one of his gifts. He needed to start paying attention to the people around him. He was so wrapped up in keeping his auxiliary energy locked down, he was missing the things that would normally come naturally to him.

Nixie stared at him. Her sitting posture meant her skirt had ridden up to show perfectly proportioned legs that ended in tidy feet with toenails painted shell-pink. He rubbed his face, and the feel of the rough bristles on his chin brought him back to the moment.

She probably thought he was an idiot. *He was an idiot.* He took a deep breath and addressed the room. Since he'd left the Guild, Feng had found one more case, which had given them enough information for a tentative hypothesis. Normally it would be too early to share without further research to back it up, but they didn't have the luxury of time.

"Here's what we've discovered so far. We have found three recorded cases in the Anahata records of what seems to be wrong with Tierra. There are likely to have been more, but given what we think causes it, they may have been kept quiet or even suppressed."

"How did they treat it?" Fintan asked.

Jeb gritted his teeth. He hadn't wanted to share this information this early. "They didn't. They all died."

The room was silent for a few moments as the energetics absorbed Jeb's horrible news. Nixie's hand had gone to her mouth in shock, Blaize paled, and Fintan's hands balled in fists at his sides. Nixie swallowed, and then as was her wont, she stepped back in her mind, withdrawing, and viewed the room as art. A black and white sketch, perhaps. The color leached from them all, strong pencil strokes, jagged lines. It would be striking. Affecting. Painful to view.

She'd call it Stricken.

Only Tierra stayed remarkably steady. "What do you think caused it?"

"We think it's to do with the fact that Tierra shared energy with Cuinn to help him find Blaize when she was kidnapped," Jeb said.

"What?" said Blaize. "Cuinn's fine."

She glanced around the room, frowning. "Isn't he?"

Nixie and Blaize had worked on the image of Cuinn, easier while both of them were distracted by Tierra's illness. In his image he held some kind of bound book, and a mist surrounded him. Blaize had thought the mist represented the ether, or the dreamscape, and they had sent the sketch over to Cuinn for his review. That had been hours ago, and his response hadn't indicated any issues.

Blaize swiftly pulled her phsone out of a pocket. She checked it, and her face relaxed a little when she saw no messages. She tapped out something even as Fintan said, with steadying hand on her shoulder, "He's fine as far as we know, Sparks."

Blaize looked up again. "Then why Tierra?"

"Because she's never been a Maven. Cuinn is. When an energetic becomes a Maven it's accepted that they will share energy with their Adherent, you in this case, Blaize. Whatever the Maven-Adherent ritual and link does, it seems to protect Mavens from any kind of ill effects."

Nixie shuddered at the idea of energy sharing. The taboo against it for energetics was as strong as that against eating meat was for the energetics. Tierra must have been truly desperate to try it.

"So the taboo about sharing energy is based on something real," Nixie said, softly.

"It seems so," agreed Jeb.

She observed him, comparing him to her prophecy sketch. It had been accurate, but to her dismay, it was the sorrowful version in front of her. Her back had been turned when he'd come in and fallen, and she had been certain she'd felt a flash of Svadisthana, but it had been gone as quickly as it had arrived. If she hadn't been so conscious of him, she'd have missed it.

He had a depth and presence that many of the men she dated lacked. Part of that was his age and experience, but there was more to it than that. But she felt that there was a wound there of some kind.

"But why did it take so long for anything to happen?" asked Tierra. "We shared energy weeks ago, but I didn't start feeling like this until I came to the island."

"Have you felt at all ill since then? Felt anything at all unusual?" Jeb said.

Fintan and Tierra exchanged a glance.

"Perhaps. Some headaches," Tierra admitted. "Nothing like this."

"Feng – that's the Anahata archivist – and I think it might be because you were in contact with people with all six of the energies at once when you came here. At Cathair Cuinn, you were missing Svadisthana and Vishudha, but with the addition of Nixie, you were in the presence of all six energies. That seems to have triggered something inside you," said Jeb.

Nixie hunched her shoulders guiltily. It wasn't her fault, she knew, but that didn't make her feel much better.

"What do we do about it?" asked Fintan, urgently. "How do we fix it?"

Jeb took a deep breath. "We're not sure. But we'll work it out. Now, I need to examine Tierra without any other energies nearby. I need to get a read on what's happening inside her, and what might be overspill energy from the rest of you nearby," said Jeb.

There was a silence, but no one moved.

"It's fine," said Tierra. She was speaking directly to Fintan, who looked sick.

"We're experienced energetics, you know," Fintan muttered mutinously. "It's not like energy is leaking out of us."

Fintan's strong Manipura, the energy of fire, meant that he was quick to anger, but Jeb appeared calm. Centered, if sad. But Nixie thought the wilder emotions and feelings, the *passion* that was the vitality and motivating force for many Svadisthana energetics seemed to be missing.

"I'll take care of her," he said to Fintan. "It won't be long."

Blaize opened the door, and Nixie got up to follow the others out, sneaking a quick look back at Jeb as she did. She'd had an idea.

Nixie might be powerless to help Tierra, but she might have thought of a creative way to contribute. Nixie was good at bringing lightness to others, at helping them lose themselves for a little while in sensation rather than having their brain switched on the whole time. Svadisthana was the energy of desire, of the soul's longings, of aliveness and sensations. She danced through life with joy, and if she avoided the more difficult aspects of the world, who would blame her? Too many people lived in the past or the future, and didn't experience the present fully.

Jeb seemed to be living in the past, and Jeb was the man who was going to make Tierra better. Nixie, then, would give him a wonderful experience in the now. She would bring out the sexy Jeb, and bring a little fun into his life to ensure he was operating at his best when healing Tierra.

Nixie would help Tierra, indirectly. She would help Jeb. And she might even help herself.

10

They all traipsed out of the room. Fintan was last out of the door, and shot Jeb a fierce glare as he did. Jeb hoped that someone would help him calm down before he came back into the room. That kind of emotion wouldn't help Tierra heal.

He turned back to Tierra. "I'm so sorry this has happened."

She nodded. "I'm glad you're here. But how are you?"

Tierra knew Jeb's story. Knew this was his first time out of the Guild in decades. And despite her illness, the first thing out of her mouth was to check on him.

"I'm okay. Really. It's strange being out of the Guild, but I'm okay," he responded. For the moment, he spoke the truth. The pressing anxiety that he'd had about leaving Egypt hadn't materialized into anything more. Perhaps the chains he and Aiko had put on his energy would work, and he could finish his task here in peace.

Then he thought of Nixie, the strange fairy creature, and his response to her, and the anxiety was back.

One thing at a time.

Tierra cocked her head to the side. "Are you, Jeb? Really? I saw Svadisthana energy flash when you came in. Have you decided to stop locking it down?"

Jeb felt his cheeks heat. "No. Aiko and I put extra wardings on it before I left the Guild."

"Maybe now's the time to let the wardings go a little," said Tierra. "Where's the harm? It's time to be a whole person again. What happened during the War –"

"It's not an option." He interrupted her before she could go further. Tierra was a true model of Anahata forgiveness. His actions in the war had the direct consequence of both her mother and aunt's death, and Tierra had managed to forgive him.

He would never forgive himself.

"Anyway, I'm here to help you, not the other way round," he said. "Let me examine you."

She nodded, and gestured to her bed. He helped her to sit up, cross-legged, and lean back against the headboard. He mirrored her position. She put her hands out palms up, and he covered them with his own, palms down.

She was the receptive party, as he would use his energy to probe her system and energies. They both closed their eyes and he got ready to work.

He felt the familiar and almost indescribable sense of energy within. It was a sixth sense to energetics, another part of themselves, another limb or function. He simply reached out with his Anahata into Tierra, as he might touch his friend with his hand. But with the energy, he could enter her system, and he didn't stop at the barrier of her skin.

He touched her energetic body, where all the other senses mixed into a synesthesia, and as he'd expected the energy of Muladhara sounded like the smell of fresh earth. That was Tierra's primary energy. He tried to separate the feel of that energy from the next strongest, Anahata, the energy of air and the heart. This was as familiar as home to Jeb, and tasted like blue and clouds.

He separated this last out too. As the energetic who had been her Maven, he was familiar with her energies, unusual in that she was almost equally strong in both. Her dominant and auxiliary energies were prevalent in her energetic body, but Jeb could sense something more.

He breathed in deeply. He centered himself and reached deeper into Tierra's energies. *Are there others?* Perhaps Heka was wrong and he was sensing the other energetics in the area.

And at first, he couldn't feel anything else. But then he caught, at the edge of his senses, a flash of the smell of heat. A little Manipura and fire. Strength and rage and willpower flowed over him, and he sucked in a breath. This was an alien energy to him.

But he'd worked through his rage many years ago. He could handle this. He gritted his teeth and moved past the Manipura.

Ajna, the energy of the mind, and Vishudha, the energy of space, washed over him and he felt as if he was falling into a great emptiness. For one moment, his mind was clear, and he saw a vision of the fairy, naked and lying on her back in front of him. Her straight hair was mussed, her back slightly arched, and her small breasts cried out to be touched.

Then the image was gone, and in his mind he tumbled over and over, losing his sense of self as his consciousness zoomed out to see the world as if from space. He could see tiny pinpricks of light, connected to each other by fine spider silk threads of energy, and he zoomed in again onto the Thai island to realize that the pinpricks were energetics scattered around the world, all joined.

Then finally his etheric body was drenched in the last, horribly familiar energy of Svadisthana. His pulse hammered in his ears. The energy of water, creativity and sexuality combined with the picture of the naked fairy to arouse his physical body.

He drew back and fled from Tierra's energetic body, and dropped her hands, breaking the connection between them. Tierra's eyes snapped open, and she caught her breath. He stumbled off the bed and sat on a chair, his head in his hands. The panic crushed him. What if he'd lost control and hurt Tierra? What had he been thinking, letting himself leave the Guild? What if he made things worse?

Tierra hugged herself and rubbed her upper arms, leaning back on the headboard. She was shivering despite the heat. "Tell me what happened there, please."

"Heka is right. You have all six energies activated. I touched all of them with my energy." He didn't mention the vision of the naked Nixie. Image, rather. It wasn't a vision. It hadn't come from Ajna, it had come from his sneaky Svadisthana energy trying to find a way out of his body. It wasn't a true glimpse of his future, and it wasn't relevant to the discussion at hand.

It was just his bloody Svadisthana trying to escape. He would take some time alone once he'd finished here, and check his wardings. He'd work out what was happening with Tierra, and keep her safe not only from that, but himself.

Tierra nodded, her face set. She looked wan, worse than before his examination. "I felt them as you moved through them. As if you were plucking strings inside me. Each one set off vibrations. But I don't know what to do with all those energies. How to handle them. My two main energies have always been part of me, always stood out. They increased as I grew, but they were always there. These feel alien. Wrong."

She paused and picked at the pillow she sat on. "Can we reverse it, Jeb?"

He wanted to reassure her, wanted to tell her this was temporary. That she wouldn't suffer the fate of any of the case studies they'd found. But he couldn't lie to her.

"I don't know. I think I can stabilize them enough so that you don't have any more fits, and so that your body is able to handle all six of them active inside you. But reversing them," he winced, "right now we don't have any information on that.

He smiled, but it was a weak effort. "Perhaps it will be a good thing. Imagine if we had access to all the energies. You could be powerful."

A crease formed between her eyes. "I'm already powerful. I don't need more. I'm happier than I've ever been."

Tierra was a strong energetic. Jeb should know – he had been her Maven for her auxiliary energy, Anahata. Tierra had proved stronger than many who had Anahata as their dominant energy. But she had no pride, no ambition. She loved to help and nurture others, never seeking positions of power in the energetics' structure.

For some, the activation of the other four Chakras within them would engender aspirations for power. But for Tierra, it meant nothing.

He sent a prayer of gratitude to Source that it was Tierra who had to bear this issue and not other energetics he knew. If – when – she came through this, and somehow ended up with all six active, she would find a way to remain steady.

"How do we fix it?" She leaned her head back against the headboard, arms wrapped around her upper body, but kept her gaze on Jeb. "We need a plan."

He nodded. "Feng is researching at the moment. He sends his love by the way."

Tierra smiled. "Thanks. He's a sweetheart."

"He's very fond of you. As am I. And, of course, so is Fintan. I'm glad the two of you got together." He glanced at her wrist, where the twin bracelet to Fintan's wrapped around the slender column. They were some kind of mysterious gift from Source, connected to the prophecy somehow, though he wasn't sure how far their research had gotten in determining what they did.

Tierra's smile turned into a beam. "Me too. I had a crush on him for the longest time, but it wasn't a real thing, a true thing. Now? The love that I feel for him, that's real."

Tierra and Fintan seemed to bring out the best in each other. Another stab of guilt assaulted Jeb. He was supposed to be one of the most powerful healers in Anahata, and he had no idea how to cure her.

"I want to talk to Heka," he said, "and then I'll find a way to stabilize you further. I have a lot to think about."

He took her hand. "But we will sort this, Tierra. We will get you back to normal."

He needed to believe it as much as she did.

❧ ❧ ❧

Nixie came into the room where Ai was slouched on her bed, fiddling with a cellphone. The girl looked up for a moment, jerked her head in acknowledgement, then went back to the screen.

"How're you doing, Ai?" Nixie asked. Tierra had asked about Ai, and Nixie had said she would check in on her. It was something she felt she could do. She didn't know the girl well, but Nixie didn't need Anahata energies to read the sullen anxiety coming off her in waves.

Nixie would try and keep it light.

Ai snorted. "Been sent to babysit?"

Nixie's eyebrows rose. Cranky much? Nixie didn't really have the energy for this. "Something like that. Better if you're not a baby though, and talk to me like an adult. How are you?"

Ai looked at Nixie with a disbelieving sneer. Nixie tried to soften her tone. "Really. I care. And I'm concerned about Tierra too."

Ai shrugged. "Tierra's cool. She doesn't deserve this."

Nixie nodded. "Do you want to talk about it?"

"Nuh, uh." Ai shook her head emphatically.

"It's going to be okay," Nixie said. "Blaize is good in a crisis."

As much as Nixie had got them into trouble over the years, Blaize had usually got her out of it. Nixie just needed faith in her pee sao, or big sister.

Ai didn't reply, but her shoulders loosened slightly. She got up and went to the wardrobe in the corner of the room. As she opened the door, a tokay gecko, one of the little lizards that frequented most houses on the island, fell out and hit Ai's arm on its way to the floor. She screamed, and it shot off into the corner of the room.

Ai gave another yell of frustration, and slammed the door shut again. "I hate this place! There are creatures everywhere. What the fuck is it with Thailand's nature anyway? Why can't it stay outside?"

Nixie winced. She liked the geckos. "It's harmless, really. They help to keep the insects down."

"I don't give a shit! I want to go back to the city," Ai snarled.

Uh. Oh dear. She was trapped with an angry teen. What was she supposed to do? She didn't love the idea of being the 'adult'. It wasn't a role she felt she played especially well. She'd never been drawn to parenthood, and had little experience with kids of any age. Maybe it was time for a different tack. "Have you ever drawn?"

Ai's brow crinkled. "What are you talking about?"

"When I'm upset, art helps me to settle myself. We could try it, if you like." Nixie wasn't exactly feeling calm and relaxed at the moment. She could do with some time in 'flow', drawing. She wasn't a huge fan of doing art with others, but maybe it would help the girl chill out. An olive branch, of sorts.

Ai squinted up at Nixie. "Really? You want to finger paint our feelings while Tierra's sick?"

The girl was a nightmare.

"I don't want to finger paint." It came out more sharply than she'd meant. "Think of it more as a form of therapy."

That went down like a lead balloon.

"Therapy," said Ai, flatly. "I've tried that. In the group home they put me in when my parents were killed. It didn't work out."

Nixie ground her teeth. This was uphill work. The girl had had a rough life, sure, but Nixie hadn't caused that. She was trying to help.

"Fun then. A distraction. You and I can't help Tierra right now, and she'd hate to think of us brooding." She'd hate to think of Ai brooding, anyway. Nixie certainly wasn't brooding. She could entertain herself fine.

Alright. One more try to explain how art could help. The teen probably hadn't had much exposure to the idea, after all. When would she have had a chance, spending most of her teenage years on the streets? "When I was a Svadisthana Adherent in the Guild, I missed home a lot. I spent a lot of time working in the sculpture room. Creating in that way helped me process what I was feeling and move past it."

One of the pieces of art she'd created had even won a Thai national art prize, though she'd given both prize and sculpture to her parents as a thank you for all their support.

"I don't want to have fun while Tierra's sick," Ai said.

"Don't be such a martyr," Nixie snapped. The child was thankless. Art was something Nixie lived and breathed, and if the kid couldn't appreciate it, that was her problem. "I'm asking you to draw, not to party. Tierra's worried about you, and I want to be able to tell her you're doing okay."

Okay, so Nixie didn't really know how to treat kids. She was going to leave her to Blaize and Tierra in future.

The girl was huddled on the bed, her face pale. Nixie had gone too far.

"At least you had parents to miss," Ai said, her tone derisive. "It's all about you. What do you do? Blaize and Fintan are Warriors, and Tierra looks after everyone else. Even that new guy has dope healing skills. But you're just hanging out drinking coconut shakes while the rest of us are trying to survive."

Nixie felt winded, as if the wounded young woman on the bed had punched her in the stomach.

It was all she could do to stumble out the door, across their wide balcony and down the stairs of the house. She threw a leg over her bike. What *did* she do? She'd even failed at the simple task of checking in on the teen.

Nixie's go-to when emotions raged inside her like this was usually sex. Today, though, when she thought about her options, the only face that came to mind was Jeb. With Jeb, though, she was the one who was meant to be providing the solace. The lightness. Right now, her frustrations were swirling inside her needing grounding, and she wasn't about to take that out on a guy who hadn't had sex in decades.

Ai had issues, she knew that. Nixie was just indignant the girl had taken them out on her. For some reason, something in Ai's criticism had shaken Nixie's usual self-confidence. She knew she couldn't be angry with the teenager, so she needed to channel her feelings elsewhere.

If it wasn't sex, then there was only one place that would do.

The sea.

A swim would help relax her, and bring her back to herself. A storm was coming, and the sands would be empty. Arriving, she parked, stripped down to her skin, and walked into the water, where she let the salt water of her angry tears blend with the warm embrace of the ocean.

CHAPTER 11

Jeb walked along the beach and looked longingly at the sea. He didn't dare go in the water this soon after leaving the safety of the Guild, but he'd missed the wild waters of the ocean, rivers, lakes. Swimming pools, baths and showers didn't measure up to the feeling of being surrounded by water in nature.

It was too soon. The Guilds were steeped in the energies of their members, the very bricks and mortar supporting any magics done there. Out here in the real world using Anahata with Tierra at the same time as keeping his Svadisthana in check was a small but constant drain, wearing him down.

His temples ached, and pressure built inside his head. His energy told him a storm was coming, so he'd stripped to his shorts to walk along the quiet golden beach, hip hop from his phone in his pocket keeping him company, the music he preferred to relax to. The skies were darkening quickly, the tropical storm coming in faster than he'd expected. Should he risk it and stay outdoors for the storm?

He took in lungfuls of the ozone in the air, relishing the empty horizon in front of him and the breeze that was building and tossing the beach's natural debris onto the sand. He felt invigorated, like something inside him was waking up.

His eyes narrowed. The view in front of him wasn't completely empty. There was a shape far out to sea – some sort of fish? No. And it was too small for a boat. He shaded his eyes with his hands, straining to see. Was it a person? They were a long way out, and taking a risk as the waves were increasing in height and frequency. It wouldn't be long before any person out there would struggle to come inland.

Rain started to fall, light at first. The figure was moving towards the shore. He was a few feet back from the water's edge, wary of it touching him. He'd need to be a damn sight surer that someone was in trouble before he went in the water.

There was no point trying to save someone, only to endanger them more.

Nixie's tears had been lost to the ocean, and she was more settled. She could feel the storm coming in, and she delighted in the air pressure building up. She loved the rain on her skin – it was a pleasure only second to swimming for her.

She ducked and dived, playing with the increasingly large waves. Her freediving experience meant she could hold her breath for many minutes so she would alternate swimming under a wave to bodysurfing on top.

The rain fell harder, and she bobbed up and down, putting her hands in the air to feel more of its punishing patter on her skin.

She loved this.

The storm built momentum, and thunder and lightning crashed through the sky. She should go back in. It was unlikely she'd be hurt by the waves, but there was always a chance for Svadisthana energetics they'd get too caught up in a storm and meld with it, losing their selfhood. She should go inland, and get back to the others. They'd wonder where she was.

She lit out for the shore. It wasn't sex, but a swim in a storm was almost as good.

She dived in a graceful ripple under the waves, and powered back with strong, sure strokes. She cut through the water, then flipped in a full roll to place her feet on the sand beneath the sea as she surged out of the water at a run, laughing.

Only a few steps out and she slammed into something solid. Dazed, she wobbled in place, then found her shoulders gripped by dry, warm hands. *What the hell?*

She blinked to clear her vision, and brought her hands up in front of her, groping the air to try and understand who was holding her. Male. A chest with a light dusting of rough hair, slick in the storm. Lean, but well-muscled.

Finally, her eyes adjusted to the dusk.

Her mouth fell open in shock as she realized who it was.

Jebediah let go and took a step back as the fairy bared fierce white teeth up at him. She might be many inches shorter than him, but in that moment he felt a sharp spike of adrenaline as to what she might do next. He turned his palms up to show he meant her no harm. He wasn't sure he could say the same for her.

It was then he realized that she was naked, her lithe light brown body showing no tan lines. His eyes were caught by a drop of rain that fell from her hair onto her small right breast. It followed that curve until it slid between her breasts, over her belly, and down into a tiny patch of trimmed hair.

He swallowed, and the adrenaline was joined by a wash of arousal so strong that his groin was filled with blood in seconds. *Shit.*

He took a step back, his hard dick obvious through the wet shorts that clung to his body. Who was this woman?

She glanced down, and her look of anger turned to one of consideration. She tipped her head to the side, and stepped into his body.

"Jebediah," she breathed. "I saw you in Cuinn's vision, you know."

He nodded. He was a fly in a spider's web. Stuck fast in place. Whoever she was, it wasn't safe. He thought about research and dusty books, about Feng and Fintan, anything to calm his sexual energy down. He could feel it hurling itself against the wardings and locks inside him.

The warm rain hammered down, and lightning flashed in the distance. They both ignored it.

"I saw two versions of you," Nixie said.

He cocked his head, his interest caught. He'd take the distraction. "What do you mean?"

"I saw lonely eyes, as if you'd spurned your Svadisthana … " She put up a palm to his cheek and he closed his eyes as her hand reached him. She touched each eyelid lightly, and put her hand on his chest, running those featherlike fingers between his nipples, and along the planes of his stomach, stopping a little above the waistband of his shorts. He stifled a groan. "…And I saw your eyes burn when you'd let go of your control."

"I can't – I don't do that."

He stepped backwards again, but she followed him, her toes pressing into the wet sand, leaving shallow footprints that the sea washed away with each new wave.

Still the rain beat down.

She put one hand on his hip, and her other slid around the back of his neck. She drew him down towards her and he was ensnared. Her mouth touched his like a brush of petals and he groaned again, but made no move to touch her. Her fingers on his cool wet skin were like a burn.

His Svadisthana energy swirled and looped inside him, looking for a way out. He needed to get away. To find a safe place away from this delicate-seeming sprite, till he figured out what she wanted.

But while it might have been what he needed, it wasn't what he wanted.

Seven decades of discipline cracked slightly, as personal desire surged inside him, and he longed to let himself free.

Instead of taking another step back, he opened his lips a little, enough for her to probe between them with a soft tongue, one that entwined with his oh-so-gently. She was wearing him down, not with a flourish of her own Svadisthana, which she could easily do, but with a serene and gradual assault on him that was making him lose his mind.

He broke the kiss with an effort, pulling his head upright and out of her reach. She really was a tiny thing. Surely he could disengage from her gracefully. "I can't do this."

She slid her arm around his waist, and then over his buttocks. "Of course you can."

She was matter-of-fact, an energetic in harmony with her Svadisthana energy. She had no issues around sex.

But her energy hadn't caused the death of innocents.

That sobering thought was enough for the hardness in his groin to subside, and he reached behind him to take her hands and detach them.

She looked up at him, those damn drops of water still falling from her hair as the rain pummeled them both. Rivulets of water drew his gaze over and over the graceful curves of her naked body.

"You're putting too much importance on sex," she said, her voice seductive. "It's just like a massage. Don't be like the humans. Don't attach shame or other issues to it. Don't make more of it than it is. And we're both Svadisthana. I can take what your energy gives, even if it's been a while."

Perhaps she was safe in that way from STIs and pregnancy, but he didn't think she quite realized what his energy might do to her.

She walked him backwards another step, and then one more.

"Sex is a gift. We can lie here on the beach, water all around us, and you can bury yourself inside me. Stroke by stroke, the pleasure will build. I can help you reclaim your Svadisthana energy. You no longer need to cut yourself off from half of who you are. You can be yourself fully once more."

The words were dangerous. Because part of him would love that. Wanted it desperately. But he knew that was a fantasy. He could never return to the lighthearted way he'd treated sex and his energy before the war.

With each sentence, she pushed him another step backwards. At the end of the last few words, he smacked into something solid, and his breath 'ouf'ed out of him. He'd hit a palm tree, and there was nowhere else to go. It broke her spell for a moment, and he tried to explain to her the danger she flirted with.

"You're desirable, Nixie, but sex with me wouldn't be safe. My energy is locked up and it needs to stay that way. My control could easily break and you could be destroyed." His body was as rigid as the tree behind him, tension in every muscle.

She put slim arms around him, and pressed her belly into his hard dick.

"What's sex without a little risk?" she whispered.

He groaned again and fisted her hair. He wrenched her head backwards, baring her neck. He leant down and kissed it, as he slid the other hand down her back to her small firm butt. He squeezed hard as he bit her neck lightly, and she moaned.

As he did, a thread of his Svadisthana slipped out and mixed with her own sexual energy. The two energies embraced each other in a shower of bronze sparks, and she gasped. He palmed her naked sex roughly as he slid two fingers inside her.

She tipped her hips up to encourage him, and he massaged her with his hand, the skills he'd learned as part of his Svadisthana training coming back to him despite the length of time since he'd last used them. Her breath came in tiny gasps, and he lifted and spun them both so she now pressed against the uneven surface of the tree. He had one hand inside her, and the other held her neck, pinning her in place.

He leaned her hard into the tree, and moved his palm and fingers, fast and light, quick and deft, following the urgent rhythm of her body and breath, until she came with a sob, her body quivering, held upright by his hands.

As the pleasure wracked her body her energy released in a rush, and swept through him in a surge.

He slammed more shields into place as his fingers curled in reflex, and stretched her neck taut as the fingers of the other hand brushed her g-spot. She cried out again.

He concentrated and kept his body a rigid fortress, while her energy and her pleasure battered at the wardings on his Svadisthana energy. He would not let go. He hadn't been able to keep all his own energy inside him, but the curls and twists that had escaped were limited, and had been mostly absorbed by Nixie as she'd writhed on his hand.

His dick throbbed in his shorts as he held his body a little away from hers. She was limp and relaxed against the tree, but he sensed she wouldn't stay that way for long.

The storm raged around them, the waves now nothing you could swim in. *Even this water sprite would have difficulty.*

After a few moments, she opened her eyes, and he removed his hand from her sex and bent slightly to scoop her up. She was as light as she looked, her skin hot.

"Where are your clothes?" he asked.

"In my motorbike." She trailed her hand over the exposed skin of his chest, face and neck. "No need for them yet. We can go to one of the beach huts."

She met his eyes. "I want you inside me. Then you'll see what letting go really means."

Lightning flashed and lit her body up. It glistened with fat drops of water that slowly gathered until they became too heavy to stay in place, and then made their leisurely way down her body until they detached themselves for the leap to the wet sand beneath them.

He carried her easily over to her motorbike a few hundred yards away, and set her gently on the ground.

"I'm sorry," he said. "You're beautiful. Wonderful. You can see that from my body's response – your skin on mine felt amazing. But

I can't risk my Svadisthana. There are good reasons I no longer use it."

He stepped back to gain a little distance between himself and her still naked, still delightful body. He felt his statement would have had more weight if his cock hadn't been visible through his shorts, the rainsoaked material clinging to it so it stood out in stark relief.

Her emotions whirled around him: surprise, disappointment, disbelief. She turned and crouched, and picked up her bike key which had been hidden beneath the wheel. The view of her curved back didn't do anything to help his dick subside. He looked away and focused on the sea behind them. Concentrating on the waves, he took deep breaths and thought about anything other than sex.

She unlocked her bike's storage compartment, and pulled out a dress that she dropped over her head. She turned back to him. "Fine. But you're missing out."

She slid a leg over the seat, the size of bike making her seem even more fragile, and shoved the key into the ignition. She turned the engine on, and with a twist of her hand, accelerated off into the night.

He was left with nothing but the sound of the rain, and a body that ached with loss and lust.

"I'm starting to realize that," he whispered into the storm.

Nixie drove like Diana during a hunt. Her body tingled all over, and she had to swallow repeatedly past a lump in her throat. She wanted to drive and drive until she was as far away as possible from that … that bastard. Unfortunately, you could drive round the whole of Koh Somdun in less than a few hours, so it wasn't an option.

She skidded onto the little road that led to her place, the combination of sand and water untrustworthy under her wheels, and jammed her brakes on to stop in front of her house. She ran up the stairs and flung herself into her hammock on the balcony. She wasn't ready to go inside yet. She wanted to be surrounded by the sound of the storm's wrath which echoed her own.

Her sobs were muffled by the sound of the weather, but after a few minutes Blaize appeared in the doorway.

"What's the matter?" Blaize asked. She pulled a chair over to the hammock and sat next to Nixie, putting a hand on her hair and stroking it gently. Being friends with a water energetic meant Blaize was no stranger to Nixie's tears.

"I had sex with Jeb," Nixie burst out.

Blaize's hand paused momentarily. "Jebediah? Isn't he celibate?"

"Apparently so." Nixie gulped back more tears.

"Wait, what? I'm confused. Did you have sex or not?" Blaize asked. "In fact – hold on."

Blaize got up and went back into the house, and returned moments later with a cool damp flannel which she handed to Nixie. Nixie swiped at her face until she felt calmer.

"Okay, continue," said Blaize. "What are you talking about?"

Nixie filled Blaize in on what happened on the beach. By the time she was finished, ending with her rush to get back home, Blaize's eyebrows were up near her hairline.

"Huh," she said. "How'd you feel? What are you going to do?"

"I don't know," Nixie admitted. "Not good. Even a bit stupid. Especially because he made me come, but never let go himself. And that's where the meaning is in Svadisthana sex, in letting go to each other."

She swallowed hard. "Actually, I feel like crap. I'm struggling with all this prophecy stuff, and sex is supposed to be the thing I am good at, but I missed something important there too."

Nixie hadn't mentioned her interaction with Ai to Blaize, though two rejections in quick succession were weighing on her.

Nixie continued. "I thought that sex with Jeb might be fun. Usually sex with another Svadisthana energetic is out of this world."

Blaize raised her eyebrows.

"I thought I could help him with his weird thing about not using Svadisthana by reminding him how great Svadisthana sex could be," Nixie continued. "And I thought if we had sex, he'd be out of my system too."

"You thought you'd forget about him after you'd had great sex?" Blaize said.

Nixie shrugged. "It happens. Sometimes I enjoy the buildup more. The flirting. The potential. Then once we actually sleep together, although the sex is mostly great, I'm less interested."

"Maybe your current approach isn't working," Blaize suggested. "Try getting to know people a bit more. Maybe if you let yourself care about them, they'd hold your interest longer."

Nixie huffed. "I do care! In general, the guys who have sex with me aren't interested in getting to know me."

She thought for a moment about Ben, who'd seemed to want something else from her, and her panicked response. She'd probably misread him.

"Anyway, thanks for listening. I appreciate this isn't a priority."

Blaize got to her feet. "I'm always here if you need me, Nix. You know that. I'm going to go and check in on Tierra before I sleep. I'll catch you in the morning. We can try another sketch."

Nixie nodded and lay back in the hammock as Blaize walked off. It had probably been a mistake to try and seduce Jeb. He was a reclusive introvert, not her type at all. There was plenty of fun, light-hearted sex available on the island. She didn't need him, and wouldn't pursue him further.

Though dammit. There was something about him.

The thunder and lightning that had surrounded Jeb and Nixie's encounter was over. She hoped that was the only storm she'd have to weather concerning him, but she worried there'd be more bad atmospheric conditions to deal with before he was gone.

It took Jeb an hour to walk back from the beach. The rain stung his bare skin every inch of the way.

He enjoyed the rain, though it wasn't comfortable. There was something else, too, some darker emotions from the night, almost a sense of being watched. He scanned the terrain around him frequently, but didn't catch sight of anyone.

He tried to open himself up to sense what was around him. His headache intensified. The encounter with Nixie had thrown him, and his energies were unsettled. He struggled to get a read on anything.

He tried instead to repair some of the damage to his wardings as he walked, building up his shields in layers. He felt a sense of urgency to talk to Nixie and apologize for his behavior. Truth was important to Jeb. Truth, and integrity. Nixie was owed more explanation as to why he couldn't be with her. Why he needed to keep his sexual energy bound tightly.

Arriving at the house, he walked upstairs to where she lay in the hammock on her house's balcony. Her balcony faced into the privacy of the forest, and wasn't overlooked by the other houses, which were all at least fifty yards apart.

It looked as if she had fallen asleep. He rocked the hammock slightly. "Nixie?"

"Hmmm?" She sounded as though she was having a nice dream.

"I'd like to talk," he said.

She opened her eyes blearily, and shook her head when she saw him standing there.

"You," she said.

"Hello." It wasn't his most scintillating conversation starter, but he was a bit thrown by the sleepy version of the fierce fairy he'd met on the beach. She looked like something from a painting, curled up in the hammock, her hands tucked under her head. She rubbed one eye with a fist and yawned. She had a perfect mouth.

"Why are you here?" She didn't sound that interested in the answer.

"To apologize."

She gave him a searching stare. "Really."

He was going to have to work harder. "I wanted to explain."

She had both eyes open, but wasn't giving anything away. Perhaps she really didn't care. But his intuition told him she did. He'd hurt her on the beach by saying no, and he wanted to explain why.

"Go on," she said. She didn't sit up.

He walked to the corner of the balcony and picked up a cushion from one of the chairs. He dropped it in front of the hammock and sat on it, facing towards her.

"I can't let my Svadisthana energy out," he said.

She tutted and waved a hand. "I know that. You mentioned it. Is that all?"

Jeb held back a frown. "No. I wanted to tell you why."

She watched him, her expression steady.

"During World War II, I used my energy to help the Allies gain information about the enemy. I was focused on saving the most lives possible. It was an adventure. I was a 'Raven' – I would seduce women collaborators for intelligence purposes. I would make sure they had a good time, and then share the information with my handler. We were careful not to burn the women as assets, and I only chose those who would have willingly slept with me anyway."

Nixie hadn't moved a muscle.

Jeb gazed off into the distance at the stars over the forest that surrounded the house. He could hear geckos chirping, and other sounds of the Thai night that surrounded them just as the warm blanket of night air did. He was grateful the humidity wasn't too bad this evening. The storm had freshened the atmosphere.

"So I thought, anyway. I fell for one. A Parisian collaborator, she ran a jazz club where she would pass on gossip to the Germans in exchange for being left alone. She was very beautiful." Men had flocked to Lucie, her infectious presence and her bewitching looks.

"We spent a week in bed, and she told me everything. I thought she cared for me in turn, that she trusted me." He shook his head. "I passed on the information to my handler after the week, and moved on. It turned out the Germans were seeking a mole. They'd passed out misinformation to find the leak. My allies used the information Lucie had provided, and she was outed."

Nixie's eyes were wide, and he could see the white surrounding her dark brown irises.

"She was executed," Jeb said.

Nixie made a sound of distress. Jeb continued on grimly. "It doesn't end there. They tortured her, and initiated reprisals in the form of collective punishment of innocents in her area. They executed another ten people, and burned businesses down. They destroyed hospitals."

Nixie took an intake of breath.

"You couldn't have known what was going to happen. I don't understand how you can blame yourself," she said, her forehead creased, her eyes soft. He didn't deserve the look she was giving him. He needed to make her understand.

He rolled his shoulders, trying to stop the muscles tightening. "After she died, I received a letter she'd written the day I left that week."

A letter that had shattered his illusions.

"What did it say?" Nixie breathed.

"It was a letter that asked me not to visit her again. That something about me clouded her judgement. That she found me arousing, but she didn't understand why. And that when I was around her, it was hard for her to think straight."

"Oh, no." Nixie understood. Any energetic with that energy would.

"Yes. Not only is all that blood on my hands, but somehow I let my Svadisthana energy manipulate her. I had convinced myself she wanted it, I wanted us to connect so much. She didn't. I might as well have forced her."

"You didn't do it on purpose," Nixie said. "It's not the same."

He shook his head. "Does it matter? I was supposed to be a Master in my energy, and I got carried away. I thought she was in control of her actions. I thought no woman could resist me. I was way over the line."

He'd stopped his actions immediately, withdrawn to the Guild. In the long months that followed, had wondered how many of the women he'd seduced had been influenced by his energy. Been manipulated into sex, which was anathema for those with his energy.

"It was War. Your work saved lives, right?" Nixie said. "You were already lying to the women."

He shrugged. "I went back to that area, and I walked around. The smoke from the burned out shops got into my nostrils. I watched children who'd had a parent taken play in the street. And I felt the pain of every person in that neighborhood. I walked around like a ghost, and realized I had a responsibility to be different. That things weren't as black and white as I'd thought, and that the great adventure was more about shades of grey than being on the 'right' side." Jeb sat up straight on his cushion. His neck felt stiff, and he rolled his head to try and loosen the kinks.

"Tierra speaks very highly of you."

He snorted. "She deserves better. Her mother and aunt were working in a Polish hospital the Germans destroyed because of information that Lucie gave them. She knew I had important connections at a hospital in a particular area, and the Germans bombed both to make sure they killed them. Tierra had to hunt for her family's bodies in the rubble. I have no right to her friendship." Yet he was grateful every time he saw her that he had it.

"I'd offer to help you with a massage, but you'd think I was coming on to you again," said Nixie. Her voice was dry, and Jeb had trouble reading her. She was still interested in him, certainly, but he also got a sense of empathy from her. He wasn't sure he could take her kindness.

"I wasn't trying to get your sympathy," he said. "I want you to understand why I chose to lock up part of myself. I wasn't able to control and channel that energy in a positive way. I wasn't in control of it. Anahata is a purer energy."

Nixie snorted. "Thanks."

"I didn't mean –"

"I know what you meant. You mean, in fact. But you're wrong." Nixie said. "Every energy can be used for good or ill. This is basic energetic teaching. I don't understand how you can be so senior in your Guild and have this giant blind spot."

She twisted so she sat up in the hammock and faced him dead on. Her feet touched the ground lightly and she pushed with the balls of her feet to make the hammock rock a little.

At one end of each oscillation, she swung over his lap. Her dress lifted with the air, and he felt a rush of arousal remembering her putting it on at the beach – with nothing underneath. He shifted on the cushion. It was fine. It was dark out here. She couldn't see.

There was a thickness in the air, almost like a syrup. Which was strange, because it wasn't humid. That darkness he'd sensed earlier was present – perhaps he was oversensitive to Tierra's illness? She was in a house not far away. He couldn't think what else it could be. His brain was so fuzzy.

He bent his head towards each shoulder, and stretched his neck out more.

She jumped off the hammock and darted round behind him. "I can't bear to see you like this. Hold still."

She put her hands on his shoulders, and he jerked a little. "The pain will help, in the long run."

She dug those slender fingers into his trapezius muscle, and squeezed and massaged and rubbed. He grimaced as she worked out kinks and knots in his shoulders and neck, and then began to dance her fingers over his skull, her body against his back.

He had to stifle a moan of appreciation at that. It was a hurt that felt good.

The thickness of the air had intensified, and he felt lightheaded, almost dizzy. Her touch slowed, her movements more languorous.

He put a hand back on one of hers and held it. "I think you should stop."

She paused in place, which was fine until he realized it meant that her small breasts rested against his back.

Her nipples dug into his back like pebbles. He drew her round, but instead of sitting in front of him on the floor or the hammock, she circled his body like a pole, and ended up sitting in his lap facing him, her legs either side of his.

He swallowed. The air was so heavy now he could barely breathe. He tried to blink away the sluggishness that pervaded his body. He wasn't sure he could move if he tried.

He needed to try. Something wasn't quite right here, but he couldn't work out what it was. All he could think about was the woman in his lap. His mind was clouded.

Her legs were loose around him, but it meant that her sex was exposed, her dress having ridden up to her waist.

He put his hands on her back to move her, but instead of encouraging her to move, his hands slid of their own volition down to her buttocks, and he cupped them, kneading and squeezing them gently. The material still covered the hot flesh, but when she tilted her butt back, his hands slid between her legs and met with the smooth slick flesh there.

She looked him in the eyes. She was as serious as him. There was little of Svadisthana's play in either of them. The dark wrapped around them on the wooden floor, him on the cushion, her on him.

He sucked in a breath, his chest expanding, and her hands came down to his nipples. She scratched his chest lightly, tracing the contours of his muscles, and he realized that he was hard. This time, though, he found it more difficult to remember why he needed to stop. He couldn't think straight. *I do need to stop though. Don't I?*

He wasn't sure. It was so hard to breathe. He felt as if he was made of thick treacle, his body hot and malleable, responding to her heat and her massaging hands. He couldn't think properly, couldn't clear his mind. It had been so long since he'd done this, he couldn't remember if this was normal. There was something at the very back of his consciousness that pinged, warning him this was a mistake, but it was a weak signal, easily ignored.

She pulled herself in tighter towards him and rested her head in the crook of his shoulder. As she did so, her hips came towards him too, and her sex met his cock, with only his shorts between them.

He lifted her up with one hand, and created enough space to unzip his pants with the other, freeing his hard dick so he could slide it in the next movement into her still slick channel.

He held himself still, lost inside her. He shouldn't move, he knew. Couldn't let himself go. Couldn't lose control.

He had enough wits about him to remember her pleasure. He slipped a hand between them and touched the area where they joined, finding her most sensitive place and tracing it, over and over and over.

Such a subtle movement.

Both of them still and silent apart from his hand working her gently, building her pleasure.

And still his head felt murky and confused.

The only thing he knew was that he wanted this woman. She liberated something inside him. He felt more free than he had for decades.

She was still nestled against him, his free arm wrapped around her. Was he holding her in place, or supporting her?

Repetitive movements.

Flesh touching flesh, softly, gently, persistently.

Her breath fluttered over his chest, warm even in the tropical night that cloaked them. It sped.

He increased the tempo of the small movements of his finger. Her clit was firm, and her orgasm was close.

The temptation to move, no, to thrust inside her, and to let go, was fierce.

He couldn't. Mustn't. Wouldn't.

Why, again?

He blinked and tried to clear his head, but as he did, she threw her head back and climaxed with a soft outbreath. Her walls clenched around his member, squeezing.

i need to keep control

Hot flesh surrounded him

dontletgo

as she contracted

controlhehadtokeepcontrol

he was almost delirious with the pleasure

control

of her tightening around him.

He tried to heed the tiny voice at the back of his head, tried to focus on what it was saying, knowing it was important, a part of him trying to reinforce his shields and keep his wards strong – even as the world exploded.

His Svadisthana energy cracked his shields, so energy escaped and rolled over hers, then spiked out into the night. He held onto the shields as much as he could, kept control in the center of the storm, but it was a battle. It tore at him, and he wrestled with the leash, trying to keep the energy in whilst his body let go. He spilled himself into her in a handful of rippling movements.

The physical was understated compared to the energy. Their Svadisthana energies entwined with each other, touching the insides of their bodies just as their flesh met outside. He tried to keep it between them, cycling between their bodies, and to keep the flare to a minimum. To ensure she, and anyone else nearby, wasn't damaged.

But he couldn't bear it. The release of pressure whilst trying to retain control was too much for him. As he came, his member jerking inside her, his energy ripping through her, his body shut down. He slumped backwards, pulling her down, and passed out into darkness.

13

Nixie slept badly, and woke up earlier than normal. She rubbed her eyes and sighed. She was going to have to face Jeb today. The night before, he'd come so hard that he'd passed out. Well, perhaps not only from his orgasm. There was also the unleashing of his sexual energy. Some of it, anyway. He'd held back most, though the encounter had been a lot more satisfying than the beach, and a lot less one-way.

Her mouth twisted. She'd had an effect on him, she knew that. So why wasn't she enough to make this man truly let go? His story had been sad, certainly, and he had a somewhat tragic past, but why was he still living in the past? Why not live for today? What he'd done had been bad, certainly, but these days he appeared to have developed iron control over his energy. He wasn't going to be influencing anyone accidentally.

Once she'd poked him in the side hard enough to wake him up, his reaction hadn't been quite what she'd been hoping for. Whilst she'd felt a tentative hope that this man might actually be someone she could connect with, and the sex had left her energized, he'd appeared horrified. Okay, perhaps horrified was a bit strong, but it had been like having drunk sex with a twentysomething guy, who'd woken up in the morning to regret it.

It wasn't a feeling she'd ever had to deal with, and she didn't like it.

While she could – and sometimes did – have sex with anyone she was attracted to, sex between two energetics with Svadisthana energy was something special. They had the potential to galvanize or soothe each other through their sexual energy. Sex with her should have made him feel good, relaxed. She knew she'd taken in some of his energy, cleansed it. She was disappointed she hadn't made him feel better. Why wouldn't he let her help him?

She sighed again. She'd get up, eat breakfast, and see if there was anything she could do to help Tierra. Nixie might as well be of some use – she'd pissed off Ai, messed things up with Jeb – who else could she upset while they were around?

She sat up in bed and wrapped her arms around her legs. Then stopped dead as her left wrist caught her eye. Wrapped tightly around it was a bracelet. A bracelet she'd never seen before. She tried to get it off, but there was no clasp, no opening, no easy way.

"Oh, shit," Nixie breathed. This looked a lot like Blaize's. And Cuinn's. And Fintan's. And Tierra's. *Shit shit shit.*

She ran a finger over it. It looked as if it was made of satin embroidery thread, with a glossy luster on each of the four colors: burnt orange, cobalt blue, fern green and a pure, bright white. It was a heck of a lot stronger than thread however, as no amount of pulling or tugging was making any difference.

She stared at her wrist for an age before she jumped out of bed and went over to her dresser. She rummaged around the jewelery scattered in heaps on the surface – she loved pretty things – until she found a large stylish silver cuff, which she put on over the bracelet. She gave her arm an experimental shake. The new bracelet was hidden, and would stay hidden until she understood properly what it was. She wasn't in a rush for bad news. She couldn't think about this right now, whatever it was.

She showered and dressed, and checked Blaize's room to see if she was up. There was no sign of her, so Nixie went across to the other house and into Tierra's room, where Nixie figured Blaize was most likely to be.

Nixie knocked softly on Tierra's door, and opened it slowly. In the room, Jeb sat on a chair next to Tierra, his fingers on her pulse. *Ah, shit.* The person she least wanted to see. Tierra looked pale and weak. There was no sign of Blaize.

Jeb rose when he saw Nixie. She saw bags under his eyes, and wondered how his sleep had been. Was it petty to wish that he'd had bad dreams too?

"I came to see how things were with Tierra," said Nixie. "I'll leave you alone."

"It's okay," said Jeb. "I need to talk to Blaize and Fintan anyway. Come walk with me."

Nixie couldn't think of anything she'd like less.

❧ ❧ ❧

Nixie held the door for Jeb, and followed him out of Tierra's room, which led directly onto the balcony. Tierra's eyes were already closing as she shut the door.

"She needs to rest," said Jeb, walking down the stairs that attached this side of the house to the ground. He was worried about her. This morning Tierra had seemed worse again. Apart from a reduction in symptoms, nothing he had done seemed to have got to the root of the issue, and Feng hadn't come up with anything new.

"Sure," said Nixie. She was subdued.

Jeb waited for Nixie to catch him up as they walked across the land between Nixie's house and where Tierra and Ai were staying. Nixie had opened up her parents' house for Jeb to sleep in last night. Not that he got much sleep. She didn't look him in the eye, but he caught her looking at his wrists several times. Eventually, he cracked.

"Everything ok? Are you looking for the time?" He held up his bare wrists. "I don't wear a watch."

"Huh," Nixie said, and her nose wrinkled. She had a pretty nose.

They found everyone eating breakfast at the shaded tables outside. Fintan half-rose to his feet as they came into view, and only Blaize's hand on his arm kept him in place.

"What's happened?" he asked.

Jebediah wasn't looking forward to this. He could feel a mix of emotions coming from the group, and few of the emotions were positive. He went for direct. "Tierra's worse."

"What? Why? I thought you'd stabilized her?" Fintan's voice rose at the end of the sentence. Jeb could feel how worn the man was. He and Tierra had barely been together for a week or two and she was sick. It was a tough burden for the man to bear.

"I thought we had. I don't know what's changed, I'm sorry. I need to go back to the Guild. If I thought Tierra was well enough to travel, I'd take her, but she should stay here. I'll be back as soon as I can." Or he'd send someone else, if necessary.

Blaize looked concerned. "Was it something to do with the energy spike I felt last night?"

"What do you mean?" said Jeb, tilting his head.

"I felt something in the air last night, a burst of something. And a strange atmosphere before I went to bed. And my dreams were –" Blaize coughed, "er, more explicit than usual. It felt like it might be Svadisthana."

Jeb's face heated while his stomach froze. Had he caused that? Had the unleashing of his sexual energy affected people who were fifty yards away?

There could be no doubt he was attracted to Nixie – and that was why he needed to get away from her as soon as possible. Not only had she got through his wards, so that some of his Svadisthana energy leaked out when he'd come, he'd been up most of the night trying to repair the damage.

His body ached, and his head swam. He had a horrible feeling that his own energetic instability might be one of the reasons why Tierra had taken a turn for the worse. She was sensitive to others' energy when she was well, let alone in the kind of situation that was happening now.

"I don't know why, Fintan," Jeb said. "That's why I need more information."

And he also needed to get away from Nixie's influence. He had let his cock get the better of him for the first time in more than half a century.

He needed to get the hell out of here.

"What happened?" Elrian got straight to the point. He paced up and down the study of his Seattle safe house. It would be time to replenish his energy again soon. He needed the boost. No, wanted, he didn't need it. He could get on okay without it, but would perform better with a top-up.

Aeros was weaker now, having served as a battery for Elrian on a number of occasions, but he was still potent enough for Elrian to drain him and benefit. Imogen was suggesting it might soon be time to make another remnant stone with him, but Elrian wasn't ready to let go of the youth until he had another energetic to replace him.

"I influenced them as discussed, and they had sex," Trent said, his voice cool even down the phone line. "The male passed out when he came."

Elrian grunted. "Excellent. Did he lose control?"

"His shields are powerful. They didn't splinter, they simply fractured, and he kept the majority of his wardings in place. He is likely to have repaired them already."

Elrian clenched his jaw. "That is…disappointing."

Elrian needed that energy to be ripped out of Jebediah, to engulf him and his lover in an ecstasy-filled feedback cycle so they had sex until they were both drained lifeless husks.

Normally, when Svadisthana energetics had sex, they energized each other. But Jebediah's moratorium meant his energy was potentially more malign than benign, pressure having built up as the energy had nowhere to go for decades, and it wasn't cleansed or filtered. He and Nixie could be consumed by it when he finally let go fully – at least that was what Elrian anticipated.

"Do you think he noticed you? Or your influence?" Elrian asked.

"I do not. However, he's going back to Anahata Guild."

"Hmm." Luckily, Elrian had Imogen inside the Guild; powerful, deadly and hidden. He ran a hand through his hair. It could do with a trim. Usually Elrian was on top of his personal grooming – outer order produced inner calm – but recently it had fallen by the wayside.

He now needed to get Nixie to the Guild along with Jeb, and Elrian could hand the problem over and focus on creating the stones. It wouldn't be long before there was one less couple to worry about. The thought brought a thin-lipped smile to his mouth.

"Do you want me to stay here?" Trent said. A faint scraping sound came through the phone. Elrian grimaced. That toothpick. Revolting.

Elrian considered what to do. The mercenary wasn't cheap, but his loyalty was assured through cold, hard cash. The Healer wasn't likely to leave the perceived safety of his Guild in a hurry for a second time, but there were a number of other…problems on the island. Perhaps it was worth investing in destabilizing those further. His whiny niece was sick, dying probably, but he needed Trent to keep hurrying things along.

"Keep the charm draining Tierra and hasten the illness. Her death will destabilize them all. Avoid any wards they have, and ensure you are not seen." That would remove one of them, and then he only needed to take Jeb or Nixie, and wouldn't need both. The risk of failure would be lowered.

"Not a problem," said Trent. "She'll be dead within the week."

C H A P T E R

14

Nixie pushed the silver cuff to the side and stared dully down at the multicolored strands around her wrist. She was in the bathroom, where she'd tried to cut the bracelet off with no success. It seemed to be resistant to energy and to human-made tools.

Normally the artist in her would be fascinated by something like this. But not this time. She hadn't mentioned it to Blaize. She didn't want to take the focus off Tierra, and she wasn't ready to explore what the bracelet might mean for herself. Was it a hope, that she might soon connect with her soulmate, or a snare where she might be trapped with someone for external reasons that weren't her own choice?

Jebediah had left the island soon after breakfast that morning, catching the first boat out to the nearest island with an airport. Which was fine, because, apparently, he didn't have the matching bracelet. If there was a matching bracelet. Just because it had worked like that for the others, didn't mean it would work like that for her.

Despite the fact she actually wanted a relationship. Wanted a lover. A soulmate.

Don't I?

She was starting to think that she'd been chasing a fantasy. She loved the sex, and the thrill of the chase, and she'd felt she needed to meet a lot of men in order to find the right one for her. But perhaps the reason no one ever measured up was that it wasn't destined to happen for her.

Perhaps she wasn't relationship material. Perhaps people were right when they'd said men were only interested in Nixie for her looks, and that what was inside her was irrelevant – or worse, a turn off for guys.

She stared into the mirror, eyes narrowed. Her usual confidence in her appearance, and gifts when it came to sex and relationships, had taken a hit. She was uncertain, a feeling she hadn't experienced much in this area. Her looks and effect on men had been a problem, sure, in her life, but not the kind of problem she was having now.

Jeb was several hundred years old. Despite the last seventy years of celibacy, he would have had a number of relationships, with all kinds of interesting women.

Whereas what could Nixie offer him? Blaize was right, Nixie had been coasting. She wasn't ready for a life of responsibilities, of adulting. It hadn't taken Jeb long to realize that. He seemed to be a man with only responsibilities, but while she'd thought to bring him some joy, she'd seemed only to bring him more difficulty.

For some reason, Jeb's leaving hurt, even though she'd only recently met the man. She winced. She didn't want a guy affecting her this way. She wanted fun, lightness, joy and delight. Great sex and play. Relationships didn't have to be serious to be meaningful, surely?

She picked at the bracelet again, frustrated. Yeah, it wasn't going anywhere. She slowly slid the large metal cuff over it again and hung her head as she rested her hands on the sink, gripping the porcelain.

She really wasn't sure this bracelet was going to lead to anything good.

"I can't believe he deserted us," said Blaize. She was oiling one of her knives, methodically and carefully running a rag up and down the blade. "He was barely here twenty four hours."

She, Fintan, Ai and Nixie were together in Tierra's room. Tierra was no longer propped up in bed, but lay, eyes closed, her dark eyelashes stark against cheeks that were no longer butterscotch but a dark vanilla. They'd opened the curtains and the shutters, so at least the air and the light streamed in and the room wasn't as claustrophobic as it had been when Tierra had been unconscious.

Nixie was doodling in her sketch pad, her pencil moving without her really thinking about it, laying lighter, darker, thicker, thinner strokes upon the page.

Tierra spoke without opening her eyes. "He's a good person. He's gone to see what else he can find."

"Why couldn't someone else do the research? Why did he have to go?" said Blaize. "I know you like him Tierra, so I'm trying to give him the benefit of the doubt, but I'm struggling. He shouldn't have run off when you're still sick."

Fintan paced up and down the room, stopping every few laps to stroke Tierra's brow, squeeze her hand, or stare down at her. Several times Nixie itched to pick up her pencil and sketch his face as he did so. She'd call it 'Devotion.'

"We needed him here," Fintan ground out.

Ai watched them all from the floor where she lay on her front, leafing through a text that Cuinn had lent her about energies.

"He has so much experience. If he reads through the research with Feng, we're much more likely to get a cure sooner," murmured Tierra.

"Can't he get help from the Guild? There's enough of them," Fintan said.

"Aiko says it's too risky to talk about until we understand more about it, and what the consequences are. It's something that no one can remember happening in living memory," Tierra said.

Nixie's stomach was like a small rock. Was she part of the reason Jebediah had left? Of course she was. He hadn't wanted to be around her. That and the comments at breakfast that indicated the sex she'd had with Jeb had loosened his energy in a way that had made Tierra worse, meant now Nixie was partly responsible for Tierra getting sicker. Should she tell them? She couldn't see how it would help, especially as Jeb had removed himself from her vicinity, and he hadn't mentioned it as far as she knew. He was a far more experienced energetic than her, and he must have had a good reason to keep it quiet. Another couple of rocks joined the first inside her.

"Why is it so wrong to share energy?" Ai asked, quietly. "Why wouldn't it be a good thing to have access to more Chakras?"

All the adults stared at her. The taboo against sharing energy was so ingrained in the energetics' culture that Nixie, certainly, had never examined it. From the looks on the others' faces, neither had they.

"In answer to the second question, I didn't think you could," Fintan said. "It doesn't happen. It's supposed to be impossible."

Ai sat up and crossed her legs, and shoved hands into her black cargo pants' pockets. "Okay. But why is sharing energy seen as so terrible? When Tierra shared energy with Cuinn, she helped him to have enough energy to find Blaize and save her life, right? How could that be bad?"

Nixie continued doodling, her hand working without needing her mind, which was partly on Jeb anyway. "I always thought it was too dangerous to share energy. Though I'm not actually sure anyone ever said what the danger was."

Blaize tapped the flat of her blade on her leg a few times. "Did we actually learn this? Or is this something that everyone just knows? I've never really considered it before."

"Is there a punishment?" Ai said, rubbing a lock of her hair between her fingers and glancing at Tierra.

"I don't know," Blaize said. "Do you, Fintan? You're closest to what's considered law around here."

Ai was asking some interesting questions, Nixie thought.

Fintan scratched his chin. "There might be. I've not heard of a case though."

"I think keeping this aspect of the situation quiet is a good plan," Blaize said. "I doubt Cuinn and Tierra would be punished in a formal sense, but there would be a lot of disapproval."

She hesitated. "Even disgust, I think, from some."

There wasn't much conversation for a while after that.

They were all on edge. Blaize spent a lot of time on the phone to Cuinn and Cara, trying to support their progress, and researching what she could with the books she'd brought with her. Blaize also dealt with talking to Tierra's work colleagues. Tierra was a syndicated columnist and was organized enough to have columns written in advance, so all Blaize needed to do was send them on. Ai looked after Tierra or helped Blaize.

Fintan reported that Adam was chasing leads in the Pacific Northwest, and had put his Protector duties on hold while he did. They were all doing what they could. More strokes joined the initial lines on her pad.

Nixie wished she could take action. Do something. The pictures, the reason the others had come here in the first place, had stalled while they dealt with this crisis. Then a thought struck her.

"Why don't…I go and help Jeb?" Nixie spoke slowly. "I'm not doing much here while Blaize is busy, but I could help with research there easily enough. I read several languages, which might be helpful, including Cappotian."

Her auxiliary Chakra, Vishudha, was seated at the throat, and an affinity for languages sometimes came as part of it. Nixie was fluent in Thai and English, and had good Mandarin, and a smattering of romance languages. Her Latin was fairly good, and she had taken to Cappotian, the energetic's ancient language, fairly well when she'd studied it at her Guild.

Fintan stopped and stared at her. "You'd do that?"

"I want to help," said Nixie. "And I can do my graphic design from anywhere."

Going to the Guild seemed pretty safe, something that would keep her out of the line of fire, and stop her messing things up further for Tierra.

"They won't let you in on your own. Well, they probably would if Jeb accepts you as his guest, but he'd be responsible for you," said Fintan. Fintan was a member of Anahata, though his trip to see Jebediah with Tierra a few weeks before had been his first trip back there in many decades.

"Can you go with her?" asked Blaize. She angled her knife to the light and studied the blade.

"I'm not leaving Tierra," said Fintan. "She needs me here more than there. Anyway, we know research isn't my best thing."

"Nixie can be Jeb's guest," said Tierra. "He'll be fine.

Nixie added a few finishing touches to the detail she'd sketched and considered it.

"Then you're up, Nix, if you really don't mind," Blaize said.

Fintan grasped Nixie by the shoulders. "And if you find out any answers? Bring them, and him, back here as soon as you can."

Nixie nodded absentmindedly, still staring down at her sketch pad. Perhaps she would bring him back. For Tierra's sake.

In the meantime, she was wondering why she'd drawn a strong male wrist. A bare one.

Jeb sat in Aiko's living quarters, head in hands. The journey back from Thailand to Egypt had passed in a blur, and once back in the relative safety of his room, he'd wearily begun rebuilding his wards. But after only a few hours, he'd realized he was struggling to put the Svadisthana back in its box, and he'd come to Aiko.

But he couldn't bring himself to tell her everything.

"It's not sustainable. The wards are going to keep breaking down," Aiko said, gently. "The only other thing I can suggest, if you must keep doing this, is that you go to Svadisthana Guild. Perhaps they have a better way of keeping the energy suppressed."

Jeb took his head out of his hands and looked at her. "No. I haven't been back there since before the War, and I don't think the atmosphere there would be beneficial."

Aiko considered him for a moment. "Perhaps you're right."

"It's awash with sexual energy. I'd step through the door and be swimming in it – I'd never keep my shields up. At least here in Anahata Guild I don't come into as much contact with that kind of energy." Jeb said. His stomach felt like lead, and his eyes were gritty. Holding the energy in wasn't easy. It was like trying to hold back the tide. Exhausting.

"I'll help you, both in my Guild capacity, and as a friend. But this needs to end." She pursed her lips. "You're sick. And I think it's because you're only half of who you are."

Jeb shook his head vigorously, and then regretted it as his temples pounded. "Please. Just help me."

She sighed. "Come here."

She walked over to one side of the room. With wooden flooring and several windows, it felt spacious and airy. The only items in that part of the room were a couple of mats on the floor and a small altar. She lit a candle, and placed it on the altar, bowing her head for a moment. Then she directed Jeb to lie face up on one of the mats, and she sat at his side, her hands outstretched over his body.

"Relax," she said. "I'll try and make this as painless as possible."

It wasn't.

She was trying to force his energy back inside him, when it wanted out. He'd been keeping it stable, but it wanted to be used. He felt comfortable with Aiko, even with this dangerous energy, as her sexual interest was women, not men. It wasn't that his Svadisthana couldn't affect her, but it was much less likely to than if she had a sexual preference for males.

He lay with his eyes closed and his teeth gritted, and attempted to keep his muscles lax. Which wasn't easy when spasms of cold fire chased around his energetic and physical body.

After what seemed like hours, Aiko paused in her ministrations. "Jeb. Something's not quite right."

Jeb felt a spurt of adrenaline. From the understated Aiko, that was tantamount to an admission that a catastrophe was about to happen.

She continued. "Don't move, please, but I want to try something."

He lay rigid. The cold fire started again, this time accompanied by a feeling of someone riffling through his body, as if he was a pack of cards being flicked through. It was a disturbing feeling.

After a few moments, Aiko spoke. "Did anything…strange happen while you were away? Was there a trigger for your shields breaking again?"

Jeb was glad his eyes were still closed. He really, really didn't want to admit this. But this was Aiko. They went back centuries. She had been there for him as a long-term friend. Plus, she was his physician in this context. He'd be a fool not to tell her everything.

"The sea affected me. So much wild water…" He swallowed. "And there was a woman."

She nodded with a grave expression. "And what happened?"

He talked her through the experience on the beach and on Nixie's balcony.

His cheeks were hot, and he was glad his eyes were closed. It wasn't shame at the sex. Energetics didn't have the same shame culture as humans about sex, and Svadisthana-trained energetics least of all. It was self-loathing at his lack of control.

"I don't know how this all connects, Jeb, but there are traces of influence in your aura. A sort of sticky energetic residue. If you'd waited much longer before coming to me, they'd have disappeared completely, but it looks to me like someone was exerting their Svadisthana on you to make you lose control."

He felt her light touch on his arm. "How much do you really know about the woman you slept with?"

Once Aiko had finished helping Jeb to lock his energy back down, they had further discussed the possibility of someone tampering with his energy. They'd discussed Nixie, and Aiko, knowing her family well, agreed it was unlikely that it was she who was influencing Jeb, but not impossible.

When he'd looked at the parts of his aura she'd pointed out to him he'd seen the taint. Where normally a healthy Anahata-Svadisthana energetic would have an aura of orange and blue, his had been tainted by subtle traces of silver-grey, as if someone had swirled cobwebs through it.

Jeb's skin crawled at the idea of anyone influencing his free will. Yet part of him wondered if this was some kind of cosmic payback for his actions during the War. Karma.

He was struggling to believe, having touched Nixie's energy, that either incident had anything to do with her directly. Someone was using them both, surely. But, why?

He sat in his study in one of the armchairs. He'd worn his favorite loose sweater today, needing the comfort of familiarity. He stared at the stained glass panel in his window. The bright sun and blue sky behind it made it pop with color. It normally soothed him, but not today.

When he thought back to a couple of nights ago, he thought about the syrupy feeling of the air, which he'd put down to humidity and sexual arousal. It had been such a long time since he'd felt either that he'd never even considered the idea that it might be a Rogue who was twisting energy to use it in such a dark way.

But Nixie was not that Rogue.

Jeb had been dealing with Rogues for centuries, and his empath energies had felt no trace of that kind of energy from her. And she didn't appear to have much guile or artifice about her. Much of her charm was in her natural allure. She had an unconscious and unaffected way of moving through the world that exuded sensuality without her appearing to make much effort. Could she really maintain that kind of deception around people like Blaize, and Fintan, who had known her for years?

Once Aiko was confident he believed her, she'd burned away the remaining traces of alien energy, and reassured him that what had been left had stopped influencing him, most likely after the sexual encounter. She'd also congratulated him for not losing his control entirely. She'd questioned him more about Nixie. He'd shared a little more detail, but he'd also told Aiko he was confident that the woman he'd had sex with – he couldn't call it making love given this new information – hadn't been the one who'd influenced him.

He was, wasn't he? She hadn't even seemed that interested when he'd come onto her balcony to apologize. Was she? He shook his head. And he had come to her, of his own free will. Or had he?

Damn it. He was tired emotionally, mentally, energetically. He needed to rest before he could sort this out in his head. Meditate, perhaps. Ground himself somehow so everything that was going on wasn't such a snarl in his brain.

Was Nixie caught up in someone else's mind games, or was she the one playing him? And what on earth would someone have to gain from making the two of them have sex?

And if it wasn't her, he probably needed to tell her. What if she was in danger?

Since his discussion with Aiko, he'd been umming and ahhing about whether to call Nixie, and he'd had his cellphone in his hand for an hour. It had grown warm from being held.

And then it rang. He almost dropped it, before he fumbled to answer it.

"Hello?" he said.

"It's Fintan. We're sending you some help. She'll be there tomorrow."

"What? What are you talking about?" said Jeb. Fintan. Of course it was Fintan. The man was relentless. Jeb had barely arrived back at the Guild.

"You need to find out answers and get back here. We're sending Nixie to the Guild to help you."

Jeb's stomach crashed to the floor.

"There's no need for that," said Jeb. He needed distance from Nixie until he worked out what was going on. When he was around her, with or without energetic influence, he was clearly susceptible.

"You can use all the help you can get, Jebediah," stated Fintan flatly. "Tierra needs you to find out answers as soon as possible. If Nixie can support you in that, that's great."

"She and I didn't resonate," said Jeb, then felt bad as soon as the words were out of his mouth. It was mean-spirited, and more than that, it wasn't true. They'd resonated far too well on some levels, that was part of the problem. He liked the woman, but she was bad for him. Possibly really bad, if Aiko's worries turned out to be true. He hurried on. "Anyway, she's an artist, not a researcher, correct? I'm not sure that she's going to be able to help. Perhaps someone else would be better?"

Please, Source, let there be someone better.

"Blaize says for all her apparent spaciness, Nixie's good at seeing the big picture. Her Vishudha isn't as strong as her Svadisthana, but it's there. Perhaps she'll see patterns that you and Feng don't see."

He needed another tack. "Is she trustworthy? There's delicate material in the archives. We can't have someone who's more, say, impulsive or capricious. She'd have to keep what she reads between us."

Fintan laughed, though there wasn't a lot of humor in it. "It's true she can be a bit fickle. But she's steadfast when it comes to loyalty to family and friends."

"I'll have to get permission from Aiko to have a guest who's not Anahata in the Guild," Jeb made one more attempt. Maybe he could get Aiko to veto the idea. He didn't want the woman here. Really. He didn't. Given the effect on his control she'd already had, he wanted to stay as far from her as possible. "She might not be comfortable with the idea."

"Cuinn has already spoken to her. She's fine with it. So tough luck, there's no problem," Fintan said. Jeb knew he'd pushed the other man far enough, especially with their already prickly relationship. Jeb rubbed his forehead. He needed to sleep. "She'll be with you first thing in the morning. Deal with it, and put her to work."

C H A P T E R

15

Nixie looked up at the entrance to Anahata Guild in some trepidation. What had seemed like such a good idea a day ago in Thailand was seeming a lot less sensible now.

The Guild was the same pale yellow that all buildings in Egypt seemed to be. She'd never seen such a yellow and blue country. The sun shone as brightly as in Thailand, but here there weren't the lush green rain forests of Thailand, or the bright colors Thais loved generally. If you went to a market in Thailand, it was a riot of color. Here, dusty yellows and bright blue dominated.

She already missed the sea. No wonder Jeb's Svadisthana had dried up, so far away from real water. Whilst the Nile would certainly count, he'd have to actually visit it. Tierra had told her that Jebediah hadn't even left the Guild in decades until his trip to Thailand last week. Nixie shook her head.

She stepped up to the door and pushed it open. A young female receptionist sat behind a counter. The entrance was neutral, with no hint as to what was in the building – it could be academic, research, an office, anything. "Can I help you?"

"I'm Nixie Lynch. I'm a guest of Jebediah Gale," she said. At least, she hoped she was.

The receptionist nodded and made a soft-voiced call. At the end, she looked at Nixie again, a more considering look this time. "Jebediah's busy. In the meantime, Aiko, our Guild Leader, asks for the pleasure of your company."

Nixie pressed her lips together. "Oh. Really? Are you sure?"

The receptionist's eyebrows drew together. "Yes. Her assistant, Sajan, is on his way down. We'll make sure your luggage gets to your room while you talk."

Nixie slunk back to the seating area, until a few minutes later a snappily dressed male energetic appeared and greeted her. He led her through a maze of corridors until he brought her into the plushly furnished anteroom of the office. "Wait here for a moment while I check she's ready, please."

Nixie kept her sigh internal. She wasn't great with bureaucracy, or pomp and circumstance, and with her recent run of pissing off everyone around her, she wasn't sure meeting one of the six Major Circle members, who was in part responsible for the political governance of the energetics race, was a good idea after such a long journey with little or no sleep.

The door behind which Sajan had disappeared opened again, and he gestured her in. She glanced at his wrists as he did. Because you never knew. Another petite Asian woman, though Japanese rather than Thai, stood to greet her. Jasmine tea in a beautifully decorated teapot with matching cups was on the table. The room was decorated in a minimalist style, with several Japanese artworks on the walls from both well-known and lesser-known artists. If Aiko herself had chosen them, she was cultured. They weren't a style Nixie favored, but they showed taste and discernment.

"I welcome you to Guild Anahata, Nixie," she said. "I am Aiko, Guild Leader."

Everyone knew the six Guild Leaders, even energetics like Nixie who didn't do politics. Whilst the Minor Circle, that is, the energetics who headed each of the thirty Minor Guilds, such as Nixie's own Svadisthana-Vishudha, weren't all known to Nixie, the six who headed the Major Guilds were.

"Svadisthana-Vishudha greets Guild Anahata," Nixie said, giving the ritual greeting of an energetic meeting any of the Guild Leaders. "May we bring balance."

She'd heard good things about Aiko. Nixie followed up by putting her hands together in a respectful wai that was all hers. "I want to help however I can. Tierra, of all people, doesn't deserve this."

They sat down at the low table, and Aiko poured out the tea. Nixie picked hers up and cupped the warm ceramic in her hands.

"I agree," said Aiko. "But it's not Tierra that I want to discuss with you."

Why else would the leader of the Guild want to talk to her? Nixie had assumed it was something to do with keeping their secrets, if they were about to let Nixie into their archives.

"Yes?" she murmured, non-committal.

"I want to talk to you about Jebediah."

Nixie's tea cup wobbled in her hand, and she placed it carefully on the table, not meeting Aiko's eyes. "Oh yes?"

What did she know? Nixie wasn't entirely innocent there. She'd tried to seduce him, and at the end of the day, he was a senior member of Aiko's Guild. Nixie had also promised Fintan she would drag Jebediah back by any means possible if Tierra needed him. Neither of these seemed like something to mention to Aiko in their first interaction.

"You may know that many decades ago, Jebediah renounced his Svadisthana," said Aiko.

"He mentioned it," said Nixie. "But even if he hadn't, it's obvious that he's not using his full powers."

That seemed safe.

"Yes," said Aiko. "With my help, and that of other senior members of the Guild, he bound his auxiliary energy. He's a strong enough Anahata energetic that he's still been a highly functioning member of the Guild."

Aiko paused and took a deliberate sip of tea. Nixie feigned polite interest, but her gut churned.

"But when he came back from his visit to the island, his bindings were in tatters. As if he'd exploded them from inside out. We've put many of them back, but I don't think they'll ever be the same."

"Oh, dear. Is he okay?" This wasn't exactly news to Nixie. She'd been there when his bindings had cracked after all. Was it her fault? Or his? He'd acted like it was something that had happened before, and had seemed to have it under control. Perhaps the fact he had immediately left had indicated something different, though she had thought it more of a reflection of his feelings about her.

"He is, to a degree," Aiko said. "However, I understand you're the only Svadisthana energetic he had contact with."

How was she supposed to reply to that? Was it a statement or a question? Or an accusation? Was Aiko saying it was her fault?

"Possibly," Nixie said. Short and factual seemed the way here. Aiko was polite but hostile, and Nixie had no idea why. Anahata were supposed to be a Guild more welcoming of outsiders than most.

"Did you access his energy?" Aiko asked.

Nixie blushed. Was Aiko asking her about their sexual interaction? Or something else? Nixie felt there was more than one level to this conversation, and some of it was passing her by. This was definitely not her Guild, where charm, flirtation and lightness was more common than this earnest civility.

"I don't believe so," Nixie said. Not on purpose, anyway. Her ears felt hot. She'd been willing, eager, even, to have sex, but so had he. Should she mention the bracelet? Her impulse was to confess everything to Aiko, but what would she say? 'I have this weird bracelet, I don't really know what to do about it so I'm pretending it doesn't exist until I can work it out.' Yeah, that didn't seem a great idea.

"I see," Aiko said. Nixie tried not to squirm. She wasn't entirely sure what she was being accused of, but her behavior wasn't exactly of the non-guilty variety. "While you're here, Nixie, I'll be checking in with you regularly."

Did the woman mean what Nixie thought? She was going to check up on her? Spy on her, even? It wasn't as if Nixie had any ulterior motivates apart from to get some kind of cure – and, Jeb, if necessary – back to the island.

"Alright," Nixie said, "though I'm not sure why."

Nixie was tired of getting it wrong recently, tired of people disliking her, rejecting her or disapproving of her.

"It's important for me to look after my Guild members," Aiko said. "Thank you for your time, and I hope you find what you are looking for in the archives."

Nixie did too. So she could get out of here as soon as possible. She'd barely arrived – and she already wanted to leave.

Jeb was in the library concentrating on a text when Aiko's assistant, Sajan, appeared. Feng bustled over to him. "Can I help? Do you or Aiko need anything?"

"No, it's Jeb we're here to see."

We?

Sajan stepped aside, and revealed the fairy. She looked a little lost amongst the stacks of books that surrounded them. She wore a short, loose skirt in a dark orange, a white short-sleeved shirt, tied over a flat stomach, and a huge silver bangle on her left wrist.

"Hi," she said. He nodded, a little at sea himself. He felt, well, something. Hmm. It was unlike him not to be able to identify an emotion. Was there any of the thickness in the air that he'd felt last time they'd, um, interacted? He took a breath, but the archive's dehumidified air felt as dry as ever. Though he was looking for it, he saw no trace of any influence magic being used.

Feng stepped over to her and gave her a little bow, and she wai-ed in return.

"Welcome to Anahata Guild," he enthused. "I hear you're going to help us. We appreciate it."

He drew her over to the table where he was working, and showed her the heap of papers he was ploughing through. Sajan disappeared silently, leaving the three of them alone.

Feng's energies might be best used in the library, but he had empathy like any other Anahata. Jeb could tell Feng had picked up on Jeb's discomfort, and stepped in. Jeb was grateful to his friend.

On the one hand, Nixie was a likely candidate for using the influence magic, if he thought about it rationally. On the other, what would her agenda be? And how could she be so trusted by Fintan, Blaize and the others if she wasn't what she seemed? Were they all taken in? She confused Jeb's emotions, it was true, but he had never picked up any negativity, or twisting in her energies, so if she was a Rogue or similar she was very well camouflaged. And she didn't seem that experienced or capable. Jeb's substantial experience with Rogues didn't align with her being one.

Feng outlined their research so far to Nixie, and Jeb went back to his text. Though he couldn't refrain from looking up every now and then to see what the fairy was doing. She seemed to be paying close attention to what Feng was saying, a serious look on her face.

They were adults. There was no need for any awkwardness, whatever his body thought of her. He'd be able to keep his energy under control. As long as they kept a polite distance between themselves. He was glad she wasn't wearing a dress. Because the thought of her in a dress, perhaps without any underwear on...

His groin twitched, and an orange spark fell from his body onto the desk in front of him. It came perilously close to setting light to the centuries old text he was reading.

"Source!" he yelped, and frantically patted the surface in front of him. It had mostly survived intact.

Nixie and Feng looked up. "What happened?"

"Nothing. A bug or something." Though not the insect kind. More like a sickness inside him. Was he still being influenced? Was she doing it? It had been harder than ever to lock down his energy this time, and Aiko had warned him once again that it wasn't going to last.

It had to last.

Although, being with Nixie hadn't felt as…wrong as it should have. There had been a sense of rightness, of completeness, when his energy had exploded and he'd once more been able to reach out and touch his Svadisthana.

Was it real?

"It's working," Trent said. "The woman, Tierra, is fading fast. She's a very strong energetic, a Master in both her energies, so it's taking a little time, but it's in progress. You don't need to check in on me like this."

They were on the phone again. Elrian was too tired to pace. He sat watching the rain through his study window. It was relentless, but it made the area very green. His Muladhara felt nourished in the woods around the house, the damp earth boosting him to some degree. But it wasn't enough. He needed to siphon energy more and more often, burning through the energy he took from Aeros in a short time. He was finding it harder to draw energy of his own from the ether, and becoming more reliant on the external sources of energy from his victims.

Trent's flat tone held a chill. "Being subtle is important in this situation. You told me you want it to look natural, part of the illness. Trust my judgement."

Elrian bit his tongue. This employee should absolutely not be talking to him like this. He was a paid worker, nothing more. Right now Elrian would tolerate it because he needed the man, and getting someone else at this stage would pose a number of risks. Afterwards, however, they would have a very different conversation.

"Fine," Elrian said. "Get the job done."

He put the phone down without further discussion, and his door opened. He looked across the room, scowling at the fact the person hadn't knocked, but his face softened slightly when he saw it was Cassidy.

She was tall for a woman, with ash blonde hair cut below her ears, and an imperious look. She had dark blue eyes and strong angular features, and she was as elegant as Elrian was dignified.

"Cassidy, good. I want to talk to you," Elrian said.

"What is it? I came to ensure you ate something," she said.

"Sit down," he gestured to one of the armchairs, and when she sat he came over to join her, sitting in the armchair next to her.

She reached out to remove some fluff from his sleeve, then put her hands in her lap and sat patiently, waiting for him to speak as he had trained her to do over the years. She was always pale, but recently her skin seemed almost translucent, thinner. Perhaps he was asking too much of her. Perhaps even the mild influence he was using on her to keep her docile was too much. He pursed his lips. There was little he could do. She had a role to play in his plans.

"I need you to dreamwalk for me again," he said.

Cassidy's eyes flickered, but other than that she did not show any reaction. "Why is that? What is it that you need?"

She had been in there before for him, perhaps more times than she realized.

"There is some information that I seek," he said. "I can brief you later. In the meantime, take the day to rest so you are in good shape, and don't forget to take your special drink. It will help you be strong."

He had trained Cassidy as an energetic himself, as her Maven, but kept her out of the Guild system. It hadn't been easy, and he had had to use persuasive methods to ensure she did not ask too many questions. She was a tool that he used, and nothing more, though one he would admit to having a soft spot for. The drink helped her to be more suggestible, and made influencing her easier.

She nodded. "Is everything okay?"

He frowned. The last thing he needed was her suspicion. "Fine, my dear. Why?"

"You seem tired. And you're still wearing yesterday's shirt," she said.

Elrian's head snapped down and he realized she was right. That was unthinkable. He nodded tightly. "Thank you. Please have dinner prepared for seven p.m. as normal. It will just be the two of us."

She nodded and stood, then glided away.

If only everyone in his life could be so agreeable.

16

Nixie spent the day with Feng. Jebediah had acknowledged her with a grunt when she came in, and then ignored her for the rest of the day, apart from another grunt of surprise when she mentioned she could read Cappotian. Feng was lovely, and had given her a good overview of where they were up to, but she could acknowledge to herself that she was hurt that Jeb hadn't paid her any attention.

Meh. He was an older energetic. Age differences between energetics weren't the issue they were between humans usually, but perhaps he was more set in his ways than most. Okay, who was she kidding? He'd been out of the Guild once in seventy years. He was the personification of set in his ways.

It was strange being in a Guild when you didn't have that energy. It felt a little bit uncomfortable. Part of it was not fitting in, that was certain, but there was also something about being surrounded by so much alien energy. Her shoulders felt stiff, and the usual grace with which she navigated the world was affected.

At dinner time Nixie went down to the dining hall. She'd thought about going out somewhere for dinner, but if she was honest with herself, she was hoping to encounter Jeb. Casually. To bump into him at the buffet perhaps. But when she went into the large hall, filled with chattering Anahata energetics, there was no sign of him, though Sajan, who she'd seen a number of times throughout the day, sat where he could see her. She wondered, paranoid, for a moment or two, if he was following her, the eyes and ears of Aiko, but this wasn't a huge Guild, and he must get around to do errands for the Guild Leader. She was sure she was imagining things. She wasn't important enough to follow.

She sat at a table on her own and forked salad into her mouth. She wished Blaize or Tierra were here. Or she'd even take Ai. Nixie's usual brightness was dulled, and she needed to get her spark back.

She finished the last few mouthfuls, and decided to get some ice-cream to take away with her. Perhaps she could befriend Sajan? Ask him to sit with her in the Egyptian night and look at the stars. Perhaps she'd feel a little more connected to her beloved island that way, and she could chat with him about the Guild. Information gathering was always useful. Or gossip. She loved gossip. Perhaps he'd know about Jeb, even. She wouldn't mind finding out more about the man.

She walked over to Sajan's table, where he sat alone. "Hi. I'm off to sit outside for a bit, and I'd love to pick your brains on the Guild. I don't know much about it."

She beamed at him, a smile that few were able to resist, though the stiffness in her shoulders had spread to her whole body and her neck was starting to ache. She rolled her head from side to side while she waited for him to answer.

"Thank you, no. I have work that I must do after dinner." He inclined his head and went back to his meal.

Ugh. What is it with this place? This was supposed to be the Guild of Anahata, love, of connection, but she was finding no emotional intimacy here at all, no inclination from any of the Guild members to reach out, or even accept her friendship advances. Her strengths of connecting to others should work well here, and yet she hadn't felt this alone for months.

She gave up. She chose a strawberry cone, and asked one of the energetics she passed to suggest a good place to sit outside. He pointed her in the right direction, and she went down several corridors until she found the external door. She pushed it open and the warm breeze, smelling of the desert, cocooned her.

She walked along a path, enjoying the well-tended hanging plants and the hint of jasmine that reminded her of home. She licked her ice cream carefully, trying to make it last. She happened across a bench that looked over a water-feature that trickled water down and along a path, a ribbon of silver in the night. She sat and looked at it as she finished her dessert.

She'd paint this in the style of van Gogh's later works, all swirls and thick paint. She rested back on her hands and looked up at the sky. So many stars. It was beautiful. But she still felt like an alien.

She'd work on the research until they found something. But in the meantime, one question wouldn't stop circling her mind.

What am I going to do about Jeb?

Jeb watched Nixie sit on his favorite bench. He'd come out for a little air, but when he'd seen her there he'd stayed in the shadows. She'd proceeded to kick her legs and lick her ice cream with apparent enjoyment, her gaze shifting between the stars above and the water feature in front of her. At first she'd appeared a little preoccupied, but by the time she seemed ready to head back inside, she'd cheered up.

He wished she hadn't had an ice cream. The sight of her small pink tongue working its way around the cone had been troublesome.

Why had she gotten under his skin? What was it about her that he found so damned attractive? He didn't know. She'd been a distraction all day, and he couldn't have that. They needed to find a cure for Tierra. He'd spoken to Fintan earlier, and Tierra was stable, but she hadn't gotten any better after her recent relapse.

Jebediah's phone buzzed in his pocket and he drew it out and answered it without looking. "Yes?"

"It's Fintan."

Jebediah winced. He should have checked it. "We haven't found anything."

"That's not why I'm calling," said Fintan, his tone a bit more upbeat than Jeb had heard since Tierra's illness began.

"Oh. Why then?" said Jeb.

"Because Cuinn's been dreamwalking, and we have more pieces of prophecy."

"Tell me," said Jebediah. Anything that might point him and Feng – and, he supposed, Nixie – in the right direction, would be helpful.

"He wants you to look into remnant stones further. Anything you can find on how they are created, and what they can be used for. He's also found a name. Iskander. You need to find any references to a man called Iskander in your research. Cuinn thinks it will help."

"I don't think I've ever come across that name," said Jebediah, disappointed. He'd hoped for more.

"It's relevant somehow," said Fintan. "Find it, and get back here."

"I –" Jebediah started, but Fintan had rung off. Was the word goodbye not in the man's vocabulary?

Back to the library Jeb went.

C H A P T E R

17

At first when Jeb had mentioned the new lead, Nixie had been excited. A message had found her, and she'd come back down to the archives, ready to put in a couple more hours.

But with no results and after working with dusty books all day and half the night she was ready to call it quits. Jeb had sent Feng — who hadn't stopped even when the other two had taken a break — to bed already. Now it was just Nixie and Jeb, alone in the library surrounded by books and a portentous silence.

She wasn't a books person. She was ready to admit that. She liked things to be more…juicy. She threw the book she was working on down on the table.

Jeb looked up. She met his eyes.

"Careful. The books can be fragile," he said. Polite. Distant. She wanted to go over there and wreck his control.

Okay. Grow up, Nixie. She'd try helping instead.

"Do you want to talk about your Svadisthana?" she asked. "Aiko told me your shields are failing. Was it to do with us?"

"I.. don't know. I don't think so. It started before I met you."

"Can I do anything to help?"

He rubbed the back of his neck. "Ah, no, I don't think so."

Gah. That was enough with trying to help the man. She picked up the next book on her pile and turned away. She was in a whole new Guild of potential partners right now, and could be socializing with interesting men, trying on possibilities for the person who had the matching bracelet to hers, and instead she was stuck with Jebediah. A guy who had rejected her.

She checked the list for why this text was in the pile. There was a reference to several prophecies that included all the energies. Which wasn't as common as you might think. She scanned the text to find it, carefully paging through the delicate sheets. This was a handwritten notebook from an Ajna-Anahata, which was how it had ended up in the Anahata library.

Cuinn, who was back in Canada, continued to look through the Ajna texts, and had drafted in Cara, as an Anahata-Manipura, to make sure he didn't miss anything from the Anahata side of things. But he hadn't mentioned the text she was holding. Perhaps this was the only copy. It certainly seemed old.

She'd gone a couple of pages more when she stopped. *Was that...?* She flicked back a couple of pages, a spark of excitement kindling in her stomach. She found the page, and traced a finger down the lines, looking for the name.

"Nixie, I'm not –" Jeb started.

"Ha!" She had it. Now to hope that it actually gave them something useful.

"What?" Jebediah demanded.

"Give me a minute." She was reading the full passage and needed to concentrate. After a few lines, she swallowed.

Oh.

Fuck.

It seemed to Jeb that Nixie was unable to focus on something for more than a few minutes, switching between books and jotting notes down in some kind of shorthand he didn't understand. Then she stopped dead, and slumped in her chair. She really was very expressive.

"Tell me what you've found." For all he knew, it could be some ancient piece of gossip. But the way she raised huge eyes up to look at him, he very much doubted it. He could feel waves of distress coming off her. He sat in a chair next to hers. He scooted it round so he sat opposite, their knees a hairsbreadth away from each other.

He reached out his hands and took her empty hand between his, the one not holding the book, and gave it a rub. Her flesh was soft, but not as much as he'd expected. Perhaps she needed a little distraction. "You have callouses on your fingers."

A look of disbelief crossed her face. He winced. Perhaps that wasn't the right distraction. Though it had worked. "I was just surprised. I didn't realize you did manual work."

She shook her head slowly, her brow still scrunched up, and pulled her hand back out of his. "I play the guitar, and I sculpt. I like working with my hands. But I'm not out digging the fields if that's what you were thinking. Nothing so worthy."

Jeb hunched his shoulders. Back to the matter at hand then. "What did you find?"

The book hung limply from her hand, but she rallied. She passed the open page to him. The book was a bound note-book, hand written in ink in beautiful flowing penmanship. "It's a translation from the original Cappotian."

He read:

From the House of Iskander
When the Twelve shall gather

Each shall have a role
But on each the work will take a toll

Twelve bracelets will give them power

Activated by pairs or all at the final hour

The pair joined in the element of mind
Will fight tooth and nail but eventually find
Dreamscape defences must be breached
If their love be found and reached

The pair joined in the element of air
Will seek far and wide for something right there
Will locate puzzle pieces made of flesh and of bone
Then find heart-magic begins at home

The pair joined in the element of water
Will battle control that has to falter
Sacrifice made and offering given
Will help ensure both are truly living

The pair joined in the element of fire
Will uncover secrets, ancient and dire
Wild energy transmits, affects and enhances
Finds solutions and increases love's chances

He frowned. "What's the gap?"

She raised empty hands. "I don't know."

There was a smudged area before the last couple of stanzas of the prophecy, as if drops of water had fallen on the page. He measured the space against previous verses. "It looks like there's room for another two verses. Which would make sense, as we have four verses about the energies, which would leave, hmm, earth and ether."

"Okay, that makes sense," Nixie said. "I wonder if it happened naturally or someone has erased them."

"We take two steps forward and one step back every time we find more information," Jeb muttered. He continued reading.

Twelve bracelets, twelve stones
Together, not alone,

In pairs they will be
And only then will they see

Without the support of them all
The Circle, the Guilds — our race — shall fall.

Jeb expelled a puff of air. It didn't relate to Tierra's illness, that was true. But it sounded worryingly as if it related to Cuinn's wider prophecy. And it didn't sound that cheery for those involved — which included both him and Nixie.

He quickly dismissed the bit about pairs. He could only worry about one thing at a time. "On each it will take a toll. That doesn't sound good."

She shook her head. "Um, understatement?!"

"Do you think that the couples joined in the elements of mind and air are Blaize and Cuinn, and Tierra and Fintan? They have bracelets, which this seems to refer to, and those are the elements they have in common."

"Perhaps," said Nixie, scratching the skin underneath her large bangle. "The verse seems to fit their stories, but we'd have to ask them."

"We should get a copy of this over to Cuinn as soon as possible," said Jeb.

"I agree. Shall I take photographs and email them to the others now, while you keep looking through the texts?" Nixie asked.

She was being very polite. Jeb wasn't sure he liked it. Usually she was more of a wildcat, spitting and hissing at him. The verses must have really affected her. What did she see in them? How did she interpret them? He nodded and walked back to where he'd been working. Perhaps Cuinn and the others would be able to fill in the gaps.

It was the first reference to this Iskander after all. Who was he? Was the use of Circle, rather than Circles, a mistake? If not, there was a minor and a major circle — which one was the prophecy referring to?

And, he thought, with a sinking heart, which verses were he and Nixie in?

It seemed the prophecy expected both of them to be in a pair, though with whom was unclear. The use of pair, not couple, suggested the pairing didn't have to be romantic, surely? Two connected energetics in some way helping each other?

He kept paging through the texts, scanning as he went, looking for more mentions of Iskander, sharing energy and the consequences, all six energies being used together, the Twelve, or really, anything that might help. His head felt fuzzy, and he needed a break. He was starting to miss things and having to catch himself and go back.

He sat back in his chair and stared into space, his eyes looking at but not really seeing the many texts around them. So many books. And yet there were many more – did they need to look in the other Guilds' libraries? Cuinn had visited Ajna, which contained most of the prophecies, if not all, that had ever been recorded, and the Anahata records contained information about Healing. But what if, like the diary Feng had found the day before, it was solely in the daybook of some ancient energetic? Not a manual or a formally written text?

They were looking for a needle in a haystack. He groaned and rested his head in his hands.

Nixie looked over. "What's the matter? Did you find something else?"

"No," he mumbled, directing his voice at the desk. "Just realizing how big the task we have is."

"Don't have such a defeatist attitude. If you think like that, we'll never find the answers. Tierra's counting on us."

Jeb's body sunk lower in the chair. "I know. That's what I'm afraid of."

"Let's lay out what we have," suggested Nixie. "That might make you feel better. Because we have made progress, whatever you think."

Jeb sat up. "Fine. Talk me through it."

Nixie got up and began to pace. "Everything started when Cuinn saw a prophecy about himself and eleven other energetics protecting our race against some great evil, which could cause the end of the energetic world. The twelve include a bunch of people he knows, and some he doesn't, but so far my drawings have helped to identify you, and once Tierra is better, Blaize and I will work together to identify the others. The prophecy snippets he has so far seem to talk about six pairs, which so far could be seen to correlate with Cuinn and Blaize, and Fintan and Tierra, but we don't have any guarantee of that. But we've sent the snippets to them to see if it resonates as a description of their relationship." She looked over at him. "Sound correct so far?"

He nodded. It was a concise summary, he supposed. In all honesty, he was fighting a little bemusement at the fact she seemed to have such a good overview of the situation. She always seemed so distracted. He blinked when he realized she was continuing.

"We seem to be fighting against what is so far a small group of Rogues, which is unusual because Rogues rarely band together. At first we thought it was Indigo working alone, but now we believe the leader seems to be the man who is Cuinn's father and was Indigo's Maven, Elrian." She stopped. "How's Cuinn doing with that, do you know?"

"I don't. I don't know Cuinn really, apart from through Tierra. It must have been a shock, although I understand they haven't talked in a long while."

"I can't imagine." Nixie shuddered. "Are your parents, or family, still alive?"

"No," he said. She waited. "But we got on fine, thanks. No dark secrets in that part of my life."

She rolled her eyes. But curiosity had come off her in waves. Perhaps he should remind her he could read emotions, even though she was a surprisingly difficult signal for him to decipher.

"So, anyway. We don't know their motives, or what, exactly, they're trying to achieve, apart from the fact it's dangerous, and risks our race, somehow. And they think we can stop it, in part by potentially killing one or more of us on our side of the prophecy."

She shifted in her seat at that, which was fair. It wasn't comfortable for him to think about either. Especially as Elrian's wife, who was also Tierra's aunt, had been one of the casualties of Jeb's actions in the war. If Elrian knew that, he might be a little keener to hurt Jeb than the others involved.

"Elrian's the leader, and there's also some blonde woman involved called Cassidy, who helped Tierra escape, but wouldn't leave herself. We don't know who she is, or what her role is, but we know she was a powerful energetic because she was able to influence Tierra and cause some memory loss, which is a strong power."

Jeb frowned. "Maybe that event was part of Tierra's illness. I'll email Fintan to ask. I think she was injured afterwards though, as she and Fintan fought a Rogue, so it might be hard to disentangle."

"Perhaps. We haven't considered that, have we? So far we think Tierra's ill because she shared energy with Cuinn, and she's not a Maven level energetic. Something about being a Maven seems to protect energetics from sharing energy, as Mavens and Adherents are the only group who seem to do it both ethically and safely." Nixie commented.

"That's correct. And we've never looked into Leeches before as they've never been that common." Jeb leaned forward. "We rehabilitate some, but many of them die. But I've never seen any information on what the ones who survive have in common, if anything."

He made a note. That would be a good thing to follow up and see if there was any research on. He'd ask Cara to check the Anahata Healers' database, and he'd also see if Feng had any thoughts.

"Tierra had some symptoms before she got to the island, but we're not sure when they started. And then we think that the fact that she was on the island with energetics with all six energies triggered a reaction in her, which then sparked the full blown illness. Whatever it is." Nixie paced up and down the small area, weaving in and out of the tables. She waved her hands around to illustrate her points as if she was lecturing. He was enjoying watching her. She was impressive.

She turned to him. "How does all that sound?"

"Good. Shall I summarize our research?" he asked, needing to contribute.

She nodded and perched on the edge of a table, the tiny skirt she wore sliding up her legs to show off an expanse of smooth tan thigh. He raised his gaze firmly up to her face.

"We've found a small number of cases where energetics have shared energy, and have been triggered by being surrounded by all the energies into whatever this illness is. Once triggered, they have – admittedly unstable – access to all the energies, unlike every other energetic alive, who only has access to a dominant and an auxiliary. And finally, we haven't found any cases where the energetic has survived unless they were a Maven." He stopped. That didn't seem like much when he put it like that.

"And then there's the name Iskander, which Cuinn also thinks is important," said Nixie.

"Yes. And also the archetypes. Cuinn thinks that snippet of the prophecy means each of the energies will be represented – Muladhara is the Protector, Svadisthana is the Creator, Manipura is the Warrior, Anahata is the Healer, Vishudha is the Communicator –"

"– and Ajna is the Sage, I know, I know."

He eyed her. He could be considered a Healer, he supposed. As could Cara. What would that make Nixie? A Creator. Again, it fit. But what could a Creator contribute to a fight? Then again, what could a Healer?

Nixie had jumped down from the table and was pacing again. "What can it be like to have access to all the energies? It must be overwhelming. How could you learn to control so many different aspects of power?"

"We don't know that anyone has. It's an anomaly, that's all. I agree, it's too much power for one person," Jeb said.

She turned on him. "But you think even two energies is too much for some people."

He gave her a sad smile. "For me, Nixie. Just for me."

Nixie glared at Jeb. "Why are you like this? How can you bear to close off such a big part of you?"

"I told you why." He turned another page in the text he was examining.

"Sure. You betrayed a woman. Yada yada. It was during the war, and you were working for a greater good. Your use of influence was accidental, and in quite a pressured situation." Nixie had been talking to Feng, and he'd confided in her that what Jeb was doing to his energy was almost always damaging for the individual. Nixie got up and once again prowled around the room. She was restless.

He stared at her, his face neutral. "It was more than a simple mistake, Nixie. It got innocent people killed."

"But that was never your intention." She was stomping rather than prowling now. "What kind of hubris does it take for you to believe that you're such a big deal?"

He started. "Hubris?"

"Yeah, hubris. It's arrogant to believe you're so important that you need to shut part of who you are away. Didn't you come from Source, like everyone else?"

A slight crease was forming on that poker face. Good. Maybe she was getting through to him. Finally.

"Who are you to believe that Source made a mistake? Why would you have access to Svadisthana if you weren't meant to use it?" She slammed her palms down on the table in front of him to emphasize her point, bending a little at the waist. Her cultured Thai mother would have a heart attack if she saw her now. Nixie was definitely channeling her Gaelic father's temper. "And what's wrong with Svadisthana, anyway? Or the energetics who have it? And actually use it?"

He put his hands over hers, and his covered hers completely. She looked down. He had strong hands, with long, nimble fingers. Good in a Healer; better in a lover. She shivered, and felt her nipples harden very slightly through the thin cotton top she wore. She wasn't wearing a bra, because no need.

She raised her head again. He hadn't moved his hands. She brought her face closer to his, and peered into his eyes, her head tilted to the side very slightly. Her back arched.

Did he feel at home in the Guild? He seemed to. "How could you hide here for decades? Didn't you miss the outside world?"

His hands tightened on hers. "I didn't."

She persisted. "And now you've been outside? Seen the sea again? How do you feel now?"

"I…" He shook his head.

He was a puzzle, that's for sure. She licked her lips. Their faces were only a handful of inches away from each other.

"You were inches from the ocean. You made me orgasm in a storm, dammit! Sexual contact surrounded by water and air, both your elements! You must be made of stone to be able to keep your control and your shields going through that kind of stimulation." She made a "pah" of disgust, and began to stand.

His fingers convulsed over hers, and she nearly lost her balance when he stopped her pulling away.

Jeb's control broke.

He cuffed both her wrists in one of his hands, put the other hand on her neck and drew her mouth to his. He did it before he'd even realized himself what he was going to do. He just knew he needed to do something. All that talk of wetness had pushed him over the edge.

The speed he'd moved at meant she gave a surprised 'ouf', and her lips stayed closed for a moment, her eyes wide, before she realized what was happening. But when she did, she gave a satisfied hum against his mouth, and returned his kiss enthusiastically.

After a few moments, she drew back for a second to look into his eyes. "Well, finally."

He growled, and pulled her back to him. She came willingly, and gave a nimble hop over the table in front of him to land in his lap. He slid a hand underneath her to cup her backside, and massaged the firm flesh there. His groin ached with need.

She skimmed her hands over his shoulders and down his upper arms, before threading her fingers through his hair. His skin felt ultra-sensitive to her touch. Or perhaps it was that it had been so long since he'd let himself enjoy a woman touching him like this.

After spending time with her, watching her, he knew she wasn't the one who had influenced him. There was no sign of the thick feeling in the air that had affected him in Thailand. Here the air around them was cool from the air conditioning, but his head also felt clear. And he had warded his shields to warn him if any trace of that energy hit him again.

He checked in. No sign. This was all him. He needed to show Nixie, who he knew he hadn't treated especially well, that he was a generous lover both in giving and receiving. He wouldn't lose control. Didn't need to. He knew he was flirting with danger, but he had confidence he could do this. He would need to tell her about the influence soon, but now wasn't the time.

He stood and took her with him. She wrapped her legs easily around his waist, adapting to their change in position. He held her in place with one hand still underneath her butt, while he walked them both over to a table that was clear of texts that were hundreds of years old. He would have her, but even in this madness, he wasn't going to have sex on texts that Feng considered priceless.

The thought of Feng gave him pause for a second, and his lips stopped moving against Nixie's. She broke their kiss, but kept a hand on the back of his head. "What? Really. Don't stop now. For Source's sake. You need this – I need this."

"I'm not stopping," he said. He pushed thoughts of anyone but Nixie firmly from his mind, and put a finger against her mouth. Her tongue darted out, and she licked the length of it.

He groaned, and pulled it away to lay her body on the table in front of him. Her legs dangled off the side. He stepped between them and hooked his fingers into her underwear and pulled it down her legs. He pushed the little skirt she wore up, and she was naked from the waist down in a moment.

He squatted and put his hands on her inner thighs and pushed slightly, enjoying the resistance as he opened her up wider. He brought his mouth to her sex and blew a little. She quivered in front of him. He breathed in the fresh smell of her, and licked along her soft folds. Her hands came to his head and massaged his scalp.

He found her clit and sucked lightly, and she gasped. He licked with a combination of zeal and finesse, and her hands convulsed in his hair, pulling him in tighter.

There was a sexual charge in the air, but he was determined to keep his Svadisthana energy reined in. He would use it – it would be almost impossible not to if he was having willing sex with another of the same energy – but he wouldn't completely let go of control. It would take finesse and some restraint, but he could do it. He would walk that line for her.

He danced his tongue along and inside her, until he focused almost entirely on that sensitive nub of flesh, taking long, slow, rhythmic licks. He paused for a moment to adjust his pants, and her hands clenched in his hair. He laughed softly into her sex. He was glad she was enjoying herself.

He was as hard as iron, his dick aching, but he was determined to bring her pleasure with his mouth. It wasn't a hardship, after all. She tasted … wonderful. Slightly more comfortable, he resumed his activity, and ran one hand up her torso, under her top, to stroke across her breasts and belly. He'd noticed her erect nipples earlier, though he'd tried to ignore them. She had tiny and perfect breasts that he could cup in a hand. The nipples puckered again as he ran his palm lightly over them.

He put his hand up to her mouth, and brushed his fingers over her lips. She nipped at his fingers, and he thrust one inside her mouth. She sucked on it hard, and he moved it in and out of her mouth in time with the movement of his tongue on her clit. She moaned.

He throbbed in his now uncomfortably tight pants.

He pulled a little Svadisthana energy, and drew his finger reluctantly out of her mouth. He wanted her to come, but he also wanted it to be memorable. He put his left hand on her belly, and stroked along her velvet folds with the fingers of his right hand. He made the strokes of his tongue a little faster, and she writhed underneath him.

Faster still.

Soon.

He lined up his first two fingers at her entrance, and then at the same time, he flooded her system with Svadisthana energy and thrust those two fingers inside her. She arched up on the table, her hands clamping his head so his mouth was pinned to her sex, and she came long and hard. He kept the energy circulating, and continued to thrust his fingers in and out in forceful strokes, whilst his tongue lapped at her clit. She throbbed and pulsed around his fingers.

After several long moments, her grip on his head relaxed, and he slid up her body to kiss her. She returned his kiss enthusiastically, and her taste was in both their mouths. She reached down to his pants to undo them, and, freed, he guided himself into her. He gasped at the hot silken sheath that surrounded him, and had to pause for a moment, his arms locked in a push up position over her, to remind himself to take it easy. He was not a boy of scant years' experience.

He began to move, gliding in and out of her as she bucked her hips to encourage him. She put her arms around his neck, and pulled him down to kiss her again as she wrapped her legs around his hips, her heels digging into his buttocks.

She broke the kiss and her head dropped backwards, and he took the opportunity to kiss her neck. She was clinging to him, only her butt and lower back on the table, and his thrusts had speeded up.

The tiniest hint of Svadisthana energy came from her, a trickle, as if her entire body had become a low level pleasure emitter. He growled, and put one arm around her back to hold her in position so he could go deeper. She let out a cry on the next thrust, and it pushed him over the edge.

His shields cracked, and orange flashes of Svadisthana sparked from him as his whole body tensed, and he came inside her with his own rough cry.

After several more hard thrusts, he squeezed her body tight, then lay her carefully down on the table. He opened his eyes, and swore.

"What?" she said sleepily, stretching like a cat with him still inside her, clearly luxuriating in the energy she'd absorbed from him.

"The energy!" He was batting at the sparks that they'd given off that had turned into water and now covered the table around them, despite leaving them in a dry circle.

Nixie turned her head to the side and bit her lip. "Oh, shit. Feng's going to be really mad."

19

The next morning Jeb got up early to swim in the Guild's pool. He ploughed up and down the length of the warm water, the pool at its best early in the day before the heat kicked in. The small, artificial body of water had been a saving grace while living here, as it didn't have the same effect as natural bodies of water.

The night before he'd asked Nixie if she wanted to come back to his rooms to stay there with him, but to his relief she'd refused. He wasn't sure why she hadn't wanted to, but on his part it was guilt that he hadn't told her about the energy that had influenced them in Thailand. He would discuss it with her this morning.

He swam faster, cutting through the water with a smooth front crawl that ate up the meters. It wasn't the same as the sea, it was true, but there was a peace in the clear blue water that he didn't find in many places.

His Svadisthana energy was escaping, and he couldn't bear the idea of going back to Aiko so quickly to rebind it. He was starting to wonder if she was right. Should he loosen the ties that kept it contained? He felt healthier since the night before, which was strange, and unexpected. He sped through the pool and did another length, diving under the water to rebound off the wall at the other end in a fluid turn.

Perhaps he could have his energy be dormant, rather than locked. Though that wasn't realistic. He was a Master energetic in Svadisthana, which had been part of the problem all along. He was powerful, and had too much energy to pretend it didn't exist. It either had to be locked up or used. There was no in-between.

But if he was going to open himself up again, he would need to have regular sex. Nixie last night had taken in some of the energy that he had leaked and made it safe as part of their sexual activity. Being with another Svadisthana energetic was a powerful experience, though he had kept his energy under control as much as he could. Of all the energetics to start having sex with, a Svadisthana was certainly the safest.

Now he had allowed himself to think about sex again, his body and his mind remembered how much he enjoyed it. Another dive under the water and another flip as he swam another length. The exercise distracted his body's attention away from exactly how much he enjoyed it, if not his mind.

And then there was Nixie. Had the sex with her been so wonderful because she was the first in decades? Or was it the influence of the energy that had ignited their sexual encounter in Thailand? Or was it her?

He didn't know. He ducked under the water again and as he came up for air he stood in the shallow end. He slicked his hair back from his face so he could see, and lounged against the side of the pool, his back to the concrete, leaning back on his elbows. Jeb's energy meant that emotions were usually an open book to him. Others' and his own.

But when it came to Nixie, he felt cloudy. As if the radar that usually meant he could pick out emotions was broken. Off.

Her emotions came through, sometimes. But not always. He'd been surprised, for example, by how much he'd appreciated her optimism the day before in the library. Sometimes she wore her emotions on her sleeve, and sometimes they were a puzzle to him.

He just wasn't sure how safe it would be to solve that puzzle.

Nixie ran along the corridors of Anahata to find Jeb. After much searching, she'd been told he was probably swimming.

She pelted towards the pool. She stumbled through the doors that led to the bright blues of the water and sky, and saw him at one end of the blue rectangle. His skin was pale – much paler than hers – but his shoulders were broader than they looked when he was wearing clothes. His hair was pushed back from his face, showing off the sharp angles of his cheek bones. There was something fragile and angelic in his handsome face.

Drops of water on his eyelashes drew her eyes to his, and finally she realized that the smoldering gaze from the second picture she had drawn had come to life. She felt a pulse between her legs and skidded to a stop, then slipped on the water on the tiles that surrounded the pool, and had to wave her arms frantically to prevent herself from falling in.

"Shit!" she said.

He was standing in the pool, but he didn't get out. She stood with her hands on her hips and looked down at him.

"Hi," he said. "Everything okay?"

She was distracted by how handsome he was for a moment, until she remembered the reason she'd come to see him. "No. Everything's not okay."

He tilted his head slightly. "What's happened?"

"Blaize called. It's Tierra. It's bad."

His eyebrows went up, and he turned away from her to heave himself out of the water, his hands on the side. Muscles corded in his upper arms.

He walked over to her, and she watched water stream down his body to pool on the floor at his feet. She really, really wanted to touch. But now was not the time.

"Tell me what she said," he asked. His voice was gentle, but there was an urgency in his tone, and the sexuality that she'd seen in his eyes had been shut down. She felt a pang of loss.

"Tierra's unconscious, and they can't wake her. Fintan's best guess is that something is draining some of Tierra's energy. They've warded her, but they can't work out how – or where – the energy's going."

Jeb walked towards the locker room. When she made no move to follow him, he beckoned her. "Come, talk while I get dressed."

That sounded like a very distracting idea indeed. She'd have to keep her eyes closed.

She followed him into the men's changing rooms, empty at this time of day. He went directly to the shower, where he turned on the water and stripped off his shorts. Nixie's eyes widened before she turned away. Yep, distracting.

"That's new information," said Jeb.

"What?" said Nixie. Her voice echoed in the changing room, bouncing off the tiles. She could hear the tap of his wet feet on the floor and him rubbing soap on his skin. She imagined her own hands helping and then shook her head.

"That she's being drained. That suggests there is something out there which is making this happen. Or at least taking advantage of it. Which tells us a lot."

"It does?" said Nixie.

"Yes. The fact that someone else knows enough to take advantage of it means that someone else is likely to know how to fix it. Given that Elrian is leeching from other energetics, and someone is trying to drain Tierra, it indicates he could be involved. He tried previously to hurt her, and failed."

"We don't know how she got away last time, do we?" Nixie asked.

"No. She was kidnapped, and then she turned up at Cathair Cuinn with massive memory loss." The noise of the shower shut off. "Can you throw me my towel?"

She opened one eye but continued to face away from him. "Where is it?"

"On the bench to your right."

She walked over to it and picked it up. The room had taken on a masculine scent of ozone and wood, and she shivered. She turned back to him and kept her eyes downwards. His feet – nice feet, for a man – came into view. She stuck a hand out with the towel.

A tug and she let go. *Is it safe to look yet?* She raised her eyes slowly, running her gaze from his feet up muscled calves with just enough hair, firm thighs, and then, thankfully, the blue towel around his waist. The planes of his stomach were clearly outlined, and she moved her gaze more quickly up to his face.

He was watching with an amused smile. "I won't ask if you like what you see, because I think we're beyond that. I didn't expect you to be shy."

She flushed. "I'm not shy. At all. But sometimes my priorities get muddled. Tierra's our focus now, and we still don't know how to help her."

The laughter lines in his face fell away. "I know. No, we don't, but every piece of information helps us. I can cross reference what we've already found with information on leeching and energy drainage. It gives us more pieces of the puzzle."

Nixie nodded, then bit her lip. "Yes. But Jeb, Blaize said that Tierra might only have days left."

Nixie didn't add how guilty she felt that they'd been having sex while Tierra got more and more ill. Nixie started. Did that mean each time they had had sex, something bad had happened to Tierra? She ran her hands up and down her upper arms. That was a crazy thought, right? Her sex with Jeb couldn't affect Tierra on another continent? That was ridiculous, right? Yet she wanted to be told it was okay, and that her focus on her own needs hadn't hurt Tierra.

"We'll have to work harder today. We both needed the break last night. I believe you were at the throwing-ancient-texts-around stage."

Jeb replied as he used a second towel to dry himself off, thoroughly rubbing his hair and patting odd droplets of water from his arms. "So I'm clear, what you're saying is that Fintan thinks Tierra is being attacked psychically, and he and the others are putting energetic shields round her, but her energy's still being siphoned off. Right?"

He pulled on his clothes, which had been folded in a pile on the bench between them. His outfit included one of the casual baggy sweaters he tended to wear in the air conditioned parts of the Guild, and something in her chest squeezed at the sight. It was so ... so him.

She nodded. "Heka is on his way back. He was only in Malaysia, working with some energetics there."

Fully clothed, he strode towards the door. When she didn't immediately follow, still trying to process everything going on, he turned.

He smiled, but she could see the strain in his eyes. "Come on. We have a puzzle to solve."

Nixie hurried along the corridor after Jeb to the archives. He seemed more relaxed than yesterday, which she was glad about. And last night had been good, really good, and he'd retained some of the control he wanted to. They seemed to be finding a way to satisfy them both, for the moment. His personal wards had fractured, but not shattered, and she'd managed to absorb some of his escaped energy as part of the natural Svadisthana sex process. Which was lucky, because Feng would have been heartbroken if they'd flooded his archives, and she'd come to be quite fond of him.

But damn.

Jeb's wrists were still bare.

Her heart shrank a little as she thought about it. She'd been making more of an effort to connect with Jeb. She'd found she was genuinely interested in what he thought about things, and wanted to share her own deeper thoughts and ideas in a way that was new to her with a man. She'd always saved that sort of emotional intimacy for Blaize.

Did he not have a bracelet because he was still suppressing his energy? Or did she get her drawing wrong, somehow, and he wasn't in the prophecy at all? Or was it Blaize's image that was wrong, and he wasn't one of the twelve, but more tangentially related? Or – and to her surprise, this one hurt her heart the most – was he going to be part of a couple with another woman? Perhaps his bracelet would turn up once he met the right woman – but that wasn't her.

She tried to shake the mood off. It was just sex between them. And hey, if there was a man that was out there who was an even better match for her than Jeb, she was excited to meet him.

She followed Jeb into the archives, where he threaded his way between shelves.

She'd managed to remain friends with most of her lovers over the years. Most Svadisthana energetics did. She and Jeb would develop a friendship, a different kind of relationship, eventually, without this heavy sexuality between them. *Right?*

Or perhaps they had this whole thing wrong, and the prophecy's use of the word pair had been very deliberate, and there was no need for romantic couples. Maybe it was each pair of the Archetypes that the prophecy referred to.

And maybe she wasn't destined to meet any kind of soulmate soon.

Perhaps that was a relief. Her brow furrowed, uncertain as she was about the idea that if it wasn't to be Jeb, she'd rather have no one. That did not seem like her at all.

Jeb paused to turn back to her, studying her. Then he pinched the brow of his nose, massaging it. It was a cute action. "Huh."

"What are you doing?" she asked. He had turned back to a section and was studying the spines.

"Your comments made me think of something I read years ago. I'm going to try and find it. You carry on with the pile from yesterday."

Nixie stifled a groan. It was going to be another long day. Then she thought of Tierra, and rolled up her sleeves.

"I need to tell you something," said Jeb.

Nixie looked up from the text she was reading. She'd made some progress in the last couple of hours, but there were still many more to read. "What?"

Jeb hunched his shoulders. There was no good way to say this, but it had been on his mind all morning. He couldn't keep it in anymore. He had quite the knot of tension between his shoulder blades from thinking about it. "Aiko found traces of influence energy on me when I came back to the Guild."

Nixie's eyebrows shot up. "Influence energy? What do you mean? And to do what? Are you okay?"

His shoulders curved a little more. "Ah, around sex. She, er, thinks it happened on the island."

Light dawned in Nixie's eyes and her mouth dropped open. "You were influenced to have sex with me?"

He shrugged helplessly. "I don't know. Maybe. It was out of character for me."

Out of character then, certainly. The times since then? Out of the character he had been for the last half century, but perhaps more of a return to the person he had been for the rest of his life.

"Okay," Nixie said, slowly. "Then… you didn't want to have sex with me when you came to visit me on my balcony?"

She pushed her chair back from the table, putting space between them, face pale. "What about last night?"

"There hasn't been any influence energy since the island. Last night was all me."

"Why didn't you tell me?" She wrapped her arms around herself.

He knew he should have told her earlier. He had been selfish. His relationship with her, whatever it was, felt so fragile he hadn't wanted to damage it.

But he had.

"You didn't tell me, and you slept with me again last night anyway," she said. "Did you really sleep with me thinking I might use my energy in that way?"

Her cheeks were flushed, and he could see her skin pale where she dug her fingers into her arms.

"No, I didn't, I don't…that's not what I think," Jeb said. How could he explain it to her?

To himself?

She opened her mouth to retort, but before she could say anything, Feng hastened towards them. She snapped her mouth shut and glared at Jeb.

Feng glanced between them, confusion on his face. He took a step back. "I didn't mean to disturb you. Is all well?"

"It's fine," Jeb assured him, hurriedly. "We can finish this later. Tierra can't wait."

He regretted it a moment later when Feng said, "You need to go and see the Hermit."

Jeb wanted to groan. How could a day that had started out so pleasantly turn thunderous so quickly?

"We've had this discussion. I don't think there's a need," Jeb said.

"Oh. No. I mean, yes, we did. But now there is," Feng said, still looking between the two them as if he could taste their emotions on the air.

Nixie's eyes were still narrowed, but she'd cocked her head to the side.

"Who's the Hermit?" she asked. "Why don't we want to see him?"

"A very annoying Anahata energetic," Jeb replied.

"He can be irascible, it's true," Feng agreed. "But he can also be very useful, if the mood strikes him."

"Which is rare. Mostly he's an arse," Jeb said.

Nixie gave a surprised giggle which she quickly tried to hide. "What?"

Jeb sighed pointedly, but in his chest, his heart turned over. Perhaps, he thought, there was hope he hadn't destroyed things entirely. "I see you didn't get a proper British education."

"An arse is –" Feng stopped mid-helpful explanation as Jeb put a hand over his mouth.

"She knows."

Poor Feng. He looked really confused now. Jeb took pity on the man. "Why should we see him?"

"Well, there is the matter of the Rogues, of course. But in addition, this morning I found some of his notes with a text on remnant stones, which suggests at some point he was doing research into them. It's possible he may have discovered how they are made."

"We know how they are made. An energetic is killed for them," Jeb said.

"We know what they are made from, but not the ceremony or ritual, or what it takes," Feng corrected. "And his research was connected to some expertise he had around healing those who had been leeched from." Feng was almost hopping in place with excitement. "Plus, I remembered that many centuries ago, he used to teach on the darker side of energy healing. I really think he could be hugely helpful."

"How can there be a darker side of healing?" Nixie asked.

"Using Anahata magic to destroy inside the body, or to take, instead of to heal," Jeb said, face grim. Dammit. That was quite a good rationale to visit the Hermit, but by Source, he really didn't want to. Plus, he'd have to leave the Guild. "Hmm. That's actually given me an idea. What if there's more than one thing happening. What if the illness was triggered by the energy sharing, but someone is draining her as well?"

Nixie pursed her lips. "Wouldn't Fintan find them? He has everything warded, and he or Blaize are on constant guard. They're barely sleeping."

"It depends how powerful they are. Elrian doesn't have Anahata, but he may have an associate who does."

"You warded her, though, right? You protected her?" Nixie said. "From that, I mean."

"Yes. Yes I did." Jeb stared at the table. He'd thought he'd had something there, but perhaps not.

"Damir, then?" Feng said, politely.

Jeb groaned.

Nixie raised her eyes to his, defiant. "When do we go?"

Nixie wasn't entirely sure who they were going to see. She'd been so furious with Jeb about hiding the influencing energy issue from her, that as soon as she'd seen he didn't want to go, she hadn't been able to stop herself, despite the fact it would only be his second trip out of the Guild in seventy years. He seemed to be handling it okay so far, she thought. Not that she cared.

Alright, maybe she cared a bit. She snuck a glance at him. His hands gripped his thighs, but other than that there were no external signs of tension.

They'd taken a taxi, and she hoped her silence was frosty and dignified.

"I'm sorry I —" Jeb started, but Nixie cut across him.

"Why were you really so reluctant to go see this guy?" she asked. Let's see how he liked his motives being questioned.

"He's difficult, and quite unpredictable," Jeb said. "Unpleasant, crotchety, and not one who likes to share information. It's not going to be easy to get anything out of him."

Okay, this Hermit didn't sound a lot of fun. It was too late to back out now, however. Plus, the scenery was stunning. She hadn't been to the Middle East before, and was enjoying the washed out feel of the city, and the strange juxtaposition of old and new. This was a city that had seen a lot.

A horn blared, and Nixie winced as someone tried to overtake on a two lane road that already had four lanes of cars jockeying for position. She couldn't believe how many vehicles Egyptians could cram into a small space. Nixie was used to traffic flowing like water in Thailand. Sure, there weren't a lot of turn signals or warning given, but drivers rarely used their horns. That wasn't so much the case here.

It was a fascinating place. And the seat of the oldest known energetic Guild, as it had been the first to be refounded after their civilization had sunk to the bottom of the sea when Atlantis drowned.

Her attention flicked from point to point outside the car, drinking it in.

"This is such a different Egypt to mine," Jeb murmured.

"Hmmmm?" Nixie said, eyes trying to absorb everything she could. She couldn't even choose what she might paint, there was so much inspiration around her.

"When I sequestered myself in the Guild, British influence was still very strong. Now the British legacy is mainly in crumbling architecture."

"And looted artefacts," Nixie said absent-mindedly. Poor Egypt. So much heritage, stolen by other more 'civilized' countries.

"I am sorry," Jeb said quietly. "I should have told you earlier."

"It's alright," Nixie said. "You wouldn't be the first to sleep with me because of my outsides even though you had a problem with my insides."

Usually, she didn't mind, as long as the experience was enjoyable for both parties. Perhaps she kept a little more distance from men because of it, but here today was a good example of why letting her guard down, and entertaining the possibility of a deeper intimacy was a mistake.

There was a sharp intake of breath from Jeb. She turned, puzzled.

"That is not what happened," Jeb said. "Aiko spotted the traces of influence when I got back to the Guild. It's true I was a little uncertain at first, but it didn't last."

"So why didn't you mention it?" Why hide it from her? It affected her, too.

"You're the first woman I've been with in a long, long time, Nixie." He twisted in his seat and took one of her hands in both his. The air conditioning wasn't powerful in this old car, and his hands were warm. "I don't know what this is, but I wasn't ready to mess it up so quickly. And truly, I'm not sure I'm good for you. For anyone."

Okay, that was a good speech. A little of the ice inside her melted.

But only a little. She was going to take a bit more time than usual before she decided whether he was worth her letting it go. In the meantime, she should really find out what they were doing.

"Why did this guy leave the Guild?" she said. "Are there other energetics there? And where exactly is there?" Nixie said.

Jeb was aware of Egypt's progress while he'd been in the Guild. He had a television, and was an enthusiastic history and culture buff who was as happy to watch the odd documentary as he was to read a book. But the TV wasn't the same as the sights, smells and sounds of Egypt up close and in person.

In this modern age the streets were as busy as they had been in the past, but now it was cars that thronged the road rather than hawkers and market stalls.

"I'm not sure why he left, but he lives on his own," Jeb said. Which was unusual. Most energetics liked to live within easy reach of others of their race. "We're going to the Necropolis, the City of the Dead."

Sitting next to Nixie in the back of the dilapidated, dented car was surprisingly soothing, despite the fact she was clearly, and quite reasonably, angry with him. On his first trip out of the Guild the week before he'd been in a daze of stimulation, all his focus as he travelled through the city to the airport on holding in his energy. He hadn't left the airport in Bangkok, had flown through to a smaller airport where he'd taken the boat. And Koh Somdun was nothing like this teeming city.

"Seriously?" Nixie said. "What is it?"

Once, Cairo had been a rich center of culture, a modern metropolis. Now, while still one of the biggest cities in the Islamic world, it felt like a faded grande dame, its revolutions and instability damaging its place on the global stage. There were fewer tourists on the streets than he had expected, and buildings and cars tended to be older and more worn.

He mourned a little for the city he had given up by isolating himself in the Guild. He had blinded himself to how insular he had become, his attention centered on his energy and the mistakes he had made in the past. He hadn't considered having a future – had felt that causing Lucie's death, and the death of the many innocents, had also been a type of death for him.

"It's a giant cemetery that dates back thirteen or fourteen hundred years," he said.

Was he ready for that to change? Being out of the Guild was uncomfortable, but he was managing so far. Was Nixie helping, or could she hinder him given her propensity to impulsiveness?

"He lives there?" Nixie said, eyebrows inquisitive. She had pretty eyebrows. Very fine and dark.

"Over half a million people do," Jeb said. So he understood, anyway. When he'd been active and out of the Guild, it hadn't been nearly that many, but migration into the city, an earthquake and poverty had increased the population greatly. "Many people live in family tombs, but I understand these days there's a medical centre, post office and even some apartment blocks. Damir lives in a large mausoleum, but Feng says he still keeps it in pristine condition."

"Okay. That's ... different," Nixie said. "Um ... who does it belong to?"

Jeb grimaced. "His human wife. She died a very long time ago. He never got over it."

"I can't decide if that's incredibly romantic or incredibly ghoulish." Nixie's face was hard to read. She shivered. "I really hope this guy can help. He sounds quite the character."

"He's hugely experienced. Feng's right. I just wish he wasn't, because it's never pleasant. But when his information's relevant, it's invaluable."

It took a while longer, but eventually their car dropped them off, and they picked their way through the dusty, dirty streets to the Hermit's house. They passed plenty of washing hung on lines, some goats, and a cluster of old men watching two even older men play dominoes on an upended plastic crate with a board laid on top. Jeb was impressed Nixie didn't comment on the filth and garbage they had to walk through to get to the house, a small, single story rectangle of grey, though not crumbling to quite the extent of some of its neighbors.

At the door, Jeb went to knock, though no one locked their door in this area as few had anything worth stealing. Anything that the Hermit did have would be under a magical lock and key that wasn't going to be something a casual thief could find, let alone steal.

As he touched the door, he knew something was very wrong. It wasn't the fact that it drifted open, but the flash of violence he got from the object. Someone had forced their way in here recently.

"Stay here," he said to Nixie, and slid in through the door. It had been a long time since he had needed any combat or stealth skills, but they were there, dormant inside him.

He needn't have bothered. It was a one room building, and Jeb was able to take the whole room in at a glance. He swallowed.

It included a very dead Hermit slumped on the floor cushions, a bloody wound slashed across his neck.

Nixie was still too annoyed at Jeb to be left out, and had followed him in, albeit quietly. She was fascinated to meet a man who could so annoy the usually even-tempered Jeb. Plus, she wasn't keen to be left alone in a giant graveyard.

When Jeb stood stock-still a few steps into the room, she peered cautiously round him, puzzled, then let out a little cry. She ran over to the body on the floor, hoping she could help.

Jeb cried out a warning, but before she could react a man in a suit stepped out of the shadows next to a bookshelf, a grim look on his face, and threw something at her.

She lurched back, already off balance as she'd been going towards the man on the floor, and Jeb caught her arm before she fell. Before either of them could react further, the man, limping, vanished out of the back exit of the simple structure.

Nixie clutched Jeb, breathing hard. She was frozen in terror. She'd never seen a dead body before. And she was pretty sure that that was what was in front of her. At the same time, she'd been attacked. Breathe. She needed to breathe.

Adrenaline winged around her body like a pinball machine ball, her system on high alert. Jeb touched her cheek. "Nixie? Stay with me. I need to check the back exit, but I don't think there's anyone here anymore."

She gestured, vaguely, weakly. "Don't you – don't you need to follow that guy?"

Her stomach gave a squeeze as she said it, as the idea of him either leaving her, or her having to go with Jeb to fight materialized in her mind.

No. She could do it. "We should. We should follow him, c'mon."

But to her huge relief he shook his head, and moved catlike towards the back door and carefully checked outside. He stepped back in. "There's no one close, and we need to understand what happened here. I'll set up a warding in case he comes back."

He placed a hand either side of the doorframe, and to Nixie's eyes it shimmered. Then he went quickly to the body, which he examined, even checked for a pulse, using the wrist – which merely had a few drops of blood spatter on it – rather than the neck. Even Nixie, with no healing knowledge, could tell that no charms or healing magic were going to bring this man back.

"It is him? Damir? The Hermit?" Nixie stuttered.

"Yes. Can you look around?" Jeb said to her. "He's dead, I'm afraid. I need to call Aiko, and then I'll study the body a little more."

Yes. A task. She could do a task. She stood in place, her eyes flicking from the threadbare rug in front of the sofa to the sink unit and single plate in the drying rack, to the well-stocked bookshelves that filled one wall. The color seemed to have been drained from everything.

She registered a marble rectangle slab at one end of the room, close to the sofa. She gulped. It was a tomb. The space was clean, that was something. Her focus skated over Damir's body, refusing to acknowledge it for the moment.

"You can move, it's okay," Jeb said.

She realized her feet had been stuck to the floor, only her gaze moving. She stepped carefully to the bookcases which dominated the room's decor. Books were piled on books, neat, but over-stuffed onto the shelves. It was almost homely, if you didn't think about the idea that the inhabitant's dead wife's tomb was at the, um, heart of this home.

She tried to work out where the man had been standing, and what he could have been looking at. Some books had been pulled out and were on the floor. She snapped a few photos with her cell before bending down to look at the titles. None seemed immediately relevant, but she might not be the best judge.

She scanned the floor around her, before catching sight of a few loose pages of handwritten script that looked like they might have fallen from a folder or notebook. She squatted next to them, afraid to move them in case she damaged them. The writing was spidery and compact, and though in her panicked state she found it hard to focus on any one part, it seemed to be in several languages. She thought she could pick out some Cappotian, and perhaps some Latin, but much of it was incomprehensible to her. She reviewed the entire page she could see, and then, with a pen from her bag, poked that page to the side to review the second.

One word jumped out at her.

Iskander.

"You shouldn't have pushed him," Elrian snapped. He and Imogen were in his hotel room in Cairo. Sweat had soaked through his shirt, and it clung to his back and underarms in an unpleasant manner.

He flicked on the air conditioning and paced the room. *Damn heat.* A cold blast cut through the close air. Blood trickled down his lower leg from a nasty slash Elrian had taken from the Hermit before he had killed him. It had been a long time since Elrian had been the one doing the dirty work in this kind of situation.

She shrugged. "I didn't expect him to be prepared to die for the knowledge. It only shows how important it is. We'll find it somewhere else."

She had fled before Elrian, as soon as they'd heard voices outside. Elrian hadn't wanted to leave without gathering more information, and had stayed, hoping they wouldn't enter. Once they'd interrupted him, already weakened, and without Imogen, he'd escaped rather than engage, but he wasn't happy about it.

"The remnant stones are critical, we know that. But we need more information about what we do with them when we have them." Elrian ran a finger over his ring. He no longer took it off. There was a palpable absence when he did, and some … discomfort. There was no need to suffer that when all he had to do was leave it on.

"We know we need to create two stones for each Chakra, draining to death an energetic who is dominant in that energy," she said. She stood by the window, leaning against the wall, watching him rage. "You need to spend more time in the dreamscape, searching for the answer. Or send Cassidy. Did you talk with her?"

He jerked his head in the affirmative. "It's getting harder to find new information in the ether at the moment. There may be something more that needs to happen for me to be able to divine new prophecy shards."

Imogen frowned. "I'm counting on you in this area. Don't neglect it."

Elrian balled a hand into a fist, then released it and ran it through his hair. He was hot and agitated. The interaction with the old energetic had been unpleasant, and, frankly, much too close for comfort. He shouldn't have been a challenge for Elrian and the woman. They were far more powerful separately than the Hermit, let alone together.

"We should have stayed and fought those two idiots. I could have taken at least one of them out, I'm sure of it," he said.

"The warding that that old fool did as he died locked my Anahata. I couldn't have fought, and I couldn't take the chance they might recognize me and survive," Imogen said, her lips flattened in displeasure. "I still need to be in Anahata Guild. There's work to do there yet."

She was right. He knew it. But he had been so close. The next couple had appeared right there in front of him, and she had called him away. Given Elrian had a wound on his leg and was hardly in perfect shape, retreat had been wise, but … Source. He slammed a fist into the wall beside him.

"We were lucky I heard Feng talking to Aiko about him at lunch," said the woman. "At least we got his notes."

She gestured to the blood-spattered thick book stuffed with pieces of paper. "There should be something in here. You will need to begin reviewing it immediately. I can't take it back to the Guild, and I need to get back quickly because all hell will break loose once news of his death gets back there."

"Your power is unlocked again?" Elrian said in surprise.

She laughed scornfully. "Of course."

She tapped the blue-green jewel around her neck. "The kind of power I have in here is far superior to his. He was lucky, that's all."

In the end, Elrian thought, remembering the limp body falling to the floor, and the sticky, hot blood that had covered his hands, not really that lucky at all.

21

Nixie and Jeb were back in the Guild a few hours later. Aiko had taken charge of the problem, liaising with Muladhara Guild and their Protectors to clear the scene of the Hermit's many non-human artefacts and make it ready for the Egyptian police. She was trying to decide what kind of warning to put out to her people, and how to share the information with the other Guilds. This was going to get out soon enough. The Hermit was known by many, and the energetics, though spread across the globe, were a small community who loved gossip.

Jeb didn't envy Aiko. Politics and leadership wasn't something for which he'd ever had any desire himself, and this was a good example of why.

The Guild was in chaos. Clusters of energetics stood in the corridors and halls talking in hushed voices. Given the looks that he and Nixie got as they walked to her room, it seemed many knew that they had been involved.

He led her to the sofa and sat next to her, taking her hand. She had barely said a word on the journey home. He had been disturbed by the scene, of course, but he hadn't been shocked in the very visceral way that Nixie had been. It's not that he didn't have faith in people – be they energetics or humans – but that faith was tempered by the knowledge that both light and dark existed in the world. He had caused darkness. Could he do more if he released himself from his need for penance and restriction? Or would it create more damage? He sighed.

Nixie started at the noise. She'd been in her own world, her hand limp in his.

"I'm sorry you had to see that," Jeb said. He truly was. Nixie was all lightness. Not very serious, perhaps, but the world needed butterflies and rainbows as much as anything else. More, maybe.

She shrugged. "I guess I needed a wake-up call."

Jeb cocked his head. "Why?"

"I was enjoying the adventure a bit too much," she said.

"Finding joy in difficult moments isn't a weakness," Jeb said. "You saw a horrible, terrible thing today. You didn't deserve it."

He put a finger under her chin and lifted it so he looked into her eyes. Tears glistened at the corners. She reached out a hand and stroked his cheek. "Thank you for that. I'm not sure you're right, but thank you."

Jeb placed a gentle kiss on each tear.

"I saw the man's face. I can draw him," she said, as he pulled back.

"That could help us a lot," Jeb said. "It has to be connected to everything else. It's too strange he would be killed on the same day we went to see him otherwise."

He'd been turning it over in his mind. "He must have known something important. I wish we knew what."

Nixie had seen a new side to Jeb today. He'd taken charge in that horrible room. And this evening, it had hit home quite how senior he was in the Guild as he'd interacted with the other members. He certainly didn't hide his Anahata energy, that was for sure.

She will still a bit pissed at him that he'd kept the knowledge of the worrying influence energy from her. They needed to find out where it had come from. She was starting to realize that he was juggling politics and responsibility as well as his own feelings.

Right now, comfort was what she craved. He had been kind to her this evening, and she'd treasured that. Unusually, she didn't feel interested in sex, so she thought she ought to let him go back to his rooms. His kisses had been gentle, but it would be understandable if he was hoping they'd lead to more.

Likely they'd get back to that tomorrow.

She let herself touch him for another moment, and then pulled back. "I'm going to have a bath, I think. I need to let some of the adrenaline inside me subside."

"That sounds like a good idea. Do you want me to stick around?" He gave her hand a squeeze.

"I'm not feeling very sexual this evening," she admitted.

Jeb scratched a cheek. "That seems quite reasonable, given the day we've had. I meant, can I make you some tea, or chat to you from either inside or outside the door. Whatever you need to make you feel better."

Nixie stared at him. Her relationships with men tended to be focused on the physical. There were emotions, certainly, but they were the highs and lows of lust and love, not this sense of, well, intimacy that Jeb seemed to be offering.

She swallowed, overcome at the idea of him caring for her, caring about her, in that way. She wasn't sure exactly what to do with it.

"You're welcome to talk to me while I have a bath," she said.

He showered while she ran a bath, using bubbles she'd brought with her, and sunk into it. He wrapped himself in a towel and perched on the toilet seat, diagonally across from her. The water was warm and the scent of roses and vanilla permeated the air. Tension began to flow from her muscles.

Jeb asked her questions about herself, from her art to her guitar playing to her relationship with Blaize. Source, the man really paid attention. He pulled her out of the dark thoughts from the day with a feeling of normal conversation. At least, the kind of conversation that was normal for her to have with Blaize or her family. Not the sort of conversation she usually had with the men in her life.

His words were an anchor for her while she felt so ragged from the day's events, and her black thoughts tried to suck her down like a whirlpool. When she got out of the bath, he pulled a towel down and tucked it around her. And cradled her for a long moment.

"Will you hold me?" she said, from the protection of his embrace. "I know I shouldn't ask, that it's unfair. I want to feel safe." She looked down at the floor, and her bare toes. "I don't feel very safe."

He squeezed her tight. "Of course I will. And it's not unfair to communicate honestly what you want or need. I'm an adult. I can say no."

He scooped her up, and carried her to the bedroom, turning the lights off on the way so the moon was their only illumination. He laid her tenderly on the bed, then shuffled into place behind her so she was propped up on his chest. He stroked her hair and his masculine, fresh scent wrapped around her like a blanket.

"I'm not saying no, Nixie," he whispered into her hair. "I'll look after you tonight."

He traced up and down her arms, the touch sensual but not quite tipping into sexual. The touch soothed her. She wanted to give something back to him.

"Jeb?"

"Hmmm?" They were in more of a reclining position now, coasting towards sleep, and Jeb sounded like he, too, was relaxing. She was glad. His day had been as tough as hers. More. She'd seen him feel responsible for the death, heard him ask one of his team for a second opinion on how much earlier they would need to have been there to make a difference. She couldn't help with that.

"I've been thinking a lot about your wards, and your auxiliary energy."

Jeb tensed.

"No, hear me out," Nixie said. "You made a mistake, and you went too far. You put a limit on yourself while you learned how to deal with that mistake."

Jeb grunted. *Damn the man and his grunts.* She pressed on.

"But we only grow if we learn from our mistakes." She twisted in his arms, and rested her chin on his chest, looking up at him. "At this point, surely it's more of a punishment than a protection?"

His hands had stilled on her body, but he didn't tell her to be quiet, yet.

"I wonder if, perhaps, your shame prevents you being who Source created you to be, so that now you've caused yourself a different issue, where your energy has built inside you, stale and destructive, and it needs letting out in a way where you can manage the release healthily."

Another grunt. She ran a hand over his chest. Up close like this, the silvery light of the moon cast shadows that she could almost imagine as shallow valleys and hills. She'd paint them as a miniature fairytale landscape, watercolor brushstrokes a mix of fine and striking.

"When you're ready to release your energy fully, I'd be privileged to help you. And in the meantime, thank you for today," she said, laying her head back down on his chest.

She liked him a lot, just as he was. But it would be nice if he liked himself, too.

～♥～ ～♥～ ～♥～

Nixie didn't sleep well. She couldn't get the scene they'd walked in on the day before out of her mind. She'd drawn the man as soon as she'd gotten up. It was Elrian, of course.

The body, the blood, the vivid fear inside her when Elrian had thrown what had turned out to simply be a book at her. She relived the moment over and over, until she'd considered going to one of the Healers in the Guild – and of course, there were many – to help her calm down some.

She could have asked Jeb, but for some reason that felt too intimate. She wasn't ready for him to realize quite how frightened she had been, and still was. She would keep her cowardice to herself, for now. He had been grounding for her last night, but they weren't in a relationship, he'd been clear about that. She couldn't rely on him in that way.

Today Jeb had invited her to attend one of his lectures. She'd asked about his day-to-day duties in the Guild, and he'd replied he'd been getting substitutes to fill in for his lectures the last week, but this current crisis meant both he and Aiko felt he should show his face to reassure the students.

Thankfully, Aiko seemed to have forgotten about Nixie for the moment.

She walked into the lecture room one minute before the lecture was due to begin. It wasn't huge, perhaps able to hold fifty students. Jeb had told her he expected it to be quite full today, given recent events, and he was right. There were no seats left by the time Nixie arrived, and she had to perch on a step near the back.

Jeb was already at the lectern, arranging papers and setting up some slides. He looked good; his stubble tidy, hair washed and brushed, wearing a grey shirt and khaki pants, with a loose navy woolen sweater over the top. The color that suited him well. She liked the look, and this version of him. She was beginning to understand that he was more than the sexy and the sorrowful she had drawn. He was a healer, and a spy, and a Maven, and a member of the Guild Leadership team. Not to mention a man who gave really good cuddles.

He began speaking at one minute past the hour, welcoming the students, and acknowledging the events of the day before, which were an open secret at this point. There was rustling in the room in response, but no one raised a hand to comment. Then he introduced the topic.

"Today, I'm going to discuss what happens when an energetic's energy twists. One way we can tell this might happen from a medical-energetic standpoint, is through the lymphatic system."

Jeb used the computer to click through to a diagram of that system. "A couple of decades ago we realized that the Chakras have a strong energetic connection to the lymphatic system, despite the fact that in general the Chakra points in the body are not physically directly correlated to these areas. Research showed that the five hundred to six hundred lymph nodes in the body, and the waste products and cellular debris it transports and drains, change as an energetic's energy twists. Measuring this gives us a good understanding of how far along an energetic might be in terms of going full Rogue."

Nixie didn't follow much of the lecture for a while after that, as it went into more technical details. She watched Jeb's hands as he shared his information, and how he used them to emphasize points. There was a sense of musicality to it which she enjoyed, as well as his voice which she loved listening to, whatever he was saying. She began to sketch him while she watched and half-listened, feeling calmer than she had for a while.

The last part of the lecture was a case study. She wasn't sure, but she thought she picked up that Jeb had been part of the team that had discovered a way of diagnosing the connection between the Chakras, the lymphatic system, and energy twisting, though it was downplayed enough she wasn't sure. He'd certainly been one of the earliest to experiment with it.

"In this situation, an Anahata-Svadisthana woman came to me to get help for her husband, a Manipura-Svadisthana energetic, who was having jealousy issues. She could see there was something wrong, and wanted a more precise way to know when to use Anahata to soothe him, so she wasn't influencing him without cause. We'd been working on the diagnostic and I was able to share the methodology with her." Jeb then described more technical detail on how they did this, and Nixie could see pens scribbling notes all around the lecture hall. The ending of the story wasn't so happy, however.

"It worked well, until the time she went on her yearly retreat. She'd done what she could to steady him before she went away, but unfortunately he refused to see anyone else for similar treatment, and his jealousy exploded. He found her in her retreat, and killed them both."

Nixie sat up straight, shocked. That sounded horribly, terribly familiar.

Jeb had been aware of Nixie's presence in the lecture hall, and had tried to ignore his tendency to want to study her. He had made a conscious effort not to look at her, but his gaze was drawn to her repeatedly. It was as if she sparkled with an inner light.

His head was full to bursting right now. He'd had to block others' feelings temporarily, as his empathy energy teetered on overload. The politics of the Guild, the death of the Hermit, Tierra's illness, the research he desperately needed to do, the prophecy, all pressed on him tearing his attention in different directions when all he really wanted to do was put his head in Nixie's lap and rest. Despite the fact he was supposed to have been comforting her last night, she'd been something he, too, had desperately needed. That sense of connection and intimacy in the dark had created a bubble around the two of them. The content of her words he couldn't deal with alongside everything else, but her voice had been pacifying.

Today, however, he needed to manage his attention better. At the end of the lecture, when the students had gone and he was packing his things, she walked over to him. He couldn't decipher the look on her face. She seemed paler than usual, and there were taut lines on her forehead, while her lips pressed together so they seemed almost bloodless.

"Are you alright?" he asked. Had something in the lecture bothered her?

She nodded. "The case study you talked about today, who was it?"

He shook his head to clear it, uncertain of what she was talking about. She seemed very different from the woman he'd left that morning. He rubbed his forehead, pressure building in his temples. Why would she ask about that?

"I try to keep the case studies anonymous," he said. It was part of Anahata's promise to its patients, and it didn't add anything for his students to know the people. It wasn't relevant.

"Was it Aria McCarthy and Aden Blackfire?" Nixie said. She clutched a sketch pad tightly to her chest.

How did she know that? She should have been a child when the incident happened. Although he supposed it was relatively well known in some circles. "It's not really appropriate for me to confirm or deny that."

"It was a long time ago, and you said they're both dead, so how can it hurt?" Nixie said.

"I can't tell you," Jeb said. Though she was right, they were dead, so his duty of care wasn't the same as when they had been alive. Why was she so focused on this? She must know he wouldn't usually give that kind of information out. Her pressing for this right now was too much. His head throbbed, pain blossoming and spreading. He squeezed his eyes tight, trying to clear it, then blinked them open again.

"I want to know more about what happened. It's them, right?" she said.

Perhaps if he confirmed that, she'd drop it? He needed a break. He needed to rest. If he didn't take some time to ground himself, he'd struggle to hold his Svadisthana in check. He was worn out from the energy it needed from him. He was confused about why she was prying about this, it wasn't her business, and it was a strange side of her to see. His role in that episode hadn't made him particularly proud.

He packed up the last of his things and straightened. "Yes, it was them. Now I need to go to my office."

He gave her a nod, then walked out of the room — while longing to be back with her in that bubble in the dark, no matter what uncomfortable ideas she might plant in his brain.

CHAPTER

22

Nixie stormed to the library. She didn't understand why Jeb had been so patronizing. There was a big hole in her family history that he could potentially fill, and he was refusing to. He had no right.

Obviously, she hadn't actually told him, or reminded him, rather, that they were her aunt and uncle. She'd thought he'd make the connection himself, and when he hadn't, she'd decided to leave it. Though on reflection, she wasn't sure quite why. Was she annoyed he wasn't interested in her enough to know?

She didn't have many connections in this Guild, but the one she did have knew Jeb quite well. And she and Feng had got on well so far, as the fussy, precise man was also kind and helpful.

She found him in the stacks, still researching the Tierra issues. He smiled in welcome, and she launched in.

"In Jeb's lecture just now, he mentioned helping Aria McCarthy and Aden Blackfire. Do you know what he did?"

Feng blinked. "Yes, I do."

Finally, Nixie thought. Answers. "Okay. Can you tell me? He said something about a diagnostic tool that he used."

"He didn't just use it, he invented it," Feng said. "And it has saved lives. The Anahata Rehabilitation Centers use it now to monitor the Rogues they are rehabilitating."

Huh. Jeb had never mentioned that. That seemed like a big deal. She'd seen he was important in the Guild, but that kind of contribution seemed like something her friends, or those she'd met in the Guild, might have mentioned.

"What happened with Aria and Aden?" Nixie said. Her stomach hurt thinking about the aunt and uncle she had only known as a small child. Aria had been loving and kind, coincidentally with the same energies as Jeb, but with full access to both. With hindsight Nixie could see she had been a very sexy woman, but at the time it had been sitting on her lap reading together, with the little Blaize in one of her arms and Nixie in the other, that made the most impression on Nixie. Aria had also been quite happy to play hide and seek with the children, either in Thailand or in Europe where her family was based.

Aden had been a more difficult man. It had been a prophecy, as far as Nixie knew, that had sown the initial seeds of jealousy that had eventually turned him into a Rogue. They had been told if they married, their union would cause both great good and great harm in the world, and a man would come between them.

"Aden was suffering, his energy flaring and twisting because of his jealousy. He lost control several times, though didn't slide into being a Rogue. Aria was worried he might be a danger to their daughter. As a healer she consulted Jeb for help. He taught her how to use the diagnostic, and use her energy, with Aden's permission, of course, to soothe him." Feng had a faraway look in his eyes. "She would come to the Guild to see Jeb, because he wouldn't leave even then, and they would spend intensive time together. What she was doing wasn't easy, especially because it was her lover she was trying to save."

He continued. "Such a use of energy drained Aria, and Jeb became her physician as well as her teacher. He kept her going during that time, which in turn kept Aden going. He gave the family a few more years together."

"But Aden still died," Nixie said, flatly.

Feng nodded, his face drawn.

"It shouldn't have happened. Aria went on a yearly retreat of several weeks, which she had done for decades. She'd been the year before and Aden was fine, because they'd spent time beforehand preparing. They prepared as usual that year, and Aden even stayed at a Rehabilitation Center for the first couple of days, so that others could keep an eye on things." He sighed. "We don't know what happened. He checked himself out without permission, and something triggered him. And you know the rest."

She did. He'd killed himself and Aria, leaving Blaize to grow up an orphan and as Nixie's surrogate sister.

Nixie rubbed her forehead. It was puzzling, to say the least, to think of Jeb playing such a role in her personal history. He had gone to so much trouble to try and save a man with a lot of problems, and his actions had probably given Blaize more years with her mother and father than she might have had otherwise.

She hadn't seen Jeb as a mystery. She'd seen him as a distraction from her own problems. As a lover, without question. But the complex man she was uncovering, who juggled political issues, invented healing practices, and saved lives, was so much more. She wondered if he'd even got any recognition or credit for what he'd done with Aria and Aden. She doubted it. He was an introvert to her extrovert.

She glowered. It seemed that Jeb was not only hot, he was a hero.

And the damn man still didn't have a bracelet.

Sitting in his office, Jeb's eyes were gritty and he was exhausted from the parade of colleagues, students and others in the Guild who wanted to extract the gory details from him as to what had happened, what it meant, and what would happen next. The care with which he needed to handle which details he gave to who made his head hurt.

He hadn't enjoyed politics before, but this current incident had stirred the pot considerably in the Guild. Incident. Source, not incident. It was a tragic death. A murder. Sanitizing it by calling it an incident was falling into a politics mindset indeed. He rested his elbows on the desk, and put his head in his hands.

He hadn't seen Nixie since after the lecture. He knew he'd been short with her, but the pressure was getting to him. He should go and talk to her. Taking her in his arms at this moment was quite the desirable goal. He needed to be careful, though. He was feeding more and more energy into his shields yet they still seemed to be weakening. He had managed to hold them through the times he and Nixie had been intimate so far, but if the trend continued, he wasn't sure what might happen. He'd injured enough people already.

He still didn't know what to think of the Hermit's death. Harrowing, certainly. But why had he been killed? And why now? The pages that Nixie had found were from some kind of notebook, presumably the Hermit's, and the variety of languages Damir had used so far also included modern Arabic, ancient Aramaic and Vietnamese, of all things. The pages were being translated as quickly as possible to see if they contained anything useful. Jeb really wished they had the rest of the pages, or the notebook that they came from. Who knows what the murderer of the Hermit had taken from the scene?

His door was pushed open without warning and he snapped his head up, shaking it to try and clear it. He felt muggy, and his brain was slow. Ah, Source. It was Maya.

"Jebediah," she said. She looked crisp in a white pant suit and matching blue jewelery. He felt creased and grubby next to her, the clothes he'd lectured in now the worse for wear after the day he'd had.

"Hi. What do you need?" he asked. He kept his tone polite, as he felt they'd always got on in the past, no matter how difficult she seemed at times. She always seemed to be laughing at her own private internal jokes, usually, he thought, at the expense of others.

"I wanted to give you advance warning that you need to prepare the information on your students for the database," Maya said. "I'm letting all the staff know."

"Okay," Jeb said, though his heart sank at yet another task going on his list. He cocked his head as a thought struck him. "How's it progressing? Is this latest release nearly ready?"

"Yes," Maya said. "I have a guy auditing the beta release right now."

"Oh, yes," Jeb said. "The audit. It seems to be taking a while? Is there a problem?"

"Not at all," Maya said, as smooth as honey. "I find technology often takes longer than planned. The modern world's conveniences can also be its downfall."

Jeb shrugged his shoulders. "Sure. Email me a reminder and I'll have the information ready for when you need it."

"My thanks, as always, Jebediah," she said. "How are you feeling today?"

"Fine, thank you," Jeb said, politely. "Busy."

"Of course," Maya said. "I'll leave you."

He could feel his internal shields and wardings stretched thin, and the pressure was getting to him.

He needed rest. Alone.

23

After supper, as Nixie still hadn't seen Jeb she decided to visit him. She'd missed seeing him that day, and at random intervals she had been struck by visions of the murdered body of the Hermit. Several times she found her eyes welling up for no reason, and had had to excuse herself from Feng and the research she had been doing with him for a moment alone.

Jeb didn't seem thrilled to see her. There were dark circles under his eyes, and he ran a hand through his hair as he let her into his living space. The revelations from Feng made her see Jeb differently. There was so much more to him than she'd realized.

She sat at the table with him. The lights were gentle, a warm breeze drifting through the room. It was simple, yes, as living quarters went, but it was calming. Peaceful. His body language was cautious. She supposed their last interaction had been a little brusque considering how intimate they had been.

She didn't beat around the bush. She needed to clear up why she'd needed to know. "Aria and Aden were my aunt and uncle. They were Blaize's parents."

Jeb looked stricken. "Nixie, I'm sorry. I was so focused on Tierra, and drained from everything that happened, it didn't occur to me to make the connection. I've given that lecture a hundred times. I wouldn't have…"

She stopped him, flushing. She could have told him what they were to her earlier. It was on her as much as it was on him. "It's fine. Feng told me more. He says you gave them extra time together, that Aden could have turned Rogue earlier had it not been for your intervention and teachings for Aria."

It was his turn to redden. "I happened to be their healer. It was a good opportunity for the diagnostic to be field-tested, and Aria was a great student. I can't take credit there."

Hmm. He really wasn't feeling very Svadisthana. Apart from Manipura, they tended to be the energetics who were least bashful about their achievements. All those artists.

She was grateful to him for what he had done for her family, however much he played it down. She stroked his hands, which were clasped loosely on the table. He didn't pull back.

"Thank you for what you did." She locked gazes with him, and ran her hand up his arm. She wanted to wipe away the tired from his eyes. The last twenty four hours had been pretty shit all round, and they both deserved cheering up.

She stood and walked over to his music system, fiddling until she found some Bach. She wound her way back across to him, and drew him out of his seat by the hand. Words weren't useful now. It was time for touch.

She wrapped her arms around his waist and swayed against him as the music changed the tone of the room to something more intimate. Her head barely came up to his chest, but she liked hearing his heartbeat as she lay her ear against it.

He stroked a hand over her hair, and she tilted her head so she could look up at him. She sighed. She enjoyed the touch, smell and look of him. He bent to kiss her, a gentle touch of the lips, a brush of the tongue.

Not to mention the taste of him.

"Let's go to bed," she said.

He hesitated a moment, then leaned to scoop her up under her legs and around her waist. She giggled in delight. He walked them both to the bedroom, and laid her on the bed reverently.

They gazed at each other, drank each other in.

They luxuriated in each other's bodies, touching without a goal. He kissed her everywhere, and she eagerly did the same.

He made her come more than once with soft licks of the tongue, and the gentle pressure of his fingers.

When he put his cock inside her, it was a tight fit at first, and she had to breathe to relax and accommodate him. He took the on top position over her – a way of having sex she'd often thought quite boring, but the intense eye contact they made with each other that night made it anything but.

She trembled underneath him, and wrapped her legs around his waist. He took long, slow strokes in and out, building the pressure inside her slowly, slowly, while she urged him on with her hips, but he was consistent, his pubic bone grinding against her clit each time he was fully inside her, and she was stimulated inside and out by his body.

He kissed her, his tongue sweeping inside her mouth as his cock did the same to her body. She wriggled underneath him, encouraging him, and moaned as his stubble rubbed against her face. Her ass cheeks clenched as she met his thrusts, and he increased the pace very slightly, driving her crazy with need. The man certainly had stamina.

It didn't take much longer before she felt that white heat between her legs. Orgasms were funny things, never the same thing twice, their final strength often difficult to predict from the way they were built. The hot ice grew inside her, his strokes kept going, until finally, finally, she crested the peak and exploded, the cold fire licking out from her core into the rest of her body.

He caught it happening, and sped up, letting go a little of his control – control that she was starting to see fade, thank Source. Moments after she came, he followed suit, burrowing his head into her neck and biting her shoulder as he did.

She saw stars on the inside of her eyelids, her orgasm prolonged by the delicious little bit of pain. He slumped, then rolled so she was on top, sprawled on his chest. She enjoyed the warmth of his body, the loose feeling inside her, the scent of sex around them, for a few minutes, then propped her elbows on his chest, and looked down at him.

"Ooof," he said. "You have sharp elbows."

She grinned. "Don't fall asleep yet."

He shook his head, eyes still shut, and drew himself out of her, nestling her onto the bed beside him. She was a perfect fit in his arms.

The sex they had that night wasn't the desperate passion they'd shared before. It was soft, gentle and connected.

She turned so she was on her back, and he on his side, one leg over her hip. "That was wonderful. But you can let go with me Jeb. I'll hold the space and keep your energies in check. You can't harm me. I'm stronger than I look."

He shook his head and slowly opened serious eyes. "I'm not ready, and anyway there's no need. I'm finding my balance with you. The place between control and release. If I keep back some energy, it's safer."

She waved her free hand, raised herself onto an elbow, and drew some Svadisthana energy, letting orange sparks leap up and down her arm. "I don't have the opportunity to use it much, but I'm a creator. I can create illusions and make fantasies come true."

She concentrated and pulled the energy through herself, and Jeb sucked in a breath. As far as she knew, he didn't have these energetic talents, despite his Svadisthana. She grinned. "Arabian princess?"

She concentrated again. "Or sexy librarian?"

Each time she created an illusion around her looks, so Jeb saw a version of her that fit the role she suggested.

Her smile faltered as he didn't look very enthusiastic. She didn't have much opportunity to practice these skills as most of the men she slept with were human, but she'd built up reasonable strengths in the area as part of her training. Her auxiliary energy helped with the illusion part.

He brushed some errant hair off her face, ignoring the illusion she had created of her wearing glasses. "Nixie, it's you I like. I don't need a fantasy. You're already enough of one of those. Do you have any idea how sexy you are?"

She glowed, and lay back down and nestled in his arms.

"Alright," she said.

Jeb watched Nixie doze in his arms, her fairy energy quieted for a change. She was usually all movement and action, chattering away to anyone they passed, though the Hermit's death had damaged that some.

He was a fool for not remembering that Blaize was the daughter in the case study from his lecture. He'd sleepwalked through the day, and the lecture had been one he'd repeated so many times over the years he hadn't thought about the content at all. Most of his mind had been on everything else that was happening.

Once again he'd held onto his control while having sex with Nixie, but his grip on it was tenuous. The strong shields he and Aiko had built were eroding, and he didn't know why. Was it Nixie? Was it simply exposure to this woman and everything she was that meant his body wanted to forego the protection he had put around it? At the same time, she felt like the safest person for him to be with – even as he cracked his shields around her, she took in his energy and cleansed it, the dangerous buildup inside him relieving slightly, the pressure diminishing.

The magic and energy in the Guild should protect him, but even that wasn't helping. He was having to invest time and energy in rewarding himself regularly through the day, and it was taking a toll on him. His whole body ached.

He put a gentle hand on Nixie's heart Chakra and felt her chest rise and fall. This woman was something, whatever else was happening.

Cuinn's prophecy surfaced in his mind. Both Jeb and Nixie were in it. Were they a pair? No. They couldn't be. They had no idea, really, how they might each be involved in the prophecy. Seeing energetics standing together had no real meaning without more interpretation, and he hadn't heard any of that from Cuinn or Blaize so far.

He ran a hand over Nixie's soft, straight hair, and her eyes opened. She sleepily stretched and then turned to hug him like a koala bear.

Should he continue this liaison? There was no real question. He shouldn't. His shields were weakening, and she was probably part of that, albeit not on purpose. She was encouraging him to use the energy he'd put away for good reason. And there were moments when he had certainly been tempted.

Being with her, feeling her Svadisthana energy, was like coming home. When she'd played with the illusions, not only had he been turned on despite just having come, but the feel of her energy had been sublime. He wanted to bathe in it. But that was a dangerous path.

He carefully disentangled himself from her grasp. "I need to go and check something with Aiko."

Her face fell, then stiffened into a mask. "It's late. Can't it wait till morning?"

"You can sleep here if you like. I might work through the night. I'm not helping enough with the Hermit investigation. The Guild's in chaos." He wanted to explain, but he knew if she tried to talk him out of it, while the room had the faint scent of sex in the air, and her lithe body lay there offering warmth and tenderness, he'd stay. That wouldn't be good for her, in the end.

She nodded, and shrugged. "See you later."

He needed to cool things off, at least until he'd worked out how to ensure his shields weren't draining as fast as he made them.

He glanced back as he dressed and exited his rooms. She lay in his bed, carnal and wicked, tan nude skin stark against his grey sheets. He wanted to run back inside and shut the door against the world.

Staying away from Nixie might not be as easy as he thought.

Cuinn's body lay on a mat in his work room in Cathair Cuinn, but his essence, his soul, was in the dreamscape. Cara was helping him with research while the others were away, was coming to see him for a couple of days here and there to slowly, patiently, fill in the gaps in the prophecy. Her no-nonsense attitude and driven nature were helpful.

They now had more information, and Nixie and Blaize had identified Jeb, a new member of the twelve, but there were still so many gaps. There were four faces missing, and several verses of the interesting Iskander document Nixie and Jeb had found were obscured.

And now Tierra was sick. She'd already been through so much. Fintan and Blaize had told Cuinn to concentrate on the prophecies rather than come to the island, but it was a hard burden to carry. Cara was a good friend and he was glad she was with him. She was close to Tierra, and worried sick.

Adam, Cuinn's cousin and Tierra's brother, was attempting to hunt the enemy here in the Pacific Northwest. As a Protector, he had skills in hunting and tracking, and he was looking into another case of leeching in the area which Fintan had found. Fintan had promised to let them both know if they needed to come to Thailand, but it seemed they could all do more from where they were. Though Adam, Cuinn and Cara were all questioning whether they should go to Thailand now. Recent reports from Blaize said Tierra was deteriorating. It was hard to know the best way to help her.

Cuinn walked out of his Haven, his safe place, in the dreamscape, into the wild energies. He wrestled with the taffy-like energies for a moment before shaping them into a place where he could open himself to the energy of prophecy. It was wearing, he'd admit. He'd done this so many times now. Sometimes information came, and sometimes nothing. But he had to hold back the wild energies each time, which wasn't easy. Only a Master level Ajna energetic could seek out prophecies like this. Other Ajna energetics could only receive what came to them.

He released the energies he'd gathered, and asked his question. *What happens now?*

His environment flickered and changed. He stood on a rock, looking out to sea. A beach was below him, with two figures who looked to be yelling at each other. A storm raged around them. They looked familiar. Were they part of the prophecy?

The smaller one gestured, and he realized it was Blaize's cousin, Nixie. He wracked his brains. If what Fintan and Blaize had told him about Nixie was correct, that might make the other figure Jebediah. Cuinn squinted. Yes. It was him.

The figures kept arguing. Cuinn could see that the man, Jebediah, was fighting an internal battle. Something was wrong with his energies. Very wrong.

The storm was right above them. Lightning cracked down like a whip. They needed to get off that beach. Cuinn resisted the urge to call down to them. This was just a potential projection of the future. Not only could he not do anything to save them, right now, there was no one to save.

The argument was reaching its peak at the same time as the storm was. If they didn't get off the beach, they were going to drown.

A huge wave was coming out of the sea. As the wave crashed over them, Nixie screamed, and the energies in Jeb exploded as he lost his final vestiges of control over his auxiliary energies.

They disappeared beneath the waves.

Blaize was on the phone, and wanted to talk to Nixie and Jeb together. Nixie had put her on speakerphone in the privacy of Jeb's study. Nixie had begun to find the books that surrounded them in there comforting rather than intimidating. Perhaps it was a form of Stockholm Syndrome.

Nixie felt a bit awkward because she'd told Blaize some of what had happened with Jeb, but nothing since she'd been at the Guild. She needed to catch her cousin up, but clearly, not right now.

Nixie sat in the chair at Jeb's desk, using a foot to push herself round in small circles. Jeb leaned against the wall. If he'd looked tired last night, now he looked shattered. His posture was slumped, the dark circles under his eyes were huge, and he could barely keep his eyes open. He must have stayed up all night. She'd gone back to her own room soon after he'd left. She hadn't slept well, but she'd done better than him.

Blaize cut to the chase. "Cuinn's received a prophecy which involves you both."

Nixie stopped, and her heart raced. Not more prophecies. She glanced down involuntarily at the silver bangle that she now never took off. "What? What was it?"

Blaize described the scene, the beach, the storm. "But it could be a metaphor. It doesn't have to happen exactly as shown. But there are two things Cuinn thinks. One is that you need to get off that beach if you ever find yourself in a similar position. And two, if you find yourselves in that situation, Jebediah needs to keep control of his energies. Cuinn thinks that given your energies, your loss of control powered the storm to rage as it did."

Nixie felt sick. Jebediah was never going to trust himself now. This was exactly what he'd been afraid of. She'd thought they were making progress – he'd opened himself up a little to his auxiliary energy, and had even used it during their lovemaking. He'd yet to use it outside the bedroom, but she'd been hopeful he might, if the opportunity presented itself.

"Nixie, we don't know what your role is here. Cuinn couldn't tell if your presence helped or hampered Jeb. Still, it's worth reminding you that prophecies are twisty," Blaize continued. "They give us hints about the future, but as I'm learning, they're a lot easier to interpret afterwards. Which doesn't really help us."

Blaize talked for a few moments more, giving them an update on Tierra's condition. Things weren't good. But Nixie and Jeb still hadn't found any answers that might help. They needed to do more, work harder, to bring something back to save Tierra.

When Blaize rang off, Nixie addressed the elephant in the room. "Using your energy again, slowly, will mean it doesn't build up so dangerously to create the problem Cuinn saw. It doesn't mean you should stop using Svadisthana again, but the opposite. You need to rebalance to be safe."

Jebediah had turned to look out the window. Nixie got up and went to him, putting a hand on his forearm, which hung loosely by his side. He put a hand over hers briefly, then moved away. The rejection hurt, but Nixie tried to hide it.

"I won't put you in danger, Nixie. Or anyone else, ever again. If that means I need to go back to the way I was before, so be it. It's a small price to pay for the safety of those I love."

Jeb's heart was heavy, but Cuinn's prophecy was all he had needed to cement the decision he knew he should have made last night. Jeb should never have become involved with Nixie. He didn't deserve a relationship with her, and the call had shown him that his small attempts at happiness with her came at too high a cost. He had to let Nixie go, for her own good.

He circled his neck, trying to get a crick out.

"There's something between us. I'm not sure what, exactly, but something," Nixie put her hands on the desk and leaned forward urgently. "And it's worth exploring. Source tells us we are responsible for balance. That means within us, as much as within the world. This is an opportunity to heal."

"I've been playing with fire," Jeb said. "I need to strengthen my shields, and that means we can't be together sexually anymore."

He felt contemptible, but this wasn't about his feelings for her. This was about the danger he posed to others.

She walked around the desk and stood in front of him, hands on hips. She had to crane her neck to look him in the eye, but the force of her gaze almost made him take a step back.

"Haven't you felt better since we've been together? Hasn't your energy felt calmer?" she asked.

"Well, yes, but my shields are crumbling," he said.

"You've developed high levels of control since the War. There's no chance anymore of you influencing people by mistake. And if that's the case, the only problem is that your energy is building up inside you in a negative way, looking for a way out." She studied him. "But if your energy is in balance, you don't need the wardings, Jeb. Think about that."

It was tempting. Source knew it was tempting. He couldn't take that risk though, especially now with Tierra's illness, the prophecy, and everything that was going on. He needed to be in control of himself, and his energy, and to be able to function around others without the fear he was going to hurt them.

"I can't, Nixie. I'm so sorry. You have no idea how sorry," Jeb said, brokenly.

Nixie nodded slowly. "All right. I think you're wrong about this, and you still have a mistaken need to punish yourself, but I accept you feel the need for it and I'm not going to try and change your mind anymore."

Jeb felt a strange mix of relief and was that – regret?

She hadn't finished, however. "I'll help you with the research, and work on the prophecy, but once this thing is done, I can't see you again."

"Of – of course," he stumbled over the words, but she had already turned away from him.

She went out of the door without looking back.

He groaned, and went to sit at his desk. The faint scent of her hung in the air and he closed his eyes and breathed it in.

Was she right, and the only reason to keep his energy bound was because he felt he needed punishing? Or was he too dangerous to others to ever let his auxiliary energy free again? He had no idea.

In the meantime he had enough to occupy him. Tierra was still deteriorating, though at a slower rate. They needed to understand and reverse her condition as soon as possible given what the research had netted them so far.

And why had the Hermit been killed? Why now? He must have known something important, presumably connected to the prophecies. But he was ancient, and his store of knowledge was huge. They were assuming it was connected to the prophecies but they didn't have proof. The mention of Iskander seemed important. But what other notes had been in that book? He needed to hurry the translation along, but part of it had been found by the linguists they were using to be in a kind of personal code of Damir's they had yet to work out.

It felt like there were a million open loops right now, and it was impossible to close them. And at the same time, he felt an ache in his chest.

At this rate, he'd have to put his heart back together as well as his shields.

25

Nixie, pacing her rooms, called Blaize and filled her in on what had happened. Nixie had managed to stay calm and mature in her engagement with Jeb, but she was a lot less chilled out now. Blaize listened and made sympathetic noises.

"The man's an idiot. An idiot!" Nixie said. She ground her teeth in frustration.

"It seems like he's trying to be responsible, Nix," Blaize soothed. "Cuinn's prophecy seemed to show a cataclysm of epic proportions if he releases his Svadisthana. You don't want to get caught up in that. Maybe after things have settled down you and he can try again with the balance thing you suggested."

Maybe. Nixie was missing the sea and wild open spaces. The Guild walls were pressing on her, and she hungered for freedom. She'd swum in the pool when she could, but it wasn't the same as the sea. "I feel like I'm going to explode into a million pieces. We're not making much progress here."

They talked about Tierra for a while and threw around various theories and ideas, mostly repeating themselves to see if anything new came up. It didn't.

"How does the bracelet thing work?" Nixie asked, trying for casual.

"What do you mean?" Blaize said.

"When you got yours, how long did it take for Cuinn's to appear?"

"They came at the same time, actually. But I think Tierra and Fintan's timing was different."

"Why?" Nixie said. She threw herself backwards on the bed, bounced once, and lay on her back.

"We don't really know," Blaize said. "We think they're from Source, but we don't understand much else about them."

She sighed. "There's really a lot we don't know right now. It's like we're drowning in questions."

Nixie shook her arm so the silver bangle slid up and stared down at her bracelet, thinking once again of Jeb's bare arms. Yeah, she knew about frustration.

She and Blaize chatted some more, then Nixie left her rooms. She needed some distraction from thoughts of Jeb which haunted her every moment.

She was full of pent up tension, and needed to do something with it. She'd checked out the Guild's training facilities, and seen they had a space for archery. It had been a while since she'd picked up a bow, but there was a point in her life when it had been one of her interests. She'd had a lot of those, she supposed. Definitely more of a jack-of-all-trades type.

She'd go to the range, and lose herself in the flow of firing arrows at a target. And she most definitely would not imagine anyone's face on that target. Nope. No matter how pissed off she was.

Jeb was back in the archives. The translation still wasn't complete, as they needed to find energetics he could trust who first recognized, then read, the various languages, some of which were dead, and some of which were in code. So far the parts Nixie had been able to read seemed to focus on some kind of tool, which was puzzling. She was poring over the Cappotian now, though it was apparently incredibly archaic, with many possible meanings. Her closest translation so far was 'tools of the conduit'.

In the meantime he was back on research.

It seemed strange that Nixie had only been in the Guild for a few days. It seemed like so much longer. He glanced across the table. She'd barely said a word to him. Feng, sensitive enough to pick up on the tension, had given Jeb an admonishing glance before being quite solicitous to Nixie's needs.

Jeb didn't like seeing Nixie upset either. Knowing he was the cause made it all the worse. There was an ache inside him despite knowing their relationship was both a distraction from what was important right now, and also hazardous to her and everyone else. He'd spent time meditating and working on his Svadisthana wardings that morning.

At one point, when Feng was off in the stacks, Jeb leaned over the desk to Nixie and said, "We can still be friends, you know. You don't have to stop talking to me."

She looked up and stared at him with such pain he almost recoiled. Without a word, she looked back down at the book she was consulting.

His heart squeezed.

They weren't getting far in the library. He leaned back in his chair and gazed at the ceiling above him. They needed a new angle, to find a different perspective.

Aiko walked up to their table and Jeb stood, surprised to see her. "Is all well?"

She nodded and sat in a seat close to him, her posture upright, her hands neatly on top of each other in her lap.

"Jebediah-san. My heart tells me you will at some point need to go back to see Tierra. If you truly wish to persist in holding your shields, you need to practice being outside the Guild."

Jeb's heart sank. Despite newly reinforced shields, and stamping down the sexual energy circulating between him and Nixie, he didn't feel ready. He opened his mouth to protest, but Aiko continued.

"I want Nixie to accompany you." Nixie, who had been studiously examining her text, snapped her head up. "She can help you to test your shields."

As both Nixie and Jeb opened their mouths to protest, Aiko held up her hand. "Carefully."

She left them. Jeb groaned. "Looks like we're going for a walk."

CHAPTER

26

Despite her mixed emotions about spending time with Jeb, Nixie's feeling of being trapped had eased some by getting out of the Guild.

Given the attack on Damir, Jeb was alert to the possibility of being followed, and she, in turn, was alert to Jeb. She tried not to glance too often at him as they walked.

"We're going to stick to quiet areas," Jeb said. "In case of problems with my energy."

She nodded. There was a tension between them, and yet at the same time she was glad to be with him. She was also enjoying looking at the local shops they passed, even if the streets were dusty. There was more greenery than she'd expected, though she wasn't used to the dry heat.

"Are you ready for me to test your shields?" Nixie said, tentatively. She saw the muscles in his neck go taut, and there was a long pause.

Nixie was wondering what else to say when a woman in dark pants and a fitted polo neck, with a hijab drawn across her face stepped out from the shadows and swept a low leg at Jeb, who avoided falling, but staggered.

The woman was tall and slender, but strong, and clearly experienced in both hand to hand combat and energy fighting. Jeb regained his balance, and defended himself as the woman continued to attack.

After her experience at the Hermit's residence, Nixie had been reminding herself about her shields, and though there had been no use of energy as yet, she pulled on her own energy to create one. The woman seemed to see Jeb as the harder target, and while she wasn't wrong, it wouldn't do for her to underestimate Nixie, she thought grimly.

Jeb was holding his own for the moment, but Nixie wondered if the binding of his Svadisthana would hinder him. Surely he would be more effective with access to both his energies?

Nixie sought a source of water in order to draw on her creator magic. Why were there no fire hydrants? Her energies discovered a stone cistern, containing enough water to support her. She pulled Svadisthana through from the ether to create a bow and arrow. It took a great deal of energy to manifest something physical, and it would take a toll, but close quarters fighting was something she was lousy at. Plus, she was terrified. Her stomach was a ball of ice, and she was shaking.

Jeb and the masked woman still fought.

Nixie's bow and arrows were basic, made from her element of water, but it was something she was practiced with. As soon as they appeared in her hands she felt lead weights land on her, as the exhaustion from the energy work hit her. At the same time, adrenaline flew around her body and kept her upright.

Energy was flashing between the two but it was hard for Nixie to work out exactly what was happening. Energetic attacks happened inside the body as well as outside.

She needed Jeb to move back for her to be able to shoot at the woman. She notched an arrow, and sighted, waiting for an opportunity. Source, she wished she'd trained more with Blaize.

Her eye followed the other two's movements. It was a quiet time of day because of the heat and there were no others about, which was lucky.

Jeb fell back against a street lamp, and cried out in pain as his ribs hit the hard surface. Before the woman could close the gap between them, Nixie let her arrow fly, then notched another one and released that.

Her first went wide, but her second scraped along the woman's left arm, tearing her sweater and opening a sharp cut which immediately produced a line of blood. The woman clutched at her arm and hesitated. She muttered something under her breath, then with a pushing motion towards Nixie, palm out, she shoved energy in her direction. Jeb yelled, and flung himself at the woman. He caught her in the side with a fist, and she let out an ooff. She shook him off, then ran, her flat shoes slapping on the concrete until she disappeared into the distance.

The energy she'd thrown had hit Nixie. Much of it had been absorbed by her shields, but the bow and arrow had fallen to the floor and disappeared, and Nixie had been caught across the top of her chest and shoulder. She had what felt like a nasty burn, and along with the energy she'd already expended to manifest the weapon, she could barely stay upright.

Jeb ran over to her and caught her as she was crumpling to the ground. His warm, strong arms coming around her and lifting her off the floor were the last things she remembered before she passed out.

Jeb took Nixie back to the Guild as fast as he could find a taxi, assessing her injuries on the way. She wasn't in critical danger, but the manifestation had taken a lot out of her, and the nasty second-

221

degree burn the masked woman had given her had shocked her system into unconsciousness.

It wasn't far, though the driver eyed them cautiously in the mirror frequently during the trip. Jeb had given the driver money hoping he wouldn't be asked questions, had covered Nixie's upper body with a coat and had briefly mentioned they'd been out for a drink.

He should have protected Nixie better. He knew she wasn't a fighter. But despite his desire to stay in the safety of the Guild, he'd seen the sense in Aiko's suggestion. He didn't plan to leave again if possible, but he should be better prepared next time if he did.

He'd been surprised to find being out with Nixie had felt restful. His Svadisthana energy had quieted. He wasn't sure what that meant, if anything.

She groaned, and opened her beautiful eyes. Her lashes fluttered as she worked out where she was. She reached up and touched his cheek.

"Are you okay?" she said.

He nodded, relief flooding his body. "I'm okay. I'll have some bruises. You have a burn, and you need rest, but you're going to be fine too."

She nodded, and lay back in his lap. "Thanks."

"I'm sorry I didn't do more," he said.

She tilted her head to the side. "What are you talking about?"

"I should have taken better care of you."

"Why? You're not in charge of me. Or responsible for me. I'm an adult, and I know what's going on. We worked together, as a team," she said, deep lines scoring her forehead and between her eyes.

Jeb knew he should have felt relief at her words, yet that wasn't what he was feeling. He had a lump in his throat and his body was heavy.

He sent word to Aiko they'd been attacked as he carried Nixie back to her room and checked her over more thoroughly. Using Anahata on her was confusing. Their energies had been so closely linked through their intimacy that it was harder than usual to get a clear reading, and he could feel his Svadisthana awake and writhing at the connection.

222

He slathered her burn with Anahata energy to encourage it to heal more quickly. It was possible she might end up with a faint scar in the area, but he'd done what he could.

Her cellphone rang and she gestured from the bed where she was resting. "Could you?"

He picked it up, and his heart sank when he realized it was Fintan.

"Just the man," Fintan said.

Jeb's stomach dropped to join his heart on the floor. He sat on the edge of the bed next to Nixie.

"Can you put it on speaker?" Nixie mouthed.

He nodded and did so. "Nixie and I are both here, Fintan. What is it?"

"Someone got through our outer wards. Ai saw them outside Tierra's window, but when she yelled for help, they ran away."

Nixie lifted her head, alarm on her face. "Is everyone okay?"

"Yes," Fintan said. "But I did a search and the person dropped something. We need to send Jeb an item to read. Tierra is getting sicker again, and we think the intruder did something, but we don't know what. She's lost weight, and her vitals aren't great. I'm worried she's going downhill, and fast. I don't know what to do. This item is our only current lead, and I don't know anyone else but you who can do telemetry, Jeb."

Fintan spoke in a rushed, jittery way, most unlike his normal laid-back self.

"What's the item?" Jeb asked.

"We're not sure. It looks like a small stick made of bone. We don't get any energy off it."

Jeb blew out a breath. "You can't send it. If it goes through the post it will pick up more memories and experiences and the reading won't be as clear. I would have to come to the island to read it. I need to think."

At every moment there was a new blow.

"I'll call you back. Let us know if anything changes." Jeb hung up the phone before either Nixie or Fintan could say anything more.

Nixie spluttered. "So?"

"What?"

"You know what. Are you going?" Nixie said.

Jeb ran a hand through his hair. The fight, such as it was, was something he hadn't been involved in for decades. His rusty skills had come back to a degree, but his body was battered and bruised, and he needed to recharge his Anahata to heal himself, having expended so much energy on Nixie.

All he wanted to do was go to bed and sleep for a week.

Ideally with this water fairy by his side.

He blew out a breath. That couldn't happen. He hadn't managed to keep Nixie safe from harm, but she was okay. Was he really going to leave Tierra to die, because he was frightened of what was inside him?

No. He was better than that. The trips outside the Guild into the city hadn't been easy, but Nixie was right. They'd been made less difficult with Nixie by his side. He wasn't going to explore why at the moment, but he was aware of it.

He wasn't going to let Tierra get worse, and he wouldn't let Nixie down. He would control his energy as best he could. But it was time to let go of some of the fear and self-hatred he'd lived with for more than half a century.

"I'm going. Will you come with me?"

27

Jeb and Nixie were back in the room with Tierra, who slept restlessly. She looked terrible, her eyes shadowed and sunken, her cheekbones more pronounced. Jeb spent some time feeding healing energy into her, but as fast as he supplied it she seemed to burn through it, her system devouring it. He'd increased the wards, yet still she was sickening.

He needed a break to think and recharge before he read the object that Fintan had found. He needed all the energy he could get right now.

He blew out a breath and turned to Nixie. She'd said she would avoid him when things were over, but they were still in the thick of things. He'd chance it. "I heard Blaize mention a lake on the island. Will you show it to me?"

There was a long pause. "Alright. Is everything okay?"

"I need a breather before I read the object." He'd have preferred the ocean, but given Cuinn's prophecy, that seemed too risky.

Nixie nodded, and she showed him the way to the lake, their walk one of companionable silence. He appreciated Nixie's quiet.

At their destination he scooped up a handful of flat, smooth stones, putting some in his pocket and rolling a couple in his palm. The water was calm, and perfect for something he hadn't done in decades.

They meandered to where the water met the shore. He didn't hesitate to shuck off his shoes and stand in the shallows. He dug his toes into the sand and let the warm water flow over his feet and ankles as he sucked air into his lungs. His auxiliary energy was under control, but he was alert.

"What were you doing that day when we met on the beach?" Jeb said.

Nixie looked puzzled for a moment, then comprehension crossed her face. "Oh. I was free diving. Well, not really, but that's why I can go under for such long periods. I was playing with the waves."

"How long have you been doing that?" Jeb asked.

Nixie shrugged. "Since I was a kid. A fisherman on the island taught me when I was young. I love going deep into the water. I scuba dive as well, but the freedom of being without equipment in the deep is amazing."

"I see," Jeb said. Though he wasn't sure he did.

Nixie seemed amused. "You don't like it? How do you like to enjoy your element, when you do? I've seen you in the pool, at least."

"I prefer to float. When I'm in the water, I love to float on the waves and stare up at the sky. It feels like I'm at one with the water."

"I don't like to be passive," Nixie said, and waved a hand. "I want to dance in the sea, to be part of the life underneath it."

Jeb grinned. "Yes, you're not the submissive type."

She really wasn't. She was vibrant, radiant, and filled with life. Even when quiet, she radiated a type of exuberance. They didn't need to have sex to enjoy each other's company. Her energy, though spirited, comforted him somehow.

"Did I hear you listening to some kind of rap on the plane?" Nixie asked.

Jeb winced and scuffed a foot, creating a small wave that he watched disappear quickly into the wider body of water. "Yep."

Nixie's brow furrowed for a moment.

"Oh-kay?" She drew out the word, and examined his face, peering at him. He kept his eyes on the lake.

She touched him on the bare arm, and his skin tingled at her touch, a light ripple going through his wards. He tried not to jerk back. He needed to watch that.

"I like it," he said.

She stepped into him, looking up into his eyes, her body not touching him, but close, so close. His groin stirred. She had dark and merry eyes.

"I'd have you pegged more for classical music," she said. She traced a finger along his arm, a gossamer touch. "I have a thing for Bach. I can listen to the cello for hours."

He needed to distract her, and him. "I don't listen to anything from before World War II. Music is a powerful trigger for me, and can bring back the horrors I saw."

Her hand covered her mouth, and her striking eyes widened. He shrugged, and hurried to move them on. "I've learned to deal with it. But that's why."

He stepped away from her, and tossed one of the stones he'd picked up in his hand. "Did you ever skim stones?"

"Sure," she said. She put a hand out and he placed a couple in her palm. "How many can you do?"

"I'm not sure," he admitted. "It's been a long time. I used to manage about eight."

She raised her eyebrows, turned, bent her knees slightly and with her arm low to the ground, let her stone fly.

He watched as it skipped once, twice, and eventually five times before it sank beneath the waves.

She beamed. "Your turn."

He only managed four the first time, but by the time they'd worked their way through the stones he'd picked up they were both on six, and laughing.

They walked back slowly.

"What is it you do in the human world?" Jeb asked.

Nixie glanced at him, eyes narrowed. "I'm a graphic artist."

She tilted her chin up, as if ready for battle.

"Okay," he said. "Comics and so on?"

He wasn't exactly sure what a graphic artist did.

"I do graphic design, and yes, I do some art work for graphic novels."

"Okay," he said. "That's how you use your Svadisthana creativity?"

She scowled. "Yes. It is."

He couldn't understand why she was being so defensive.

"Okay," he said.

She spun to face him, and he stopped short as words burst out of her. "Art and creativity are a lot more than oil paintings in a gallery chosen by some old white man in the nineteenth century. Art can be anything that expresses our thoughts, desires, feelings, ideas to others. And creativity can be applied anywhere, anyhow."

He nodded, bemused, unsure where this was coming from but interested. "My education around art was a long time ago, and more formal."

"Exactly!" she wagged a finger at him. "But that's only one aspect of art!"

"I'm not an artist," he said. "My energy, even when I used it, never came out that way."

"Huh." She dropped the finger, but put her hands on her hips. "Beauty and good design can be used anywhere. Art can be graffiti on the street, a child's pencil drawing, or a sculpture in a gallery. People's definitions are too narrow. It pisses me off."

"I see that," he said, dryly.

"Aesthetics are important. Art can make the world a better place. It ignites our imagination, creates shared values, and is a way to explore and question the world around us." Her face was alight with an earnest passion.

"I've never really thought about it that way before," Jeb said. She certainly made him look at the world in a different way.

On the way back she talked about some of her projects, creating brand images for NGOs and sculpture projects for large organizations. She had works inside some major buildings in New York, London and Vancouver. He was impressed. She was diverse, that was certain, in her creativity, but there was a coherence and vision behind it all that he hadn't expected. She truly wanted to create things that inspired people.

And he realized her enthusiasm had kindled yet another part of himself that had been quiescent. It had engaged the part of him that enjoyed intimacy and connecting with a woman. Building a true relationship.

He'd enjoyed talking to her. Watching her passion and animation. Initially, he'd thought they hadn't much in common apart from the sexual tension that simmered between them, but perhaps they could be friends after all.

He could use a friend.

Back in Tierra's room Fintan looked almost as bad as Tierra, his hair wild and unwashed, his usual stubble now an unkempt scraggle.

Jeb felt refreshed by his time at the lake, and was ready to work.

"I'm going to need to do this outside. I don't want to do it around Tierra, just in case," Jeb said.

Fintan, Jeb, Blaize and Nixie trooped outside, leaving Ai to stay with Tierra.

"How can we help you?" Fintan said. The man was desperate for action and running on empty. Jeb would try and handle him with kid gloves, though he didn't have a lot to spare when he was doing telemetry as it was very wearing.

"I have it under control, though we'll go a bit further from the house. Don't touch me while I'm reading the object," Jeb said.

Fintan had watched him do this before, and had brought a traditional-style straw mat with him for them to sit on.

Jeb arranged himself into a cross-legged position on the mat and breathed deeply. He needed to center himself before he touched the object. He put his hands on his knees and deliberately relaxed his muscles, maintaining an upright posture.

He pulled Anahata energy through from the ether, and felt his heart Chakra tingle. This kind of energy work was difficult, because it carried risk. When you touched an object to read it, you never knew what might have happened to that object. As you lived through those experiences, albeit in a flash, when you were reading it, you had no idea what you were inviting into your psyche.

"I'm ready. Can you drop it into my hands?" He held out cupped hands in front of him, eyes still closed. A touch from someone else would confuse things, and he wanted a clean reading.

He pressed his tailbone into the ground and wriggled slightly so he was solid in place.

Then something light and cool fell into his hands, and he opened himself up to it in a rush of sensation.

He jerked, and images and scenes hurtled through his mind.

He was on a nineteenth century pirate ship, the toothpick — because that was what it was — between the captain's teeth. He'd carved it himself out of the penis bone of a racoon, and he loved the look on pretentious ladies' faces when he told them what it was made from.

Blood. A lot of blood. The pirate rarely took it out of his mouth, even when murdering his victims.

Rape.

Death.

Destruction.

Arson.

Jeb took a breath, his heart racing, his chest heaving, face full of disgust. But this wasn't what he wanted. These were images from the first owner. The pirate was not an energetic, and would be long dead. The challenge with telemetry was that it had a tendency to pick up more easily on events with high emotion, and this toothpick apparently had seen more of that than most objects.

He dived back into the swarm of emotions and scenes that were connected to the toothpick.

A safe being opened by a terrified man. Twentieth century dress. A more recent scene, but not current day.

The toothpick is spotted by another man, who is methodically clearing out the safe, and he puts it in his mouth to chew on while he takes money, bonds, jewelery.

In the doorway a woman is slumped, arterial blood splattering the walls.

The terrified man is on his knees.

The new owner of the toothpick grabs him by the hair, lifts his head so his chin is up, and with a swift left-to-right movement, slits his throat.

Murder.

Many murders.

But strange. From here on in, all the emotion was from the murder victims. The owner of the toothpick was cold and impassive, even when he slaughtered his victims. It was rare for anyone to show no emotion. A psychopath? A sociopath? And yet, an energetic, because in the scenes, the murders that the man had committed sometimes involved energy use. Jeb thought Svadisthana-Ajna, though the latter energy was slender.

Jeb was sick to his stomach at the visions passing through his senses.

The iron tang of blood in the back of his throat.

The rattling gurgle as a victim died.

The feel of hot blood gushing down a chest.

The harsh smell of urine and worse as a victim released their bladder and bowels in death.

Ah ha.

The sight, from the victim's perspective, of a tall white man, with dark, neat hair, and a relatively unprepossessing face. Not unattractive physically, he clearly trained his body to be in peak condition. Watching the murders he committed, Jeb could see death in his eyes, combined with indifference.

Jeb's gorge rose.

But he needed more information.

He drew energy harder and faster, trying to find the more recent emotional memories on the toothpick, something that would tell them where the man who was trying to hurt Tierra was hiding.

Prickles ran up his arms and legs as magic raced around his body. He focused it on his hands where he cradled the toothpick.

There had been no murders on the island as yet. Which was a blessing, but it also meant that the emotional memories here were harder to trace. The psychopath emitted very few feelings of any kind, and so Jeb's only chance was where others had had emotions he could 'catch'.

That meant increasing his sensitivity, which meant the deaths that the toothpick had seen pressed in on him, crowding his mind with images of brutality and nightmares. His head pounded. He couldn't keep this up much longer. But he needed to find something. Anything. Some kind of clue to find this bastard and bring him down.

Ah, here. A faint – compared to all the blood and executions – emotional sense memory which was recent. The man with the toothpick had rented a house here, and Jeb suspected the woman he'd rented from was a sensitive of some kind, given her reactions to the man – reactions which Jeb experienced for himself.

Cold fear. Ice in her veins. She froze when he walked up, asking for rentals on the island.

Which was less dangerous? Telling him she was fully booked? Renting to him?

Showing any kind of fear was dangerous with this kind of predator.

An evil man.

Casually threatening though his words were sweet.

She'd rent to him, as the easiest option.

She hoped she wouldn't regret it.

Jeb shuddered, and released the toothpick to the ground. He had what they needed, the image of where the psychopath had rented his accommodation. All they needed to do was find it.

He staggered to his feet, lurched a few feet away into the bushes, and threw up.

Nixie had watched Jeb read the toothpick with her heart in her throat. The distress on his face was evident as he read the object and pushed out words. She jotted down notes as he did so, glad to have a task.

When he threw up, she jumped up and grabbed a bottle of water. He unbent and stood, scrubbing an arm wearily over his face. She offered him the water carefully, not touching him. She hated herself a little for checking his wrists yet again, covering the big silver bangle with her hand when his were still bare.

Was there someone out there with a matching bracelet? She'd really thought Jeb might wear the corresponding one. It had the right colors, after all – her own orange for Svadisthana, and blue for Vishudha, white for Sahasara, which was the color of the energy of the Source, or the divine, and then one final color. Green. The color of Anahata. Which Jeb had.

And yet.

The walk by the lake had been intimate in a way she wasn't used to. After he'd taken sex off the table she'd expected him to be less interested. She was perplexed, but intrigued, by this interaction. She was a bit embarrassed about the intensity with which she'd shared her views about art, but she'd wanted to explain, to show him, how important it was to her.

She had found it was nice to be listened to. To be really heard.

He took the water from her, swilled it round his mouth and spat it out. "Thanks."

"What do we have?" Fintan demanded. He'd been silent for long enough, but was bursting to do something.

"I saw the place he rented his lodgings." Jeb looked as though he might collapse at any minute.

"Where is it?" Fintan said.

"I don't know. It seemed familiar, like something I'd passed in town, but I can't remember exactly."

"Right," Fintan said. "Let's go. I'll drive us round until you see it."

He hesitated, then met Jeb's eyes with his own. "Thank you."

Jeb nodded, and the men drove off, accompanied by the throaty roar of Fintan's bike.

Nixie looked at Blaize. Jeb set an example that was hard to live up to, but she could show him she too could contribute.

"I'm ready to do more sketching," Nixie said.

Blaize tilted her head from side to side and stretched. They'd done little on the sketches while Tierra was ill, as both Nixie and Blaize struggled to focus with everything going on.

"I don't know," Blaize said. "I'm not sure I can hold an image for long. And we don't have a spotter."

"We'll set an alarm," Nixie said, more confidently than she felt. "Small periods, with breaks. I need to be doing something, Blaize."

Nixie wanted to throw herself into helping. Blaize nodded slowly and Nixie felt lighter.

She'd told Jeb art could change the world. This could be an opportunity to prove that.

Elrian reviewed the Hermit's papers, but couldn't concentrate. The words swam in front of his eyes. He sat at a desk in the dusty apartment he was currently inhabiting. There were plenty of empty apartment buildings on the outskirts of Cairo. It was an excess of housing created by a country where high inflation and limits on sending cash abroad meant the Egyptians had needed internal, local investments that would maintain their value. But most were priced outside the ordinary Egyptian's means.

Whole streets stood half-built, or built but empty, waiting for better times. It had been simple for Elrian and Imogen to find a quiet place for him to heal from his wound after the fight with the Hermit, while she went back to the Guild.

Elrian needed more energy to heal and complete the task she had set him. He tried to draw from the ether, but his connection was sticky, blocked. He needed an external source.

His head was in a fog. He left his papers and he went out.

He needed energy.

Elrian wandered aimlessly in the streets near the Guild. Not too near, he had some sense of self-preservation, but in the places Guild members frequented.

A youth crossed his path. A younger energetic, with no Adherent markings, the single stripe an energetic gained on their shoulder when they were bonded to a Maven. He seemed to be on some sort of errand, an empty bag in his hand. He was a higher risk abduction, but Elrian needed what he had.

Elrian stalked him, purpose infusing him. He could impress Imogen. That morning he had found a suggestion about a shortcut to create a remnant stone. This youth would be perfect to try it on. Elrian would gain energy for himself, and he would show Imogen he had power, that he was able to create the stones as she did, on his own. The papers had seemed to show him a way.

He stalked the prey till he crossed to a quiet street. Elrian came up behind him, placed a hand on his shoulder and began talking. His prey was weak, easy to influence. It took only a minute to have the boy under his control.

Elrian brought him home. He didn't waste time. He leeched enough energy to heal his wounds and find clarity through the murkiness that kept clouding his mind.

Next was to show Imogen he could create a fifth stone on his own. As far as they knew there were only five or six people in the world who had the knowledge to create new remnant stones – one fewer since they'd killed the Hermit – and perhaps only he and Imogen who were able to combine that knowledge with the power and the will to create them.

She'd had to go back to the Guild to maintain her cover. He had plenty of time before she returned.

The boy was unconscious from the leeching, so there was no issue there of him trying to get away. He lay the boy on the floor and set up the ritual around him, preparing him as a sacrifice.

They needed twelve remnant stones for the final ritual. Each one took a great investment of power to create. So far, they had the original stone, the one that had started everything. Then she had created two more, and they had created one together. That last stone Indigo had had charge of, and had been lost. They would need to find it, or create another to replace it, but that was a problem for Canada, not Egypt.

He breathed in deeply, and opened the channel. He poured himself into the ritual, ready, eager to offer the youth in exchange for the power of another stone.

The energy built up inside him, painful in its intensity. He guided his energies as they cascaded into the ritual, and he grew ready to draw the energy out of the boy to create the stone.

A flash. The boy screamed, long and loud, then slumped back, his eyes burned out.

Elrian's gorge rose, and shaking, he stared down at the corpse.

He'd failed.

And wasted another source of energy.

He'd failed.

Time passed as he stood there, frozen in place.

He'd failed.

A blow hit him across the face and he staggered, his head snapping back. He blinked, and Imogen came into focus. He lifted his hands in front of his face, palms out. How much time had passed? How was she back already? He must have been standing there for hours. The eye sockets no longer smoked, which was a blessing.

"What have you done?" she snarled.

Failed.

"I wanted to show you – to create – I wanted to make a new stone," he stuttered.

"The Guild is in uproar, and you abduct and kill a member? What is wrong with you?" She was furious, eyes cold, lips curled, her body taut, as if she was keeping herself under tight control. "What if you were seen? What if they use a Tracker? You're going to have to get out of town."

His head was muddled again, the clarity of the energy rush draining in the face of her fury.

He'd failed.

They'd have to create the next stone together. Somehow she was more powerful than him. He needed her. Did that matter? He didn't want to be without her, after all. They needed each other, surely?

Or perhaps he could still make one without her. Perhaps he'd got the shortcut wrong. He'd study the notes more. He'd been tired when he'd tried today. He should have spent longer preparing. He straightened, and tried to pull himself together. His hands dropped to his sides. He had no need to defend himself from her. She'd slapped him to bring him back to himself. He'd needed it.

Perhaps Cassidy and he would have enough power to create one together? Though it would cross a threshold with her he wouldn't be able to reverse, involving her in that. He might not be able to hold her under his influence while managing such a tricky magic. Cassidy was something else he was worried about. The balancing act of protecting her from the blonde and yet using Cassidy's still growing powers to help their cause was a strain.

His cell phone beeped, and he glanced reflexively at it. Imogen hissed, but he snatched it up gratefully.

"It's Trent." He read the message. "The charm is working. He's checking it twice a day, and he doesn't think she has much longer."

"Good. That will help. Then we still need to deal with either the healer or the flighty chit." She stepped across the body that lay on the floor between them without appearing to notice it. She put a hand flat on Elrian's chest. "Perhaps it's time for you to go there. The girl is hardly a rocket scientist. She's not a fighter. Separate her from her friends, and she should be easy to pick off. She's vain, proud, and emotional. And Source knows we need to get you out of here."

He didn't know the girl well, but perhaps Imogen was right. He put one hand on her shoulder, and texted Trent with the other.

Get Nixie to the beach at midnight in two days. I'm coming.

The response was fast. *Roger that. How?*

Elrian's jaw clenched with irritation. Wasn't that his problem to figure out?

Tell her we want her bracelet in exchange for Tierra's life. She will believe she is giving up the chance for true love.

The prophecy slivers he'd seen indicated Nixie was ready for some kind of self-sacrifice. He might as well play to that. While in fact, he'd end up with the two energetics he needed to end the prophecy at this stage, Nixie and Tierra.

"It's done. I'll burn this place and leave." He bent down and kissed her, threading a hand in her hair. She tasted of honey and lemon, sweet with a bitter aftertaste. It was addictive.

He'd read and research more in the Hermit's papers, he'd center himself, and next time, he'd make the remnant stone correctly. He'd show Imogen he was as valuable as she was. That they were equals.

He wouldn't fail again.

Nixie hopped on her bike to get fruit smoothies for those at the house. There was a woman with a bamboo stand who made them a kilometer or so away. Nixie could have walked it, but she'd been in creative flow, and didn't want a long break. She was keen to get back to her sketches as quickly as possible. They'd completed Fintan, an easier image for Blaize to hold while tired, as they'd known each other a long time. He had a long sword of fire sheathed on his back. Nixie wanted to see herself, but they'd realized they should focus on Tierra next, in case her image provided any clues to her illness. Nixie was annoyed at herself for not thinking of it before.

With four drink orders and only one blender, she'd be at the drinks stand a while. She wandered a few meters from the woman while she worked, and gazed into the green of the jungle. Home.

Her skin tingled, and she turned. A man stood there, sunglasses propped on his head, neat and handsome, yet there was something off about him. Something unpleasant.

She shifted her body and decided to walk back to the fruit shake stand.

He shook his head. "Uh uh. I have a message for you."

"I'm not interested." She tried to push past him, but he grabbed her wrist. She broke the grab by jerking her wrist through the weakest part of his hold, between his first finger and thumb, and backed out of reach.

He sighed in an exaggerated fashion and gave a forced smile. "Just stay there. All I want to do is talk."

She gestured. "Talk. Then fuck off. Or fuck off first. Either way."

She feigned indifference, but inside she felt sick. She was barely preventing her whole body from shaking from the massive adrenaline dump caused when he grabbed her. Who was this guy? The one Fintan and Jeb were out looking for? He matched the limited description Jeb had shared. Or was there more than one enemy on the island?

She shot a glance over to the fruit stall to check the woman was still there. She was, unconcernedly working on drink number three. At least there'd be a witness, she thought. But to what?

"A friend of mine wants to offer you a trade. Your bracelet for Tierra's life." The man was a kind of bland handsome, yet managed to exude menace. He was overdressed for the island, a shirt and chinos. A predator in smart casual clothing.

"Why would I do that?" she asked. She was proud that her voice didn't waver.

"Because Tierra is only one or two nights away from death. And because the only reason Jebediah wants you is because I encouraged him through Svadisthana influence. Whereas your feelings for him … " he shrugged. "Well, those I didn't touch. Your bracelet doesn't have a match."

Nixie felt tears prick her eyelids. She knew it. That was why she had a bracelet and Jeb didn't. The answer was as simple as that. Jeb had been manipulated.

She'd hoped after all this hellish situation was over, she'd be able to persuade him that they were good for each other. She'd wanted to believe that their growing relationship was somehow more real than other relationships she'd had with men.

When in fact, it was the most fake of them all.

She wouldn't cry in front of this jerk. "And what would it mean to give the bracelet up?"

"You'd come with me. Willingly. We only need one bracelet. We'll remove it in a ritual, then you can go. It won't be pleasant, but once we have it, we'll leave Tierra – sweet, warm Tierra, who has contributed so much to the world, with a partner who loves her – alone."

"When do I have to decide?"

"You have till sunset tomorrow. If you're not with me by then to go through the ritual, Tierra will go downhill quickly. But we'll leave her alone for now, as a show of good faith." He took his sunglasses off his head and cleaned them diligently, then handed her a white card with a phone number on it. "Text this number to confirm. I hope, for her sake, you make the right decision. Personally, I have no problem killing you all, including that man you wish was yours. The bracelet seems an easy trade for the lives of those you love."

He put the sunglasses back on. "I suggest you keep this conversation to yourself. Don't think we're not listening. If we hear you tell your friends about it, it will be easy enough for us to end Tierra."

He slashed a hand through the air in front of her, sharp and fast. Then turned on his heel and stalked off, leaving her clutching the paper, eyes wide and pregnant with tears, her heart cracking inside her chest.

Nixie waited till he was out of sight before she went, mechanically, to collect and pay for her drinks. She hooked the little plastic bags they came in to her bike, then drove a short way away before pulling over to the side of the dirt road. She walked into the trees that fringed the road, and sank to the dry, sandy dirt as if her legs had stopped working.

The tears she had held back overflowed down her cheeks, and she swallowed compulsively to try and rid herself of the burning lump in her throat. She rubbed at her eyes angrily. She didn't have time for this. *What am I going to do?*

She was the weak one in their group. She'd thought she'd spent her life searching for love, but she was beginning to realize love wasn't what she'd thought. The bracelet had offered her hope that might change, and now she needed to give it up.

What did she have to offer? She was a quick study with a pencil. It was hardly a talent that was needed to prevent the end of the world.

It was better for Jeb they weren't a pair. If she got rid of the bracelet, and stopped being so attached to him, perhaps he'd finally shake off the traces of the influence energy, and choose someone for himself who he could really let go with. Who he'd feel comfortable enough to loose his Svadisthana energy with, confident his partner would be there to hold the space for him.

Tierra was good, and kind. And at the heart of the group of energetics who had been called to this great task. If she died, it would tear them all apart. You only needed to see Fintan and Blaize right now to realize that they would be devastated by her loss. And Ai. Tierra was the closest thing to a mother that the girl had ever had.

She knew it was probably a trick, but she couldn't live with herself if she didn't try. These people had tried to kill Blaize already, and had kidnapped Tierra. It was likely they didn't simply want Nixie's bracelet, but her energy, or her life. And yet, what if it wasn't a trick, and she could save Tierra?

If something happened, while Nixie wasn't so stupid as to think she wouldn't be missed, the loss would be bearable. She knew that she wasn't as reliable a friend as she could be. She was impulsive and self-centered and easily distracted by the world around her.

She laughed grimly. A week ago, Nixie had been full of herself. This has been one of the longest weeks of her life. She stood slowly,

242

wobbling, and walked back to her bike in the darkness. She rubbed at her eyes with her sleeves, and ignored the aching lump in her throat.

She got out her cellphone and the white card. She texted the number written there with a simple: *Yes.*

She knew what she needed to do. She just hoped she was brave enough to go through with it.

29

Jeb and Fintan had driven round the small harbor town for a couple of hours before Jeb had been so exhausted he'd nearly fallen from the bike. Fintan had driven them back to the house for rest and food.

Jebediah had slept for an hour, then they'd all gathered for food in Tierra's room.

She'd seemed to rally this evening, and he hoped it had been the energy he'd poured into her earlier. It was so frustrating not to understand what was going on with her.

He sat on the floor with Ai, Nixie and Blaize on Thai-style cushions, with the food on several low tables Blaize had brought in. Fintan sat on the bed with Tierra, feeding her as much as she would let him.

Nixie seemed withdrawn, her usual sparkle dimmed. She'd been polite to Jeb, but the solicitude she'd shown earlier wasn't present. Fair enough. He hadn't exactly covered himself in manly glory by puking in the bushes. He grimaced. It had been a long time since he'd cared what another thought of him in that way.

"Thank you for reading the toothpick, Jeb," Tierra said. "I know how much it takes out of you. I wouldn't have asked."

She shot a look at Fintan, who shrugged innocently.

"It was impressive," Blaize said. "And useful. If I'd known I'd have brought something Tierra found in the remains of Indigo's house."

"The remnant stone?" Tierra asked.

Blaize nodded.

Jeb shook his head. "That's not something I could read. Well, I might be able to. But it would almost certainly send me mad. You know what has to happen to make them?"

"A death," Fintan said.

"The negative emotional potential in them is so great that even low level, prolonged exposure to them would drive you slowly out of your mind," Jeb explained. "An intense, active engagement like the kind I do with telemetry would dump the experience of that death into me, not just into my brain as a thought, but as a sense memory – I would literally go through that experience of dying."

Blaize grimaced. "Got it. No reading the stone."

With a meaningful glance at Ai, Tierra turned the conversation to lighter topics. There was a little more color in her cheeks, and Jeb could see the relief in Fintan's posture as he nagged her to eat more food.

"How will you stand up to all that ravishing I'm going to do to you when you're better if you're not properly fed?" Fintan said.

"You won't be doing any ravishing unless you trim that caveman beard," Tierra retorted, though she ate another few spoonfuls of tom yum soup.

The room's shutters were open, and the night breeze, along with the occasional light-seeking moth, blew softly through. Six in the room was a bit of a squeeze, but there was a warmth and connection in the group that felt good. He wished Nixie wasn't on the other side of the room. She alone seemed a bit off, and he would have liked to have checked on her, but didn't want to draw attention to her if she wasn't feeling good.

They were a very diverse set of individuals, with energies that were quite different, despite the various ones they had in common. The way Tierra's Muladhara-Anahata was very different from Fintan's Manipura-Anahata, or his own Anahata-Svadisthana, despite the heart energy in common. Such was the way with combinations of energies. And even then, there were different abilities within each Guild.

His brow furrowed as something tickled his brain. He'd had the inkling of something, there, something relevant. But he couldn't quite catch it.

Jeb was glad of this respite, but he knew he'd done nothing that was likely to have cured whatever was wrong with Tierra. All he'd done was slow the symptoms. And unless the illness was something that spontaneously resolved itself – possible, but unlikely given the pattern so far and the evidence they'd found in the archives – they still needed to understand what was happening and solve it.

He might have bought time, but he still needed to work out how to use it.

After the meal, Jeb paced the beach with a manic energy. He could protect Tierra, he knew it. He could save her. He would. He was wracking his brains to try and come up with ideas that might help her. And there was something – something that might help that had tickled the edge of his brain earlier when they'd been talking and eating, family and friends gathered together. Something that would help, Source damn it.

He couldn't grab it. Couldn't make it surface from his tired-wired brain. He was pacing because it helped him to think, and the noise of the sea soothed him. The closest beach wasn't far from the houses, and he had his cellphone so he could be back in under ten minutes if there was a problem. He'd needed some silence to think.

Fintan had agreed to wait till first light to try to find the rental place again, while Jeb's brain worked on Tierra's illness. Jeb felt the weight of expectations and hope pressing on him, his stomach tight, his body fizzing with nervous exhaustion as it ran on fumes.

It was strange being here, where Nixie had been brought up. He'd like time for her to show him around at some point. When all this madness was over. To talk to her parents, when they came back from their current trip, and learn more about who Nixie was.

What he and Nixie had was valuable. He'd thought it was merely a sexual connection, but even when he'd paused that, he had still enjoyed being around her more than any woman in decades. Had found himself wanting to share parts of himself that hadn't seen the light of day in forever, but which he wanted to dust off and offer to her.

And, like a miracle, he seemed to be able to be with her without unleashing his Svadisthana completely. He did feel better with some of that energy present once again in his life.

However, he couldn't, wouldn't release it entirely. Cuinn's prophecy had reinforced that. Source knew his self-control could manage to hold back. But there was the possibility that perhaps, after this period was over, he could have his cake and eat it too, although he planned never to unchain that energy fully. He didn't trust himself.

Still. He felt a sense of optimism about his personal future for the first time in a long, long time.

He stopped and looked out to sea. The squid catchers were out there, with their strange fluorescent lights that apparently brought the squid to the surface, ready to be caught. Poor creatures. Going to their deaths happily, without realising they were chasing their own mortality.

He turned away from the water and began to walk once more, his bare feet sinking into the damp sand and leaving a trail of footprints behind him.

Elrian had been heading to the Thai island when he'd received Trent's text that Nixie had confirmed she would hand herself over in exchange for Tierra's life.

Elrian had been beside himself with relief and anticipation.

Once their adversaries in the prophecy were taken care of, that would leave them free to create the rest of the remnant stones, and once they found the place required for the final ceremony, power would be within their reach. So much power.

Then Imogen and he could remake the energetics into the race they had once been. And prune the humans, teaching them their place.

Thinner, perhaps, than he used to be, he had taken care to dress for the travel in a well-cut bespoke suit and shirt, top button undone.

The girl had agreed to sacrifice herself as the shards of prophecy Elrian had gathered predicted. Tierra would die either way.

But the best part was, Nixie was both prize and bait. Elrian's reading indicated a willing sacrifice made a stronger remnant stone, and it would help him get round the issues he'd had without Imogen there to support him with her energy. He knew if circumstances stopped working against him, he could make this stone alone.

They needed two individuals from the prophecy to die at this point. Elrian planned for Tierra to die anyway, but this time, he was putting in place a contingency, and aiming for the deaths of three of his enemies.

When Nixie volunteered herself, Jebediah would almost certainly come after her.

And when he did, given the instability of his energies, and the storm that was predicted, they would both die.

A romantic death, true, as they'd die together. And with two of them removed, the prophecy would be ruined and he would be able to continue with his activities unchecked.

It was perfect.

30

Jeb's walk hadn't worked. He knew— knew— there was something that could be done, but it kept slipping through his mind, a fish through water that he couldn't catch. He'd come back into Tierra's room to watch her, to see if he could work out what it was by monitoring her symptoms. And perhaps a small part of him thought that he could prevent her from being drained if he was in the room. Though it was strange, she did seem to have stabilized.

He stood, his hands clasped in front of him. Tierra lay, her normally vibrant energy dimmed, her body small in the middle of the bed as he studied her. She opened her eyes and stared at him. "What's wrong?"

He gave a strangled laugh. "You're asking me what's wrong? While you lie there, being drained? And we can't find who's doing it? Everything is wrong, my friend."

They both spoke in hushed voices. Fintan was asleep on the mat next to her bed.

"Pft." Tierra waved a hand weakly. "I hear Nixie has been helping with the research."

He gave a small nod. Tierra was empathic enough to be able to read more than he'd like from him. *But perhaps she was too ill to notice?*

Tierra cocked her head to the side and narrowed her eyes. "How are the two of you getting on?"

Perhaps not. "We're fine. We just met."

Tierra shook her head. "No. The two of you are meant to be. I saw the spark – the literal spark – when the two of you met. You practically fell over when you first saw her."

Jeb came close and gripped the end of the wooden bed frame. "Something had been happening with my Svadisthana for weeks. It was a coincidence."

She gave him a direct look, calling him on his attempt at self-deception. "I don't think so, Jeb. She calls to something in you. You haven't been a whole person for a long time. None of us can suppress our true selves for so long – energetic or any other part of ourselves – without consequences. You've been as sick as I have in your own way. Nixie is a gift. She's helping you to be the person you were before the war."

"I can't erase what happened in the war. I have to live with it. And I don't want it to happen again. I have to be careful. Cuinn's prophecy shows that." He walked over to the large open window, covered with the mesh screen that let the air circulate around the sick room without the insects getting in. The air was sultry today. There wasn't much of a breeze. Tierra had a fan in the room, and the hum of it felt loud.

"I know I'm dying," said Tierra. There wasn't any emotion behind her words, rather, it was a statement of fact, as if she'd said 'I know the sky is blue.'

Jeb spun round and walked over to her side. He perched himself on the side of the bed and took one of her hands in his. "You're not dying."

Not if I can help it, he added silently.

"You haven't got any worse today," he said.

She shrugged. "It's the calm before the storm. It happens, sometimes, with patients before the last, we both know that. I've accepted it. But if I'm going to die, I don't want my friends missing their chances. And you might have been my Maven once, but now you're my friend. You deserve happiness. You did what you felt was right after the war, and I know that you needed time to heal. But that season has passed. You need to be back out in the world."

She looked out the window. "And Fintan is going to need friends. You and he can be friends, I'm sure of it."

Jeb struggled to get his words out past the thickness in his throat. "We need you for the prophecy."

"Perhaps. Perhaps not. Perhaps I've served my function, or perhaps there'll be someone who will take my place in the prophecy. I've been around Cuinn and Adam and their Ajna long enough to know that no prophecy is set in stone, or we wouldn't have so many interpretations of each one by different Sages."

She coughed, and lifted a hand to her mouth to cover it. When she brought it away, Jeb saw the brightness of blood on her palm. He took in a breath. She hadn't been drained any further, but damage had already been done to her body.

"I can heal that." He pulled Anahata and putting a hand on her chest, closed his eyes. He drew on his energy to heal the blood vessels that had ruptured in her lungs.

She swallowed but didn't cough again. "It's like giving blood to someone who's bleeding out from an artery. You can't just keep healing me while I'm drained elsewhere."

"Yes. I can." And he would.

Early the next morning Nixie came into Tierra's room and found Jeb holding Tierra's hand. He looked broken, and she looked pale and fragile. The man at the beach was right. If Nixie didn't act, Tierra didn't have much time left. It made Nixie fiercer in her resolve to go through with it.

She'd always avoided pain. She was a sybarite. A pleasure seeker. And that had served her well for many years, while she thought she had been looking for her soulmate.

But now, finally, she'd learned what real love was. It was about compromise, and sometimes, choosing to put someone else's needs before your own.

It was Jeb leaving the safety of the Guild to come and help Tierra. It was Cuinn risking madness searching for Blaize in the dreamscape. It was Fintan sleeping on the floor by Tierra's bed. It was Nixie's parents, who she'd called before she came into the room to hear their voices one last time, living together and creating a life out of small, everyday moments of connection.

It wasn't Nixie's grand romantic notions of love. Of flowers and candlelit dinners and sex. That might be part of it, but it was just the surface. Love was kind, and it didn't ask, it gave.

Love was also brave. Which she wasn't, really. But perhaps she could be brave when it was for someone else, not for herself.

She knew that at the very least she might be giving up the opportunity for love with the bracelet. The prophecy hadn't guaranteed a match, and if it wasn't going to be Jeb, there could still have been someone else. Without the bracelet, she might lose that, forever. Even if she lived, Source might not give her a second chance.

She stepped up close to the bed and stroked Tierra's hair. Tierra smiled, a true smile, as if she was genuinely pleased to see Nixie, with no thought for her own illness. Nixie fought back tears. "Hello, love."

Jeb didn't look up at Nixie, but he did rest a hand briefly on her free arm. She nodded at him.

"No news," Nixie said. "Thought I'd come say hi."

"Thanks for coming," said Tierra. "Nothing to report here either."

She laughed, but neither Nixie or Jeb could raise a smile.

There was a grunt from the floor, and Fintan came to a sitting position. "What happened?"

Tierra turned her head towards him. "Nothing. Get more sleep."

He rubbed his eyes, and pushed himself to his feet. He pressed a light kiss to Tierra's palm before stumbling over to the coffee machine in the corner of the room. Something twisted inside Nixie's stomach at his gentle gesture.

"No need," Fintan said. "I'm up now. We can go search again once I'm properly awake."

Jeb glanced over at that other man. "We'll leave you alone."

Fintan waved a hand back at them, still focused on the coffee. "S'fine."

Tierra looked up at Nixie then across at Jeb. "No. Fin and I should have some time alone. You two go and get some food. You must be starving."

Nixie couldn't remember when she last ate, and she wasn't interested in food now, but she also realized that Tierra probably wanted some time together with her man. And Nixie and Jeb weren't doing anything useful here.

Nixie stroked Tierra's hair back from her forehead one more time. "We'll see you later."

She hoped so. But there was no guarantee.

❧ ❧ ❧

When Nixie drew him out of the room, Jeb was annoyed at first, as he was still trying to remember his idea. But when she had looked meaningfully between Fintan and Tierra, he'd realized why. It was strange, his sensitivity to emotions really must be confused by Nixie, because he'd missed that entirely.

He followed Nixie out after a final squeeze of Tierra's hand and a sympathetic slap on Fintan's shoulder, who'd jerked his head in acknowledgement.

They stepped out into the warm day and went down the bungalow's steps to the scrub and sand. He was grateful Nixie still seemed to be talking to him, and hadn't followed up on her threat to not interact with him. He'd try and enjoy her company while he could.

"I got close to an idea last night," he said. "Something that might help. But I can't remember it."

It was giving him a headache trying to work out what it was.

She looked up at him, the shade making her dark eyes luminous. "Can you remember what was going on when you thought it? Maybe that will remind you."

He shook his head and rubbed his temples to relieve the ache there. "Something triggered during the meal last night, when everyone was together."

She gave a stifled snort. "Yeah. It was pretty awful. Like a wake. And people taking it in turns to spend time with Tierra. The poor woman was probably worn out with all our visiting."

"Everybody cares, and wants to do something for her," he murmured.

Nixie nodded, and they walked aimlessly in a companionable silence, though Nixie seemed distracted. It was rare she didn't chatter at him.

Tierra's words about Nixie and him nagged at him. Perhaps it wouldn't hurt to touch each other.

He put a hand out to capture her hand. She didn't pull away.

They walked until they came upon a hammock slung between two trees. She tugged him into it, and after some shuffling and a little inelegance – mainly from him, Nixie was as graceful as a cat, as always – they were both nestled together in the hammock. He yearned for the warmth of her body against his. He gazed upwards at the blue of the sky and took a deep breath, grounding himself. This felt … right. She connected him to the now.

And, he realized, her presence no longer automatically pushed at his wards. No longer shook his control. Carefully, he focused on his Svadisthana. He examined his shields as best he could. There were cracks, but nothing was leaking. However, there was some kind of link between him and Nixie. Some of her energy was entwining with his, and soothing his wards, a balm, of sorts. Somehow, they had become attuned to each other. Her energies seemed to complement and support him.

Source. He felt a thrill of something down his spine. Fear? Excitement? He couldn't tell.

"I'd really like you as a friend," he said. He needed her to stick around until he worked this out. And, of course, until they'd solved the deadly and mysterious threats hanging over all of them. "Don't bail on me yet."

She didn't say anything.

He tried not to beg. He really didn't want her to leave him alone. "Maybe, one day, once this prophecy is done, we can be something more."

He knew, now, he wanted that, though who knew what the future held. He wasn't convinced about her argument about balance, but he would try whatever it took to both keep her, and keep his energy in check.

She shrugged in his arms and twisted in the hammock so she could kiss him. It was a soft kiss. Gentle. Caring. On the edge of friendly and, well, not. He returned it just as carefully.

"Sometimes I can inspire other people's creativity. I can spark them," she said. "You want me to give you a little of that energy? Maybe it will help you to remember or to find a solution. It's not my strongest gift, but it might help."

He tried to sit up and failed, as there was no purchase in the hammock. "Yes! Yes. I haven't come across that very often. I don't have it and my Svadisthana Maven didn't have it. I didn't realize you could. Usually those who have it are teachers, or muses for other artists."

"Like I said, it's not a strong gift. But it can't hurt, right?" she said.

"Definitely. How do we do it?"

"Can you sit up in the hammock? It might be stronger if we were near water, but I'm pretty sure I can do something where we are. We don't want to waste time."

They shuffled around until they were both sitting cross-legged in the hammock, facing each other. She took his hands in hers. "Close your eyes, and wait. You should feel something, I think, and then you need to go and work on the problem straight away. Just head off, no need to talk to me. See what happens. I've been told it's like a shot of caffeine, or those smart drugs, what are they called – nootropics?"

"Okay," he said. She was over-explaining – was she nervous? "It doesn't matter if it doesn't work. I'll keep working anyway."

She nodded, and they both closed their eyes. He could feel a ripple of something, presumably as she drew on her Svadisthana, and the greenery seemed to still around them.

Out of nowhere, her emotions smashed into him. He hadn't been expecting that. He tried to pick them apart, to distinguish all that she was feeling, so they didn't engulf him. The emotions hacked at his hard-won control, and he wavered in the stream, not so much a rock as a bit of flotsam caught in the weeds, that any moment could be torn loose and be lost forever.

He caught hope, sadness, fear, love and altruism before his whole body was hit by the next phase, a shockwave of energy that drenched him from head to toe. He felt electrified, and a flood of thoughts, ideas, inspiration and visions galvanized his brain. He could feel that the answer was in there. He just needed to find it.

She squeezed his hands and let go.

"Write it out," she advised. "Go back and write everything down you can think of, and connections might come. Or take a shower. Sometimes a shower helps – it's weird but whatever works, right? Good luck."

She closed the short distance between them and kissed him. He couldn't concentrate on her perfect mouth right now. It was almost a sensory overload. He broke the kiss before her, and fell out of the hammock, leaving her swinging.

"Thank you. I'll see you later." He ran his hand over her silky hair once before he turned and ran back to the house. The solution to protecting Tierra was on the tip of his tongue. He could taste it.

Nixie was amazing. Her 'spark' might have saved Tierra's life.

C H A P T E R

31

The day passed surprisingly quickly. Nixie lay in the hammock a little longer, savoring the last kiss she and Jeb had shared, before gathering her courage. She'd been glad to give the spark to Jeb, to leave him with a positive memory of her. She wanted to know there would be another option for Tierra, if this didn't work.

She really hoped it would.

She had drawn on the sense of security and strength that Jeb had provided, one last boost of courage before she left. She was a constantly moving creek, and he was a pool, still and deep.

She and Blaize had completed the image of Tierra that afternoon, while Jeb and Fintan continued to scour the island. Tierra's sketch showed her with an olive branch wrapped around one arm and the faintest smear of color at each of her Chakra points.

Blaize had frowned at this. "This wasn't in the image Cuinn passed to me. Are you sure you saw it?"

"Yes," Nixie said. "It's there. And the colors correspond to each Chakra. But they're not the wheels you would usually expect if they were representing Chakras. They're more like paint splodges, or splashes, uneven with torn edges."

It seemed that Nixie's creative Chakras saw more in the image than Blaize and Cuinn had. They hadn't come to a conclusion as to what it might mean, and she had left the drawing for Blaize and Cuinn to argue about over the phone.

As the day waned, and shadows started to grow longer, she drove to the meeting point Trent had given her. It wasn't quite sunset, but she wasn't rushing. She left her bike by the road and walked the last few hundred meters onto the beach.

She wasn't sure how they would take the bracelet – Source knows she had tried to cut it off herself – but it was unlikely to be easy. She wondered why they wanted it. It felt like the lesser evil, compared to Tierra's death, but could they use it as a weapon? She paused a moment in her walk then resumed. She had to have faith that her friends were strong enough to overcome any negative side-effects of her actions.

It was strange, but she felt calmer than she would have expected once she'd made the decision. Being surrounded by water would help with whatever came next.

A wind arose, whipping dry leaves and sand past her legs. She smelled ozone on the air.

A storm was coming.

The man had asked her to meet him at an outcropping of rocks on the beach that jutted into the water, where several sturdy coconut palms stood.

Her feet dragged as she got closer. She realized there were two men, the cold one she'd met, who stood, feet planted apart, solidly watching her approach, and another thinner, older energetic, who was drawing with chalk on the bare rock. He was incongruously well-dressed for a man crawling on his hands and knees.

She swallowed. He was setting up some kind of ritual. It was overly complex if they were simply removing her bracelet. There were symbols written on the floor, and physical totems that she couldn't make out, though they likely represented the Chakras, amongst other things. Fire was easiest to spot, and there were several torches stuck into the ground, their light flickering wildly.

"Good," the cold man said.

"I want you to heal Tierra," Nixie said. She kept a couple of meters away, out of arms' reach. The other energetic glanced at her, but kept on with his work, his mutters drifting away on the wind.

"After. We gave her a reprieve. You must have noticed," he said.

She nodded. She needed more. "It's not enough."

"We'll stop the illness once we're done here," he said. "Still. I thought you might ask, so as a token of good faith, your friend should be a little better now. Text your friends, and ask."

Nixie fumbled for her cell, and texted Blaize for an update on Tierra. The answer came quickly.

She's looking better. I think she might have turned a corner. We're chatting, it's nice. Come join us!

Some tension left her body. It was real. She could do this.

So Tierra didn't lose her life.

So Fintan didn't lose his lover.

So Jeb didn't lose his friend.

So Nixie's friends would be able to resolve the prophecy, and save their world, and their lives.

"Throw your cell into the water," the man said.

She bounced it in her hand a couple of times, then flung it as far as she could. It sailed over the rocks and dropped into the sea.

She was alone.

Jeb ran back to the tiny bungalow where he was staying. He would take a cool shower first, given he needed waking up rather than relaxing, and let the ideas percolate.

Nixie had seemed subdued today. Jeb's empathy was still off, but he thought it had been sadness that he'd sensed from her most clearly. She must be worried about Tierra.

As was he. Tierra didn't have much time. She'd rallied some, but if her illness continued and she was also drained remotely, and he wasn't able to protect her, she would fade away within days. He swallowed. He couldn't let that happen.

He'd go sit with her after the shower. Perhaps that would help trigger his memory.

He reached his place and bounded up the steps and inside. He stripped off and went into the shower, turning it to cold.

He reached out a hand to grab the soap, and paused.

What is that?

Oh, no…

His heart sank, and for a moment he felt trapped, unable to breathe as he stared.

A bracelet was wrapped around his wrist, the twin to the ones he'd seen on Tierra, Fintan and Blaize, though with different colors.

But – it was a bracelet he hadn't seen on Nixie, the person who'd finally opened his heart again. She tended to wear a big silver bangle on her left wrist, which must have some sentimental value, as she never seemed to take it off. But he'd seen no sign of a Source-given bracelet.

He stared at the plaited cords on his wrist for a few more moments before he made a decision about what to do. He'd meditate and ask the Source for answers, on the off-chance it was related to Tierra.

He finished in the shower in less than three minutes, and roughly toweled himself off. He dressed in loose pants and a long-sleeved shirt and went out onto the balcony, where he sat cross-legged on the wooden floor.

He took a deep breath and closed his eyes. This was a form of prayer for him. Energetics didn't have a religion, as such, because there was no need. Source, their divine, was an easy and self-evident part of their lives. They were connected through energy. Every time they pulled energy from the ether, the energetic plane, they were connected to Source.

But that didn't mean they understood it. Or her, as Jeb liked to call it. Each energetic connected to Source in their own way. For a dominant Ajna energetic, it might be through a dreamwalk in the ether. For a dominant Svadisthana, it might be through a piece of art. For Jeb, as a dominant Anahata, it was through the embodiment of love.

For him, he personified Source as a feminine figure. Divine, loving and always there.

He took another breath from his diaphragm, and connected to Source. He pulled both his energies, Anahata and Svadisthana, and held them inside himself. The energies bounced around his body, and he felt wired, alive. They mixed inside him and he addressed Source as if she were there with him. As if she were a person.

Source, I ask you. What is this bracelet you have given me? Who has the other?

He waited. He stayed still, and kept his breathing steady. He opened himself up to receive as much as was possible, while still holding both the energies within him. His cracked shields were more of a hindrance than a help at this stage. Was he going to have to let go of them completely? *No.* He shut that thought down. He could use a little of his Svadisthana, but not all of it. He wouldn't open himself to temptation again.

There wasn't always a response from Source. And even when there was, it was hard to tell at times if it was from one's own subconscious, or from the divine.

This time, after twenty minutes of meditating, holding his question and Source in his mind, a cryptic answer came back to him.

Embrace your full self. Then help the others to understand their bracelets' gifts.

That didn't really help him. He had embraced his full self. Hadn't he? Then he thought about his Svadisthana. Surely she didn't mean for him to fully open himself up around that? He shook his head. And what could the bracelets do?

He considered it a moment more, then boxed the whole problem up for later, sliding his sleeve over the bracelet. He couldn't deal with it now. They all had enough to worry about. Tierra first, then the bracelets.

He got to his feet. To try to recall his earlier idea, he'd sit in the room with Tierra and free-write, to see what came. His brain felt alive. He grabbed a paper and pen before he walked across the yard between houses to where Tierra was. As he entered the room, Fintan glanced over at him before he turned back to Tierra. He was talking to her in a soft voice, their heads close together.

They weren't alone. Ai was here, her arms wrapped around her knees so she took up as small a space as possible in the corner of the room, listening to something on her cellphone, earbuds in. Blaize paced backwards and forwards, her energy barely contained. With this many upset energetics in the room, the air was thick with power.

His mind bubbled with thoughts and ideas, the creative energy that Nixie had sparked still lively inside him. He got out pencil and paper and jotted down anything that came into his head, while keeping an eye on the room.

Fintan was amusing Tierra by playing with a flame that he made flicker over his hands and dance up and down his bare arms. She chided him and he grinned. She asked for water, and Fintan walked across the room to refill her glass.

Jebediah frowned. Something wasn't right about what he was seeing. He shook his head to clear it. Was he seeing an after-image?

He narrowed his eyes. It was still there.

A flame, rippling with oranges and yellows, rested on Tierra's palm. But Fintan, the fire energetic, wasn't anywhere near her. Yet the fire didn't seem to be hurting her. She stared down at it, a confused look on her face.

"Uh, Fintan?" Tierra said.

He turned, and nearly dropped the water. He ran over and smoothed a hand over hers, and the flame went out.

"Um. I don't think I should be able to do that," Tierra said, weakly.

"You really shouldn't," Fintan said.

They both looked at Jeb.

And it came to him, finally, that last click as the thing that had been tantalizing him slid into place.

That was it. The solution to keeping her protected. They'd only been warding her with Anahata, the usual healing wards and protection. And Tierra had her own Muladhara wards and protections which he knew were active.

But Tierra was something new. She needed protection across all the energies. That's what he'd thought of the night before, when the handful of energetics had been present and all the energies had been represented.

At the moment the energies that were new to her were loose and unbound within her, and the Leech, whoever it was, was able to siphon energy from her from a distance. Maybe he was Ajna – which of course, if it was Elrian, he was. And Tierra now had Ajna too, so that could explain how he was able to take her energy from a distance.

He could test this. "Fintan. Use energy to see if you can see Tierra's new Manipura energies. What can you sense?"

Fintan looked at him, his forehead creased. "I don't –"

"Just look," Jeb urged.

Fintan shrugged and closed his eyes. After a couple of long minutes, he opened them again, wide. "I can see it. She has Manipura energy like a Dormant. It's there, but not active, not really."

He puffed out a breath of air. "She's going to need training."

Jeb nodded and turned to Blaize. "Can you do the same for Ajna?"

She stepped over to the bed and closed her eyes in the same way, touching her fingers to Tierra's forehead. After another few tense minutes, she breathed out, "Oh, shit."

"What?" Fintan and Jeb said at the same time.

"She's a Dormant in Ajna too, but there's a gaping tear there where someone's draining energy from her. We need to get shields and wards up around her asap."

When Tierra had shared energy with Cuinn, she'd somehow both awakened her other Chakras, and become a Dormant in all the other energies, but it had also left energetic weaknesses in her that someone had been able to exploit. He could kick himself for not thinking of this earlier. He could ward her to some degree across all energies, but ideally they needed a stronger energetic in each specific energy to help her with the new energies that she was Dormant in.

Jeb nodded grimly. "She needs warding for all the energies. Not the usual healing Anahata, or her dominant and auxiliary. She's open through them all."

Blaize nodded decisively, clearly happy to have a task. She glanced around the room. "We can cover everything apart from Vishudha. We need Nixie for that."

"Ai, could you go find her and bring her back?" Jeb asked.

The teen sprang to her feet like a colt and shot out of the door.

Jeb felt something that had been tight inside him relax. They'd done it. They could have Tierra warded in an hour. She'd be safe.

On the plane Elrian had pored over the Hermit's notes, revising, cross-checking and reviewing the information against what he already knew about remnant stone creation.

He'd had the chance to begin his preparations for the ritual as soon as darkness fell, on this isolated part of the island's coast away from the tourist hot spots. He was taking her Svadisthana, so completing the ritual on the beach, near her element of water, would strengthen the final stone.

He was impressed Trent had managed to get the girl here of her own accord. All his notes said a willing sacrifice would create a much stronger stone. It was also likely to be less difficult for him.

He'd try and keep her willing, but he'd planned to restrain her anyway, in case she changed her mind. Either way, she'd make a stone.

Currents of air lashed at him, and he had to grab the dried flowers he'd put out and place a stone on them to hold them down. The storm was natural, but Trent's energies, which included an affinity with the weather, meant he could influence it to some degree. They'd agreed rain would shelter them from prying eyes further, and was to their advantage.

At the moment, it was still dry.

Elrian was prepared, but he didn't feel well. Pulling energy was much harder than it used to be these days. He had always been a strong energetic in both his energies, Ajna and Muladhara, and at points in his life had been a Maven in both. He had a lot more inner resources to draw on than the average energetic.

He wanted to show Imogen that he was equal to the task of making a stone on his own. Did the fact she'd let him come alone mean she believed in him? Or was she playing some kind of twisted game where she set him up for failure? He was never quite sure where he stood with her. Which made her all the more alluring. Plus, the power she wielded was an aphrodisiac indeed. But that was why he needed to make a good showing himself.

He flicked a glance over to where Trent and the girl stood. She was quite tiny next to the mercenary. Her power, happily, was a lot greater than her stature might indicate. He shot out a thread of his Ajna, assessing her power levels, tasting her. She shivered, but it was unlikely she knew what he was doing. Yes. With the right training, she could eventually have been a Master in Svadisthana, and a Practitioner in Vishudha. That was fine for his purposes. It was the former he was interested in harvesting for the stone. It was a shame he couldn't leech from her first, but with no energies in common, that wouldn't work well.

Trent, however, had Ajna as his auxiliary energy. Elrian assessed the big man. Clearly, Elrian had no chance against him physically, but energetically – could Elrian take from him without him noticing? Siphon a little from him. The man wasn't a talker. He was more than muscle, but he wasn't an intellect. Given the weather, and the need to influence the storm, Trent's attention would be on his Svadisthana, not his Ajna. It would be an extra service the man could unknowingly provide for his exorbitant fee.

It might work. A dangerous balancing act, tonight was another step forward in their plan to ensure the prophecy went in their direction.

And the eventual rewards?

He'd remake the world.

32

Ai came back into the room ten minutes later. Tears streaked her face. She thrust a piece of paper out in front of her, biting her cuticles and staring down at her feet.

"Nixie's gone."

"What?" Jeb took the paper from her, while Blaize put an arm around the distraught girl.

It was a note.

Jeb

A man offered me a trade, my bracelet for Tierra's life, down by the water. I took it. She's worth a lot more than I am to the prophecy. I hope to be back soon, and Tierra will be well again, but if not, for what it's worth, I'm glad I met you.

I think I even loved you a little.

Nixie.

He read it out loud, blinking at the idea she had a bracelet. Why had she hidden it from him? And what the hell did she think she was doing?

Ai buried her head in Blaize's shoulder. Blaize comforted her, but at the same time, her eyes were hard and flat. Blaize and Nixie were like sisters.

"Where has she gone?" Blaize snapped out. "What has that crazy girl done now?"

Jeb turned the note over to see if there was anything else. He shook his head.

"Call her," Blaize ordered Jeb. He fumbled for his phone, and did so. It went straight to voice mail.

"The phone's off," he said.

Jeb pushed a hand through his hair and squeezed his eyes shut. They had two serious problems now. They needed to find Nixie urgently, but Tierra was also in danger.

Without Nixie, they had no Vishudha energetic to help complete the protection and warding of Tierra. And he was also the only Svadisthana energetic. They could ward four of her Chakras without him using his Svadisthana, or five if he was prepared to open his wards further, which posed a different sort of risk.

Thunder cracked close by. There was no rain yet, but a storm was on its way. That wasn't going to help.

"We need Nixie to keep Tierra safe," Fintan said.

"We need Nixie because we need Nixie," Blaize stated. "Battle plan?"

They were all looking at him, despite the fact two of them had more military understanding than him, being Warrior-trained. Jeb was the one with the healing knowledge. His war days were long behind him.

He tried to tap into the Jeb of old. The devil-may-care, confident spy. The supposedly wise guru of the Guild.

The person who got people killed.

He shook that thought away.

This was a chance to do things differently. To use his energy carefully, appropriately.

To save, rather than to slaughter.

Tierra had rallied this evening. She had more color in her cheeks than she'd had since he'd been back.

"We're going to ward Tierra in all her Chakras apart from Vishudha. I'll use Anahata to give her a patch in case the draining starts again while I'm out. You'll stay with her to keep her safe." His jaw clenched. "Then I'm going to bring Nixie home."

It wasn't that simple, and they all had questions. But there wasn't that much time to lose. He chopped through all their initial arguments and focused them on warding Tierra. Her biggest danger areas were Ajna, where the tear had been, and Vishudha, where all he could do was give her an Anahata patch, which anyone with the right energy could probably rip through pretty fast.

Tierra was sitting up by the end of the treatment. Without the drain, she was able to pull her own Muladhara from the ether and boost herself.

"Right," she said. "Blaize. Go get me something important to Nixie. I'm going to track her. Jeb, you can't go off half-cocked. You never found the landlady, so you need a place to start."

Blaize darted out of the room. Tierra was an expert tracker. She was also ill. Jeb put a hand out then dropped it to his side. "Tierra, you're not well enough for that."

"Don't be silly," she said briskly, and for all his worry, he was pleased to see a little of the old Tierra back. "How will you find her otherwise? She hasn't been gone long, it's a small area, and I have a good connection with her. Conditions for me being able to narrow down the area she's in are good. We know she's by the water, so it's either one of the lakes or the coast. Plus, the sooner you bring her back, the sooner you can complete my wards and I'm safe."

Blaize came back in with a slim, elegant lighter in her hand and gave it to Tierra.

"What's that?" asked Jeb. "Nixie doesn't smoke."

"No. She uses this for her art," said Blaize. "It was part of a gift from her parents when she won a national art prize in her teens. It's part of her finishing techniques for many of her pieces. She loves it. Also, I'm coming with you to find her."

"Perfect," said Tierra. "Now everyone give me some peace to work with the energy. I don't have a lot to waste."

They tied her to the rough bark of one of the palm trees, facing out to sea. She didn't resist. It was her choice to do this.

Elrian had examined her bracelet initially, and bound her so her arms were in front of her, and the bracelet accessible.

The ritual seemed to involve a lot of stuff. The two men had very different roles. The cold one, the younger one, Elrian had called Trent. He was some sort of guard or soldier. Less interesting if she was to draw him. Handsome, but somehow blank.

The older one had introduced himself as Elrian, but she'd known who he was as soon as she'd seen him. The man from the Hermit's house, who'd thrown the book at her.

The heavens had opened not long after they'd tied her. It seemed to be causing Elrian some challenges. His torches fizzled out, and as neither of the men had any Manipura, he struggled to relight them.

There'd been some weirdness between the men, she'd thought. Something strange that she couldn't quite make sense of. The dynamic between them wasn't exactly friendly.

She wondered about using her own power on them, but Trent had told her that Tierra's life was on the line for her compliance. For perhaps the first time in her life, she'd obey all the rules. Slivers of doubt slid through her mind as she wondered if she was doing the right thing, if she was in over her head, but she crushed them.

To calm her nerves she considered how she might paint the scene. A sort of Andromeda chained to the rocks. Not in the classical style though, too dull. Cubist? Perhaps she'd take inspiration from the region and try some Malaysian-inspired batik. She'd seen some beautiful examples there last year when she'd gone for a weekend break to Kuala Lumpur.

Focusing on the way she'd create art from the scene helped her to ignore her racing heart, flickering pulse, the metallic taste of fear in her mouth and the very real fact that the two men in front of her appeared to be preparing to kill her.

"Why are you doing this?" she asked Elrian.

"I'm going to take your bracelet, and use your death to create a remnant stone," Elrian said.

Despite the fact she had considered the possibility they might do this as well as taking her bracelet, her blood ran cold and her pulse sped up, fluttering inside her. She had hoped she was wrong, it seemed. She wriggled her torso, checking how secure her bondage was. Was she still prepared to die? To sacrifice herself, not simply her bracelet?

Elrian was less elegant now, with his hair plastered to his head from the rain, but he was studiously ignoring it. Nixie, with water in her blood, reveled in it. With the sea and the storm, power washed through her veins, begging to be used. It would take her a moment to pull power, she thought. Just a moment.

Elrian caught something in her eye, and reached up and slapped her in the face. Pain smashed through her, and she froze for a second, then blinked, her eyes watering. Her jaw snapped shut, her cheek throbbing. Ouch. Her body shook, and her tears mixed with the rain.

Could she paint pain? She'd never experienced anyone deliberately causing her that level of physical pain before. What would it look like? A red smear? Black tones?

Her head swam. She was going to die here on this beach. She would become one with her element, and her soul would roam the waters. She chided herself for her romantic notions, even in death. She'd never really thought much about the afterlife, only that she'd somehow go back to Source. It had always seemed so far away, when energetics could live hundreds of years.

Whatever Elrian needed to complete his preparation seemed to be done. He was pulling in a great deal of power. He bent to squat inside the circle he'd created, and placed his hands on the runes and symbols he'd drawn.

They lit up with power. And that power shot straight to her, at the center of it all.

Fuck, the pain.

She'd never known such pain. White-burning-ice-fire-intense. A laser beam installation so bright that viewers couldn't look at it directly. That would be interesting, to create a piece that couldn't be seen.

It hurt so much.

She kept up the narrative in her head, even while her body bent in cramps from the agony that Elrian was inflicting on her. It gave her strength to disassociate from what was happening, to see it as art.

She didn't feel as powerful anymore. He was draining that from her. Taking her energy. Leeching. But the pace was fast, faster than she'd expected.

She wished she'd had the chance to tell Jeb he'd taught her about real love. That love was made up of a thousand tiny touches, not just the flash and bang of the sexual peak. That she didn't only love the sex they had – although she did – but she loved the way he pinched the brow of his nose when he was thinking. That she adored the baggy wool sweaters he wore, which had a touch of old-fashioned about them, whilst his torso was slender but as well-muscled as any athlete. That she loved the way his body cut through the water when he swam.

That she loved him. All of him.

She held onto the thought of that love as the pain burned through her, and weakness began to enervate her system.

Something small and orange glowed on the floor in front of Elrian, and all the lines from him to her and around them led to it.

It was beautiful.

It was her death in the sand.

Elrian's exhaustion had fallen away as the runes he'd made on the sandy rock lit up.

It was working.

His knees and shoulders ached as he held his position on the floor, the conduit of the energy from the girl into the stone, but it was working.

He was exultant. He could do this. He needed to hold until the girl was fully drained, which could be four minutes or it could be forty. It seemed to be happening quickly so far.

But the pace was taking a toll on him. He'd taken the merest touch of energy from Trent before starting the ritual. Trent had shuddered, but hadn't seemed to catch what he was doing. It had been helpful, that boost.

Elrian consciously slowed down the rate at which he was draining the girl into the stone, unsure he could take the flow of energy for much longer at the same rate.

With things more under control, he glanced around him. The sea heaved behind Trent now, the waves high. They were above beach level, and their rocky outcropping had some shelter, but occasionally spray reached them, adding to the constant rain.

Elrian frowned. He needed to keep the pace up if he was going to drain her before the storm caught them. He shifted his gaze to Trent. The man stood at ease, but his eyes ranged around the landscape for threats. He was alert and ready in case of an attack. Trent checked in on Nixie too, infrequently, but he rarely looked down at what Elrian was doing.

Good.

Maintaining his position as the channel for the flow of Nixie's energy to the stone, Elrian put out the merest thread of energy towards Trent, aimed at scraping more off the surface, like a cat skimming the cream.

It was a delicate balancing act. Lightning cracked through the sky and lit up purple clouds, and the rain sheeted down harder.

"Can you take the edge off the storm?" he shouted to Trent.

Through the energy wisp, he felt Trent pull energy from the ether and feed it into the storm. His face had a wild joy on it, an expression Elrian hadn't seen before. Actually, he'd barely seen any expression from him before.

The rain was cut by perhaps ten percent, and the next gap between thunder and lightning was longer.

Elrian kept holding the connection. The girl, despite her natural skin tone, was pale and bloodless, and he wasn't sure what was rain and what was tears as water poured down her face. She was limp in the wet rope, but she was still conscious, the whites of her eyes stark and vivid. She glared at him, but her power was dimmed.

There was a rumble in the earth, far, far away, and Elrian's Muladhara pricked even with everything going on. Trent shouted something, but Elrian couldn't hear.

Then Trent was at his ear, yelling urgently. "A tsunami's coming. We have maybe fifteen, twenty minutes. We need to get the fuck off this beach, now."

"Calm it!" Elrian shouted back.

"I can't. Come on. We need to go."

Elrian shook his head. "I don't need long. Calm it."

He needed more from Trent though, if he was going to speed up. He reached to take a little more from him, but he was clumsier, his tiredness tripping him, and Trent's eyes widened.

"Tell me," he said, "that you didn't leech from me."

A shiver ran through Elrian at the very matter of fact way Trent said it.

Trent leaned down, and spoke very close to Elrian's ear. "I could kill you in a heartbeat. And it would not be an easy death."

He stood straight again. "I'm going. Come with me, or you'll die here on this beach. I've earned my money, so I'd prefer it if you were still breathing tomorrow to pay me."

Elrian was so close. So close. He shook his head.

Trent shrugged. "Leave, or die. Personally, I'm leaving."

"Then we need to take her with us! I might be able to finish the ritual later," Elrian said, desperate.

"No time," Trent said. He began to jog inland. "I suggest you leave her, and you do it now."

Inside Elrian's head he was screaming, screaming with rage at the disrespect, and at the opportunity loss. Trent was correct. The girl's bonds were sodden, getting her out would take precious minutes he no longer had.

He couldn't believe he'd failed again. He'd been so close.

He disconnected from the runes with a hot wrench, scooped the topaz from the floor, and lifted Nixie's hanging head by the hair. He hissed into her ear, "Leave here, and I will drain Tierra. Nothing's changed. Your life, for hers."

The tsunami would take her. He might not get a stone from this debacle, but he would get a death. He would be one step closer to stopping the prophecy.

And when he drained Tierra, they would be impotent to stop him, and all he would need to concentrate on was the stones.

33

It had taken longer than he'd wanted, but Tierra had narrowed down the area that Nixie was in. Jeb and Blaize had split up, she starting inland at a freshwater lake, and he starting on the coast, and they planned to work their way towards each other.

There was an ominous feel to the air, the rain pouring down, thunder booming and lightning cracking down far out to sea. But the storm was coming in.

Where was she, damn it?

Jeb got to the beach and ran along it, his gaze raking the wild and empty expanse of sand.

He ran until his lungs burned. Finally, up where the shore rose to a low platform, he saw the first person since he'd hit the beach. Only a silhouette at first, but when he was within a hundred yards it resolved itself into Nixie's petite form, slumped against a palm tree. There was no sign of anyone with her, though as he got to her he saw the signs of a ritual disturbed.

He intended to lift her over his shoulder and take her back. But when he got to the tree, he realized she was tied to it with rough ropes that were wet and swollen from the spray of the sea and the rain. The waves were already higher than the usual tide line. And the tide wasn't going out.

He tugged at the ropes ineffectually, trying to release her, but they were stiff and unyielding. Damn it. Why wasn't he the sort of man who carried a knife? He bet Fintan carried a knife. He shouted her name. "Nixie! Wake up! We need to get you out of here."

He barely noticed the water now, though it thudded into his body like a hail of tiny spears. He cupped her head in his hands, and she groaned.

"What…?" She opened her eyes and looked around her, her eyes going wide and then squeezing shut as she drew in several rasping breaths.

"We need to get you out of here," Jebediah said urgently. "But I don't know how to free you. Any ideas?"

She shook her head and swallowed. Her voice was breathy with fear and she was trembling. "We need Blaize and her fire. I don't think any of our energies are going to help here, are they?"

"No. But we'll get you out. I'll get you out." He promised. He looked around the beach. What could he use? How could he help her?

"Wait, no! You can't!" Her eyes were huge, pleading. "They'll drain Tierra. I promised I'd stay here so they wouldn't. You need to go."

The waves were higher, and the sea washed around their feet as it teased them by coming in, and then retreating. It had crested the rocks, and the spray was up to her calves. They didn't have much time. He ignored her words, focusing on the problem at hand. He could solve this.

She was bound around the tops of her arms, above the elbows, her hands in front of her. She reached out as far as she could, and he reached back towards her even as he continued looking around for a way to free her. The silver bangle caught in her drenched clothes, and he pulled it off her wrist and shoved it in one of his pockets. He

280

might be able to expand the loops of the rope enough for her to pull her wrist through, but not with that giant bracelet on it.

He cupped her face in his hands, briefly, to comfort her, and she closed her eyes for a second and leaned into them, then shook her head. When she opened her eyes, she caught sight of something and stopped dead.

Jeb's head pounded, the pressure and exhaustion of the last few days pressing on him.

What new danger was happening now?

She'd taken the comfort of his hands, and was ready to tell him to get out of there and leave her to die.

And then she'd seen his wrist, and had frozen.

When Nixie realized that Jeb's bracelet was the twin of her own, she didn't know how to react. To laugh at the ridiculousness of seeing it now, as all they were and could have been was about to be destroyed, or to cry because of all that they could have had, could have been.

"Look," she urged, and used her head to indicate their wrists.

His mouth dropped open, and wonderingly, he put his wrist next to hers so they touched. She clasped his right hand in her left.

She felt her Svadisthana and her Vishudha rise up in her. She wasn't even drawing on them, but out of nowhere she knew that both were inside her, ready to be used.

Her energies had somehow been amplified by the bracelets.

"Do you feel that?" she yelled over the noise of the storm.

He had his eyes closed, fighting something inside him. Fighting his own energy, she guessed.

"You need to go!" she yelled. "Leave me!"

"I won't until you come." He didn't open his eyes. "We can protect Tierra. I worked it out. We need your energy to do it though. The way to save her is to come with me, not stay here."

Something rigid inside her relaxed, and hope flooded her. Perhaps…there was another way? Her impulsive nature surged and she made a split second decision.

"Get me out of here!" she shouted.

His body shuddered, and his grip on hers tightened. "Are you sure?"

She knew that Source wouldn't have given him a bracelet if his feelings for her hadn't been his own, and not the product of influence. And if Jeb was able to save Tierra without her death, there was no need for her to give up.

"Yes!" she said. "Yes."

She felt a touch of his Svadisthana. What remained of his wards, the last remnants, were being assaulted by an energy that wanted to be fully free. Would it help them, or kill them faster?

Cuinn had seen them like this in his vision, but he hadn't seen that she would be bound. *Did the fact that I chose this willingly change anything?* Had Cuinn been right that Jeb needed to keep control? Some primal instinct deep inside where her sparks of inspiration came from said he was wrong. And what did they have to lose?

"Let go!" she screamed. The sea pooled around her knees now, and the spray hit her chest. "You would never hurt me! I trust you! You need to trust yourself!"

"There has to be another way," Jeb said, vehemently. "Otherwise, I'm going to end up killing you myself."

34

She was wrong. He couldn't trust himself. Didn't. He needed to keep her safe, and he wasn't safe. But the words of Source came back to him. 'Embrace your full self.' Did she mean now? What would happen if he let those last pieces of control go?

He could feel his energies inside him, battering him on the inside as the sea was battering his physical body. The storm was elemental, made of air and water just as his own energies were. He felt almost as if he could take the storm and make it his own. He could become the storm. What would happen to him if he did? Would he lose himself? What would happen to Nixie?

Everything was unknown. But he had no other ideas. If he could control the storm, if he was one with the storm, maybe he could direct it back out to sea. Away from Nixie. But it would take more power than he'd ever had before. It had been many decades since he'd experimented with influencing the weather.

But this surge of energy throbbing inside him made him feel powerful. As if he could do anything. If only he was prepared to let go, and embrace all his energies.

And if it destroyed him and left Nixie alive? It was a sacrifice more than worth making.

He leaned in and cradled her head in his left hand, his right still holding hers, and kissed her mouth. Water ran down their faces. The sea was up to Nixie's waist, and every other wave sprayed their faces with the sting of sea water. Their touching hands and wrists were under the water.

It was now or never. He'd run out of time.

With a roar, Jeb finally tore down the last of his wards, and released his Svadisthana from its bonds. His shields exploded into shreds.

His long suppressed energy flooded his whole being, both agonizing and invigorating, but his scream was lost to the crash of the storm that pounded the beach around them. Nixie clung to his hand, her hair plastered against her head, her hand in his like a tether. She gripped his forearm so their bracelets still touched.

"Focus on me," she yelled. "Don't lose yourself!"

He tried, but the energy that he'd freed was almost too much to bear. It ran up and down his body in a pleasure-pain combination that was on the wrong side of too sensitive.

He was fading in and out of consciousness. A pain in his hand brought him back to the moment. Nixie was digging her nails into his palm. The surf pounded on the beach, the waves rising and rising.

"We need to get you to higher ground," he rasped. He leaned against the tree next to her. He didn't think he could move, but she needed to get away. He should have broken her bonds first. He couldn't control the energy. It came through him from the ether without him pulling it. He was merely a conduit. He had the fleeting thought he should have cleared away the remnants of the ritual, as who knew how they were interacting with the energies. He had no idea what the ritual was for, but he wanted to be sure they didn't feed it further.

How would he halt the energy exploding within? A dam inside him had burst. All the suppressed wants, needs and desires from the last seventy years had exploded at once.

Nixie, who still held his hand tight, stretched out her arm as much as the ropes allowed her to. The sand was gritty underneath his feet. They were both soaked to the skin. Lightning cracked across the sky in the distance, and the thunder came quickly after. The storm was almost directly over them.

She dug her nails in again. "Focus! Take control of the storm!"

Could he? The energy could destroy him. Consume him. Could he find the strength to dominate it, and save them both? If he didn't, when the storm was above them, the energy and the storm would become one, and he would be annihilated. A crack of thunder and barely two seconds later, the lightning came, and indicated he didn't have much time left.

He blinked and her face wavered in front of him. He needed to keep her safe. If she was here she'd be destroyed along with him. And she was still tied up. The beach was otherwise deserted, but she needed to get out of here.

Her voice came into focus again. "Take control of the storm! Or we both die!"

It was the 'both' that did it. The energy spun through him, out of control, but he had to fight it, and control it, if they were going to live.

If she was going to live.

"Don't let go of my hand!" he shouted. She nodded. Her face was pale, silver-lit by the moon and each strike of lightning, strikes which were coming more and more frequently.

He closed his eyes, still propped against the tree, one hand in hers. He was going to try and command the storm.

He reached inside himself to connect with the energy. To become the energy. He'd never felt his energies as powerfully before, and given he was already one of the most powerful energetics in the Anahata Guild, that was a terrifying thought. He took the energy of air and water and expanded his consciousness outside his physical body.

The storm had no personality, no agency, but nonetheless, he could feel the weight and power of it in the air. He searched blindly to find the point at which the temperature differed – where the heated air rose, cooled, and the moisture fell back to earth.

His physical body told him the sea was up to his waist now. Up to Nixie's chest. They didn't have long.

He found it. He drew on all his energy and calmed the sea breezes that had caused the air to lift. He thrust his energies out into the unstable warm air that kept rising, causing the storm to continue. He felt a shift and the storm calmed.

But it wasn't enough. The waters, the tide, kept rising.

And a giant wave was coming. His connection to the sea and storm showed him a tsunami on its way, a growing wall of water that would not simply take him and Nixie, but destroy much of the coast here, smashing into it at high speed and dragging houses, cars, bikes and people back into the sea.

No.

He needed to calm the tsunami, then the storm. He pulled energy from the ether to add to the huge wellspring of power he felt inside him, and with an enormous effort of will, threw up a gigantic wall of water in front of the wave, mimicking the sea walls the Japanese used to protect their ports from the same. It was over fifty feet tall and a hundred miles long. It took tremendous effort.

The wave smashed against his wall instead of the coast, and he waited for the drawback, the wave's trough, which lowered the sea level in that area by meters for minutes. The wave built into another ridge, and once again smashed into Jeb's wall.

He clutched Nixie, her touch and the connection with the bracelet somehow amplifying his power. He needed it. It was the biggest single use of energy he had ever undertaken. He was burning through energy at a shocking rate, his body electric with the energies flowing through him.

Dissolving the tsunami took time, but eventually it was done, he released – gently – his wall of water, and he was left with the storm, still wild and savage.

He focused on the wind. He coaxed it and soothed it, the energy in him thick and plentiful. It was like spreading balm onto a burn. The balm cooled the waves, and they began to drop. He sighed in relief. He could do this. A few more minutes and the storm was dying down. The lightning whipped, and the thunder cracked, but it was further out to sea.

It was done.

He had a moment where he hovered between the energetic world and the physical one. He could follow the storm. Become the storm. He could leave his physical body and chase it, and he would no longer be bound to the physical plane. He'd be free of the guilt and the shame of his past actions. As the storm, he could take the pain of the war and be part of the cycle of natural disasters that affected the world, and forget all about control. He could let go entirely, and dissolve. Become a natural force of destruction.

He wavered, his senses alert to the disappearing storm, his energies still part of the wind and the waters, poised, ready to be assimilated and subsumed.

But he could feel the heat of Nixie's hand in his, their bracelets still touching, tethering his physical body to the world. If he left his physical body, he would be leaving Nixie. She'd asked him to stay.

It was hard, living in the world. Vanishing into the elements might be easier.

But, Nixie. Beautiful, light, fun and talented. With a depth most didn't see. If he faded away, he would never have the opportunity to experience love with her.

Her hand went limp. Their connection broke, and the decision was made. He needed to ensure she was okay. She wasn't saved yet.

He flew like an arrow, his essence hitting his physical body in a rush. The power was still there, coiled inside him, but he was in control of it. His Svadisthana was no longer a liability.

Moreover, there was something missing inside him. The guilt and emotional pain he'd been carrying for decades had been left out in the ocean with the storm. His body was light, despite the pain from the power use.

He opened his eyes and saw Nixie slumped over the ropes that tied her, her eyes closed. The waves were now back at his thighs as the tide began to go out. He had no way to judge how long it had taken, but for Nixie to have breathed in water, it must have been more than a few minutes.

"Nixie!" he shouted.

He couldn't give her mouth-to-mouth standing up, but she needed it now.

He had a crazy idea. He threw his energetic essence out again and called a part of the storm back. He drew the smallest lightning strike he could from the clouds and aimed it at the tree. A tingling and a hiss, and he threw shields around both himself and Nixie. This was going to sting a little.

The lightning struck her bonds at the back of the trunk, and chunks of the tree exploded outwards as the moisture in the bark was super-heated even by this small lightning strike. The tree provided a path for the lightning to hit the ground, and it would have left a scar on the tree. But the ropes were burnt through, and Nixie fell into his arms.

He carried her several hundred yards inland, her body light in his arms, to where there was no longer any sea, and laid her on the ground. He checked her pulse, but her body was limp and lifeless. He administered CPR, willing her to breathe again. Nothing.

She was so pale. He tried not to panic. He kept up the CPR, and drew on his energy. This time, instead of rescue breaths, he put his hand in the air above her mouth, squeezed his hand into a fist, and threw his healing energy into her body. He jerked the water out of her lungs, and used his energy to increase the oxygen flow through her blood. Then went back to rescue breathing.

He blended human and energetic methods of lifesaving, willing her to live, to breathe.

He needed her.

An eternity passed. An eternity considering a life without her.

He'd braved the storm for her. She couldn't leave him now.

Her body jolted, and she coughed and spluttered, water coming out of her mouth. He turned her head to the side, until she was ready to sit up. She was shivering.

He put his arms carefully around her to warm her. The skies were clearing, the seas receding, and they were finally safe.

35

Nixie faced Jeb over a supine Tierra, who Jeb had made lie down on the bed. She was much recovered since she'd been able to draw on her own energy from the ether, but her new Vishudha needed warding, and for that they needed Nixie's energy. He'd already removed the Anahata 'patch' he'd put over it.

They hadn't rested since the beach, where Blaize had found them, bedraggled and staggering to Nixie's bike. They'd come directly to Tierra's room. Nixie was still dripping wet, but thankfully, the island was warm.

She didn't have much left in her at this point. She was ready to collapse into bed and sleep for a week.

Jeb placed Nixie's left hand on Tierra's lower abdomen, and put his right hand over the top so their wrists, and bracelets, touched. She felt him draw on his energy, and she opened herself up, sending the blue of her Vishudha to mix with the greens of his Anahata. Together, they warded Tierra's last Chakra, weaving their energy together into something that would last until it became second nature for Tierra to do it herself, as any new energetic coming into their powers would be taught as a child or teenager. Tierra herself had taught Ai only a couple of weeks ago.

"It's done," Jeb said. Nixie nodded, tired to her very bones. She slumped into a nearby chair.

Tierra sat up, energized. "I'm going to track down whatever was draining me."

Nixie cocked her head. "You can do that?"

Tierra nodded firmly. "It might take me a while, but I think I can."

"She's a tracker," said Blaize without looking up, as she read through some material Cuinn had sent on her phone. "Now we know more, she'll find it."

"Don't overdo it," Jeb warned, stretching. He yawned, and beckoned to Nixie. "Let's go."

She shuffled over to him and he held out an arm. She tucked herself under it, and burrowed her head into his warm chest. He smelled divine.

"Wait, we need you to tell us what happened," Blaize protested, finally looking up. "We need the details to send to the others."

Nixie almost cried. She needed to rest. She could barely stand.

"We'll tell you later. We need to sleep first. This one –" Jeb gestured to Nixie, who was using him to stay upright, "– needs rest."

"You too," Nixie mumbled, not bothering to move her head from where it nestled against him. Rest sounded nice. In fact, for perhaps the first time in her life, it sounded better than sex.

There was no longer any rush. She had all the time in the world with him.

Jeb and Nixie retired to her bed, and, exhausted, slept wrapped around each other. He loved holding her in his arms. She felt so right there. They slept a long time.

They got up to eat, and Nixie worked with Blaize on another sketch while Jeb filled Aiko in on what had happened. Neither of them had the energy for much more, withdrawing to her hammock after only an hour or two.

She lay between his legs, both facing forward, her back resting on his stomach, his legs outside hers. He stroked her hair in wonderment, the texture lustrous. He loved to touch the thickness of it.

Though at this point, despite having slept the night and much of the day away, he was so worn out he could barely move a muscle. The gentle sway of the hammock was soothing, lulling him into a semi-doze.

The air was sweet and clear around them, stars sprinkling the sky above. There was little light pollution on the island to cloud their view. There was a hint of lemongrass in the air, a scented candle Nixie had lit to keep the bugs away. Noisy crickets kept them company.

Nixie ran a hand up and down his thigh. They touched as much as possible, their bodies stacked on top of each other. He was shirtless, and her top was half a shirt only, stopping a fraction below the smooth swell of her breasts. She wore no bra.

He wrapped an arm around her, and traced circles on her bare, flat stomach.

"You nearly went with the storm, didn't you?" Nixie said, eyes shut.

"Hmmm?" Jeb said. It was hard to concentrate on her words when he had her body in his lap like this.

She turned, and his body stirred in response as her breasts pressed against his legs, his groin, and she crawled up his body to sit on his torso, her legs either side of his chest. His arms were free, and he rested his hands on her thighs. She had dug her toes into the hammock netting to keep herself in place.

She was as agile as one of those geckos she loved so much.

"I felt the call of the tempest through the bracelets. I thought you might leave. Did you want to?" Nixie said. She looked down at him, her dark eyes serious.

He thought about lying to her. Did she need to know the truth? He lifted his hands, palms up, let them fall and blew out a breath.

"There was a moment when I did, yes," he admitted. "It would have been so easy. I've never been so at one with the elements."

Nixie dropped her head for a moment, then gazed at him directly. "Do you regret the choice you made?"

He raised his eyebrows. "Not for a second. I came back for you, and I will never mourn anything I lost because of that. Besides, there's nowhere in the world I want to be more than in this hammock, with you."

She cocked her head and then jerked it in the direction of the bedroom, suggestively. "Nowhere?"

He grinned. "I want to be wherever you are."

She had no idea that she'd liberated him far more than losing himself to the storm would have.

She nodded and bent and dropped a swift kiss on his lips. "And your Svadisthana?"

His lips twisted, rueful. "It's as much part of me as anything else. My wardings are all gone. It's time to remember how to use it, and to put it to good use in the world."

Nixie gave a short laugh. "It looked to me like you remembered how to use it pretty well on the beach. I've never seen power like that."

He shrugged. "I think it was a one-off, a combination of circumstances. The buildup of my power and me letting down my shields fully for the first time in decades, the ritual and runes that Elrian left, and –" he hesitated.

"Yes?" she said. She was kneading his chest.

"Our bracelets. Did you feel anything?" He was fairly certain some of Source's message to him had been untangled in the use of the bracelets, but he wanted external confirmation.

"Sure," she said. "Connecting them makes us stronger. It's obvious, really."

She made it sound so simple. She shifted her left hand to his right, and interlocked their hands, then pressed her wrist against his.

An instant shock of energy invigorated Jeb, and he jerked in the hammock, setting it swinging. Nixie almost purred.

His energies twanged inside him like plucked strings, his Svadisthana finally as free as his Anahata.

"We're stronger together,' Jeb said. He'd been alone so long, he'd forgotten the power of having someone in your corner. Someone on your side no matter what. Someone who believed in and accepted your, good and, well, less good bits.

"You don't have to fight yourself anymore," Nixie said. "You're fine as you are, a man who's made mistakes, like everyone else. You have dark and light in you, as I do, as everyone does. Our mistakes help us choose the light the next time."

Nixie was a source of light for him, that was certain. He'd misjudged her initially. She had a personality that was light, and fun, and the sensual fairy was part of her, but that didn't mean she couldn't be serious or thoughtful.

Watching her concentrate while drawing as she'd completed another sketch with Blaize that day, and get lost in the flow of putting pencil strokes on a page, had made him realize she had stronger powers of concentration than most. It was a time he'd enjoyed, when he could study her without her realizing given how absorbed she was in her work.

The damage from the war hadn't gone, but a burden had been lifted from him, and this amazing woman was part of that. He couldn't believe how lucky he was that she was his.

He drew on his Svadisthana and sent a pulse of it through their bracelets. She shivered delightfully and his groin responded.

He suddenly found he wasn't quite as tired as he'd thought.

Nixie wanted to roll herself on Jeb like he was catnip. Wanted to nip and nibble, to rub herself on his scent, and generally stay as close to him as possible.

She'd grown up a lot in the last couple of weeks. Her entire outlook on love had changed, as she'd realized what she'd previously been chasing in love was selfish, a mirror for her own vanity, rather than something more solid and selfless.

She responded to his pulse of desire by running her hands down his bare chest, using the merest touch as she skated her fingers over his nipples. He let out a groan.

Jeb wasn't the kind of man she'd been looking for. He was serious, damaged, scholarly, steady, much more experienced in the world, and involved in highlevel Guild politics.

Yet his solemnity complemented her more mercurial temperament. He grounded her, and she uplifted him.

She bent down and licked along the shell of his ear, then bit the lobe very gently. He sighed and she felt his cock harden between them. She moved her hips slightly, rubbing, encouraging, daring.

And Source, the man had power. Exhilarating, impressive, terrifying power. When he'd taken control of the storm, she'd thought she'd lose him. Or that he'd lose control and destroy the island. She'd seen the possibility in that moment.

He'd stayed with her though. With his matching bracelet. Source had paired them together. Through good times and difficult ones, she'd be there for him now. Whatever else this prophecy threw at them.

He scooped his arms around her and swept her into a horizontal kiss. She wriggled on top of him, and got her hand between them, deftly undoing his pants. He spluttered and laughed through their kiss, but didn't stop her. She shoved them down and he kicked them off. They ended up in a heap at the end of the hammock, but she didn't care.

She shimmied her shorts and underwear off, writhing against him delightfully as she did. He skimmed hands over her naked ass.

She was wet for him, ready, and she sat up, gazing down at him. His hair was as unkempt as usual, but his mostly-dark stubble was neat, around a mouth that curved up a little either side. She ran a finger down his neck and along the lean muscles on his shoulders and arms that must come from swimming.

It was his eyes that caught her, though. Blue like a storm, blue like the sea, they held a world of promise and desire for her.

The heat and thickness of his cock was gratifying.

She lifted her hips, and, slowly, without dropping eye contact, she slid him inside her. It wasn't easy, and the effort showed in her face, and she could see the idea pleased him. Men.

His smirk dropped once she'd sheathed him fully inside her, and began to roll her hips. She rode him, bit him, scratched him, and he met her action for action, deed for deed.

Their energies danced between them, enhancing sensation, curling around each other, twisting and winding until they melded completely, and there was no separation in their Svadisthanas.

The pleasure built and built in her, and she squeezed her pelvic muscles, spurring him on, and he met her thrust for thrust, despite the limited purchase he had on the hammock.

The hammock swung faster, side-to-side just as they moved up and down. The movements complemented each other, hypnotic and primal, until with a howl she came, and her pussy contracted around him, her nails digging into his shoulders. Mine, she thought. Mine.

The orgasm went through her like waves on the sea, taking its time to calm. When it had finished, she was hyper-sensitive, and his movements inside her felt disproportionately huge.

His eyes had darkened as he'd watched her come, and he reached two fingers down to stroke her clit gently as she continued to circle her hips.

"Again," he said, insistent, and she linked her hands behind her head, her small breasts thrust out, and rode him harder, harder, till the perfect and continuous pressure he was putting on her clit pushed her over again, and she clenched and squeezed and asked and took and he came inside her, while their gazes stayed as locked as their energy was.

36

Elrian stalked through the dawn in Seattle, cold wet rain running down his neck. He'd lost more weight, and he'd had to tighten his belt a notch. He was shaky. He needed energy.

He had been livid about the beach, and losing Nixie. Worse still, Imogen had told him the Guild's latest gossip. Tierra and Nixie had both survived, and Nixie and Jeb were a couple. He'd failed again.

Three couples down.

Three to go.

A man and woman, clearly on a date, blocked his way, and he covered a sneer by stepping aside to let them pass. He turned the collar of his long black raincoat up as he did.

He'd spent a great deal of the last couple of weeks in the ether, searching and seeking as to who the next couple would be, determined not to fail again. He'd decide then whether it would be easier to focus on one of this couple and one of those already bonded, or simply kill both members of the next pair. He still only needed to kill two of the twelve, but if he somehow bungled this next two, and his adversaries managed to have four couples together, he would need to kill three of them.

Inconceivable.

Cassidy had been worried about him, and forced food and drink on him that were irrelevant. The only thing he needed was energy.

It was so hard to pull energy from the ether these days. So much easier to take it from someone else.

He'd kept the stone that he'd part filled from Nixie, and tasted a little of her energy now and then. It kept the edge off. But he needed another victim. And he needed to show Imogen that he was a capable partner. She had responded with disdainful silence to the disaster at the beach. He wondered what Trent had told her. He'd had to pay Trent extra, as the man had noticed Elrian's leeching from him, despite the fact he had no proof. Elrian supposed he was lucky Trent didn't murder him in his sleep, but the other man was unlikely to cross Imogen.

He strode on, passing endless coffee shops and anonymous office buildings.

Happily, the male of the next potential couple worked right here in Seattle. Some kind of tech geek, he didn't seem likely to cross paths with Cara, the female, anytime soon. Especially as she lived on some godforsaken island off Canada, managing a Rehab Center.

Elrian had time, but he wanted the man. He would use him for a remnant stone, as the man was a strong Vishudha-Manipura. Elrian had let go of the need to find energetic matches to drain energy from. While his own energies were Muladhara-Ajna, and energetics with these nourished him the best, Nixie's Svadisthana had still given him something worthwhile. So he'd kill two birds with one stone, and take this male for both purposes.

He'd been shadowing the man, Archer, for days, watching his habits. He was a runner, and every other day he did a three mile loop around the city at dawn. Elrian planned to grab him at the end of this, when he was tired and off-guard. Elrian would use his influence energy to move him, and had prepared a space for the ritual in a hidden spot nearby.

Archer always parked his mountain bike in the same place at the edge of a park. He'd head off, do his three miles, run back to the bike, do a couple of stretches, take out an energy drink he'd stashed on a clip near the handlebars, drink it down, then hop on and cycle the two miles home.

Routine could make you stronger, but could also make you sloppy.

In this case, Archer being sloppy would make Elrian stronger.

Nixie dropped a kiss on Jeb's palm, then flicked on the video call, and her friends' images slowly came into focus on the laptop screen.

Despite the constant sense of menace and threat they lived with, the connection between the different members of the team – for Nixie had begun to think of them that way, though, perhaps, family was a better word – was strong. There was even back channel chatter in the text chat scrolling along, with Blaize messing with Fintan, who messed with everyone, while Tierra scolded him, and worried about her brother and cousin.

Nixie had taken a lot of scoldings and recriminations herself from everyone for her actions. For the first few days, Jeb had flickered between anger and an inability to leave her side. It had worked out, but Nixie had learned she wasn't alone, and the value of real connection. There would be no more superficial hook-ups for Nixie. She had found her match. Her soulmate.

It had been a couple of weeks since the events on the beach, and the group had scattered to the winds.

On screen the video boxes lined up.

There were Blaize and Cuinn, both now at Cathair Cuinn, outside Vancouver. They were back to the research, dreamwalks, and trying to put everything together. They were looking into Iskander, what Elrian might be doing with the remnant stones, why Atlantis burned, and the many other mysteries that were still unresolved. Cathair Cuinn was still HQ, no matter how dispersed they all were.

Nixie had been able to draw the majority of the twelve energetics from Blaize's mind-pictures. Eight energetics they'd already identified, there was one male she'd drawn who none of them yet recognized, and there were three she, Blaize and Cuinn were having trouble with. In the meantime, she was part of the small team finishing the translation of the Hermit's notes, which Jeb was convinced held some kind of key.

Back on the screen, she saw Adam, Tierra's big brother, in Seattle, investigating a recent leeching in case it was connected. He was also checking with his human contacts in the various governmental agencies around the world to see if they had any knowledge of Elrian's whereabouts.

There was Cara, at Vancouver Island's Rehab Center, with Ai hovering behind her, the girl staying with Cara for her first lessons in Anahata energy.

There were Tierra and Fintan in Cairo, at Anahata Guild, where Tierra was healing and being examined by Feng and Aiko, and Fintan was keeping a worried eye on her. Something bigger was going on at Anahata, Jeb felt, and he'd sent Tierra on ahead to check it out.

Cuinn began to speak, and everyone hushed. Nixie smiled. Jeb would nudge her if there was anything she really needed to pay attention to.

She sat curled up next to him as he watched the screen intently, the tinny voices of the others coming through their laptop's speakers and fighting with the sounds of birdsong and gecko on the island, where she and Jeb were taking some time to recover before they went to visit Svadisthana Guild. Jeb wanted to spend a few days there to refresh himself now that his energy was in harmony again.

She smiled, capturing the scene in her mind, another group of contrasting portraits, full of color, light and love. She was looking forward to it. There was a hell of a lot of sexual energy around the Guild. And she intended to take full advantage of that.

Glossary

Adherent – Once an energetic is taken on by a Maven, they are called an Adherent as they train for their Chakra trial. As part of the ritual when they bond with their Maven, they receive one thin black band around the top of their arm (left arm for females, right arm for males).

Ajna – The Third Eye Chakra, associated with the element of the Mind and the color indigo. The energy of imagination, of visualizations, and insight. Of clarity and wisdom. Of dreams and intuition.

Anahata – The Heart Chakra, associated with the element of the Air and the color green. The energy of healing, and of balance, located in the middle of the body and the seven Chakras. The energy of love, of relationships, of devotion. Of compassion and empathy.

Auxiliary Chakra – Energetics have two Chakras activated in them, that is, energy they can draw upon and use as power. Their auxiliary Chakra is the weaker of the two.

Chakra Trial – When an energetic wants to move up a power level, they are trained for several years by a Maven, and then tested by a Chakra trial (e.g. From Adherent to Practitioner, or Practitioner to Master).

Dormant – When an energetic is born, their energies are Dormant. At birth, their strongest Chakra is almost always identifiable and they are named after this.

Dominant Chakra – Energetics have two Chakras activated in them, that is, energy they can draw upon and use as power. Their dominant Chakra is the stronger of the two.

Dreamscape – Another name for the ether, where Ajna energetics can create their Haven and use Ajna to search for prophecy shards or do other activities related to their energy. The ether is also the place where raw energy is drawn from by energetics, so all energetics have some kind of internal connection to it.

Dreamwalker – An Ajna energetic who can go the dreamscape and gather prophecy.

Ether – Also known as the dreamscape, where Ajna energetics can create their Haven and use Ajna to search for prophecy shards or do other activities related to their energy. The ether is also the place where raw energy is drawn from by energetics, so all energetics have some kind of internal connection to it.

Haven – The space in the ether/dreamscape that an Ajna energetic creates for her or himself that is 'safe'.

Guild Leader – The energetic who is the leader of either a Major or a Minor Guild. A Guild leader has to 'balance' a Guild's energy so it takes an energetic of some power.

Practitioner – Once an energetic has passed a Chakra trial, they are a Practitioner, and receive a second thin black band around the top of their arm (left arm for females, right arm for males). This is the most common level of power for energetics.

Leech – An energetic who has turned into a Rouge, and is draining other energetics of the energy (not all Rouges are leeches).

Major Guilds – The six Chakras have one Guild each (e.g. Muladhara, Svadisthana etc.).

Major Circle – The Major Circle is the highest form of government with one powerful energetic representing each Major Guild, making decisions on behalf of the race.

Manipura – The Navel Chakra, associated with the element of Fire and the color yellow. The energy of the individual; of confidence, of proactivity and of drive and passion. Playful and proud.

Master – If an energetic passes a Chakra trial at the end of their Practitioner training, they become a Master energetic, and receive a third thin black band around the top of their arm (left arm for females, right arm for males).

Maven – This is the name for those energetics who take on an Adherent to train in an energy. An energetic has to be at Master level to become a Maven, but Mavens are outside the power structure. Their symbol is an owl on their robes, but there is no tattoo as it can be a position only taken once in a lifetime, or a Master can take on many Adherents consecutively.

Minor Guilds – These represent each dominant-auxiliary Chakras. There are thirty Minor Guilds representing each combination (for example, Manipura-Ajna is a separate Guild from Ajna-Manipura).

Minor Circle – The Minor Circle is the energetics' second tier of government, and is made up of the thirty energetics who lead each of the Minor Guilds.

Muladhara – The Root Chakra, associated with the element of Earth and the color red. The energy of nourishment and home, family and safety.

Remnant Stone – A stone that can store the energy of an energetic who has been drained to the point of death.

Rogue – An energetic whose energy has 'twisted' into the negative version of the Chakra.

Sahasara – The Crown Chakra, not associated with an element. The purest of all the energies. Only experienced through the Grace of the Source (the energetics' name for the creator, the divine).

Svadisthana – The Sacral Chakra, associated with the element of Water and the color orange. Fluid and adaptable, the energy of movement and connection, of practical and physical creativity. The energy of pleasure, sexuality and sensation, and emotions.

Vishudha – The Throat Chakra, associated with the element of Ether (Space) and the color blue. The energy of communication, of conceptual creativity, and of truth. Of expression, and of listening.

The Guilds and Circles

The energetics' power structure is Guild based.

There are six Major Guilds, one for each of the six Chakras:

- **Muladhara** (The Root Chakra – Earth Element)
- **Svadisthana** (The Sacral Chakra – Water Element)
- **Manipura** (The Navel Chakra – Fire Element)
- **Anahata** (The Heart Chakra – Air Element)
- **Vishudha** (The Throat Chakra – Ether (Space) Element)
- **Ajna** (The Third Eye – The Mind)
  (Sahasara, the Crown Chakra, does not have a Guild.)

Each energetic has two activated Chakras, one dominant and one auxiliary, and it is the combination of these that influences their power, and to some degree, their personality.

Because of the huge differences between an energetic like Blaize, who combines her Manipura dominant with Ajna auxiliary, and one like Fintan, who combines Manipura dominant with Anahata auxiliary, a system of Minor Guilds also developed. There are thirty

Minor Guilds representing each combination of powers (for example, Manipura-Ajna is a separate Guild from Ajna-Manipura).

Each individual energetic therefore belongs to two Major Guilds, and one Minor Guild.

For example: Cuinn has Ajna dominant, and Muladhara auxiliary. He therefore belongs to the Ajna Major Guild, the Muladhara Major Guild, and the Ajna-Muladhara Minor Guild.

The Major Circle is the highest form of government with one powerful energetic representing each Major Guild, making decisions on behalf of the race. The Minor Circle, the second tier of government, is made up of the thirty energetics who lead each of the Minor Guilds.

List of Minor Guilds:

- Muladhara-Svadisthana
- Muladhara-Manipura
- Muladhara-Anahata
- Muladhara-Vishudha
- Muladhara-Ajna
- Svadisthana-Muladhara
- Svadisthana-Manipura
- Svadisthana-Anahata
- Svadisthana-Vishudha
- Svadisthana-Ajna
- Manipura-Muladhara
- Manipura-Svadisthana
- Manipura-Anahata
- Manipura-Vishudha
- Manipura-Ajna
- Anahata-Muladhara
- Anahata-Svadisthana
- Anahata-Manipura

- Anahata-Vishudha
- Anahata-Ajna
- Vishudha-Muladhara
- Vishudha-Svadisthana
- Vishudha-Manipura
- Vishudha-Anahata
- Vishudha-Ajna
- Ajna-Muladhara
- Ajna-Svadisthana
- Ajna-Manipura
- Ajna-Anahata
- Ajna-Vishudha

Want More?

The story of the energetics continues in Cara and Archer's story, **Cara and the Hacker**.

To be first to hear when it's out, visit my website:
EllenBardAuthor.com/sign-up
for updates, giveaways and inside information.

Discover Your Energetic Profile!

Want to know what your Dominant Chakra would be? Which Guild you would belong to? What your archetype is?

Take the Chakra Quiz, and find out!

EllenBardAuthor.com/chakra-quiz

Make a Difference with a Review

If you loved the book and have a few minutes, I would hugely appreciate it if you had time to leave a short review where you bought the book, and / or on goodreads. For instructions, go to the link below.

EllenBardAuthor.com/how-to-leave-a-review

Your review will help other readers discover the series, and is greatly appreciated in spreading the word. Authors like me rely on amazing readers like you to share their love of books with others.

Thank you!

About the Author

Ellen is an author who writes paranormal romance full of enchantment, intrigue and action. Her writing blends a background in psychology and her experiences traveling the world, with a love of magic, fantasy and a happy ending.

She's a Chartered Occupational Psychologist with the British Psychological Society, and continues to work as an international management consultant, which she has done for the last 18 years. She's worked all over the world in countries such as China, Saudi Arabia and Malaysia. She writes non-fiction under Ellen M Bard.

Her passion for other lands and cultures helps inform her writing, as does her desire to try new things – from art classes to Krav Maga, the self-defence system.

She's a passionate and dedicated reader, speeding through 80-100 books a year – find her on goodreads to see what currently has her hooked.

Born in the UK, she currently lives in an apartment nest in Bangkok, Thailand where she (almost!) never has to feel the cold.

Connect with Ellen:
Facebook: facebook.com/EllenBardAuthor
Twitter: twitter.com/ellenbard
Goodreads: goodreads.com/ellenbard
Instagram: instagram.com/ellenbard

Acknowledgments

The character of Nixie is, of the heroines so far – Blaize, Tierra and even the next in the series, Cara – the one who shares fewest traits in common with me. She grew from experiences with acquaintances on the Thai islands, and from a desire to embody a character who was a lot more relaxed and enthusiastic about sex than many of the heroines I read about in romance. I want my heroines to display a diverse set of women, who show up in the world with strength from all kinds of sources.

That also means I struggled a lot more with getting her character right. My sister and alpha reader, Sarah Bard, and my editor, Claire Taylor Nelson, helped a lot here – and in many other places! – and I'm very grateful for their notes on this and other aspects of the plot and characters. My mum, Mary Bard, was another great alpha reader, spotting a lot of my consistency errors and typos, and bringing her own unique commentary to her editing notes.

Eléonore Chaban Delmas, friend, writer and beta reader extraordinaire, turned round a reading of this book – with more than a hundred useful comments and notes – overnight. For that, and her generosity and constant warmth as a friend, I have immense gratitude.

My friends Anna Charbonneau and Graham Morley have provided much cheerleading and support, and I'm lucky to have them in my life whether we're in the same country that week or not.

Thanks also to Peter Bainbridge and my aunt, Ellen Dunne, who helped do the final proofs of the book.

The soundtrack to Nixie and Jeb's story was Jasmine Thompson, whose many covers and original songs I had on loop while writing. Her haunting voice and danceable beats were of great help in getting me in the right mood for writing the book.

Finally, as ever, thanks to my Fox. Life-partner and accountability partner are just two of the ways that you show up in my life, providing inspiration and motivation and so much more. Thank you for all the support, encouragement and pad thais, not to mention sharing an office with a coworker who has all the questions, all the time, and expects you to be able to answer.

Ellen Bard, May 2019

9 780993 439445